ON SUNDAYS SHE PICKED FLOWERS

ON SUNDAYS SHE PICKED FLOWERS

YAH YAH SCHOLFIELD

solstice

London · New York · Amsterdam/Antwerp · Sydney/Melbourne · Toronto · New Delhi

First published in the United States by Saga Press,
an imprint of Simon & Schuster, LLC, 2026
First published in Great Britain by Solstice Books, an imprint of
Simon & Schuster UK Ltd, 2026

Copyright © Mariyah Scholfield, 2026

The right of Mariyah Scholfield to be identified as author
of this work has been asserted in accordance with the
Copyright, Designs and Patents Act, 1988.

1 3 5 7 9 10 8 6 4 2

Simon & Schuster UK Ltd
1st Floor
222 Gray's Inn Road
London WC1X 8HB

For more than 100 years, Simon & Schuster has championed authors and the stories they create. By respecting the copyright of an author's intellectual property, you enable Simon & Schuster and the author to continue publishing exceptional books for years to come. We thank you for supporting the author's copyright by purchasing an authorised edition of this book.

No amount of this book may be reproduced or stored in any format, nor may it be uploaded to any website, database, language-learning model, or other repository, retrieval, or artificial intelligence system without express permission. All rights reserved. Enquiries may be directed to Simon & Schuster, 222 Gray's Inn Road, London WC1X 8HB or RightsMailbox@simonandschuster.co.uk

Simon & Schuster Australia, Sydney
Simon & Schuster India, New Delhi

www.simonandschuster.co.uk
www.simonandschuster.com.au
www.simonandschuster.co.in

The authorised representative in the EEA is Simon & Schuster Netherlands BV, Herculesplein 96, 3584 AA Utrecht, Netherlands. info@simonandschuster.nl

Simon & Schuster strongly believes in freedom of expression and stands against censorship in all its forms. For more information, visit BooksBelong.com

A CIP catalogue record for this book
is available from the British Library

Hardback ISBN: 978-1-3985-4542-7
eBook ISBN: 978-1-3985-4542-7
Audio ISBN: 978-1-3985-4545-8

This book is a work of fiction. Names, characters, places and incidents are either a product of the author's imagination or are used fictitiously. Any resemblance to actual people living or dead, events or locales is entirely coincidental.

Interior design by Lewelin Polanco

Printed and Bound in the UK using 100% Renewable Electricity
at CPI Group (UK) Ltd

*To my nana, Lydia Olivia Coulston,
who blessed me with her fire
and my warped mind.*

On Sundays She Picked Flowers engages with topics of physical, verbal and emotional abuse, as well as anti-Black violence, cannibalism and semi-explicit references to incest, self-harm and child death.

PART 1

I am the shape you made me.
Filth teaches filth.
—SOPHOKLES

1

Autumn
1965

Ma'am cracked Jude's skull against the wall for talking back, and the realization that no one was going to save her struck Jude like a revelation from God.

Smack of bone against plaster, brick. Sudden darkness, sudden flash of white light—was it the act itself that schooled her, or was the pain her teacher? Or maybe it was the apathy of her audience, her mother's quilting circle (religious women, saints in knee-length skirts and compression socks) glancing briefly at Jude's crumpled body before returning to their sewing. Ma'am stepped over her, sat among her friends as Jude stumbled to her feet. Her face was wet—blood, thank God, rather than humiliating tears—and she knew she could no longer live in her mother's house.

That it took Judith Rice forty-one years to come to the conclusion was proof of only a hopeful nature. Or was it naivete? Jude certainly felt naive when she bowed to pray to her mother's god, as silly as a little girl wishing on shooting stars, dandelions. What could he give her that hadn't already been denied? Strength? Resilience? Mercy, maybe, if such a thing existed.

No paintings of God were hung in the Westmoor house, so Jude imagined her grandfather, stern and humorless as he glared from his position on the living room wall. It was to him that she directed her prayers for freedom, pious and patient, and then her curses, though these she quickly corrected with apologies. If ever once Jude pleaded with the Lord to strike Ma'am dead, strike her *dead, strike the bitch dead*, only Jesus knew it, and he knew her heart, didn't he, knew she didn't mean it, not really. He alone knew that Jude wasn't as spiteful as her prayers, that she'd rather there be peace. On her knees, she asked for patience, time—if only she and Ma'am had time away from each other, time to think and let the bitter sentiments settle, then things could be sweet between them. Normal, familial; friendly, even, like the mothers and daughters on TV.

Jude couldn't say which blow it was that knocked the prayers from her mouth like teeth. Only remembered chasing after them, running her hands through the carpet to find this or that plea, all the while knowing it was useless. Of course, God wasn't listening to her. Of course, Jesus wasn't *her* friend. They were her mother's men, and all the time she was on her knees, begging, crying out for her freedom, they were at work with Ma'am, whispering in her ear, colluding on crueler and viler punishments.

Up in her bedroom with the lights off and the curtains pulled, a wad of gauze pressed to her gashed head, Jude nursed thoughts of escape alongside her concussion. She could get a bus out of town, but wait—how would she get the ticket, never mind leave the house? And if she did, somehow, manage to leave her mother's house, where could she go? So cagey were the Negroes of Vine City, so protective of themselves and nervous of outside influence. Nothing entered and nothing left. Jude recalled her past attempts to escape, each of them thwarted by neighbors, nosy folk from church—once Jude had gotten as far as Ashby Street before a minister her mother knew had corralled her, protesting, into his car and returned her home. Ma'am had wept and bought locks for the doors that could only be opened by keys she kept on her person.

Her mind was a tangle, bus routes and city names and paths of egress muddling, twisting, knotting. Pressure on her chest, weighing on her belly; she panted, fought for breath. The corners of her bedroom, childish and pink, folded in and in, squashing her, and a voice like wasp's wings beat against the glass of her brain. *The only way out is through, and aren't there spiders who eat their mothers, and can't you just— Wouldn't it be easier to just—*

Jude flattened the thought. She waited until her mind felt clear to slowly lift the hand, peeking underneath to see the idea, oozing and twitching, a cockroach near death.

She was not a violent person, Jude. When she felt the need to be ugly, when the meanness was too much for the frangible cage of her body and her hands itched to break something, someone, she broke only herself. Tailoring pins in the palm of her hand, needles jammed into her thighs—she alone took the brunt of her ire, the copper of her blood, as she lapped at an injury, as comforting as the cut itself. But to turn the blade outward . . .

Well, said the wasp-wing voice, *it isn't like you'd be hurting anything real.* Hadn't Ma'am long ago severed their ties? Hadn't she made it so clear to Jude that the blood that bonded them meant nothing to her? Jude's rage would touch only what little of the bond that remained—the terrific physical form, the birthing body that resisted and resented. It was only the afterbirth, and like the placenta, it needed to be expelled lest it poison the body. It was up to Jude to decide what to do with it afterward, whether she'd discard it or burn it, bury it in the garden.

It was near dark when Ma'am brought her a bowl of greens and two aspirin. Jude took small bites of the cabbage, swallowed the pills, and half listened as Ma'am talked her way around a non-apology. When her plate was clear, Ma'am set it on the nightstand and put a warm, wrinkled paw to Jude's forehead.

"How's your head?"

Splitting, aching. "It's alright, Ma'ammy."

"That aspirin gon' take the pain out." She hummed, picked lint off Jude's comforter, did anything but look Jude in the face. "Want anything special-like for dinner tomorrow?"

This was her way—cruelty and then candy. No more able to parse the kindness than she was able to stomach the meanness, Jude learned to take each act, sweet and bitter, as they came, never once growing accustomed to the shifting ground on which she stood.

A verbal apology, a *real* apology, was out of the question. One did not apologize to a child, especially not if that child was one's own. Instead, there were invitations to run errands, permission to pick out any fruit she liked at the market. Flash of light, ages of pitch darkness; hands roughly shaking her awake, icy water shocking her back to consciousness. Scars were salved over with baby dolls, broken skin and bones by good food, collards or cornbread, the stickiest pig's foot set aside for her.

Now that they were older, Ma'am was less likely to play at making nice and Jude was less likely to be appeased. Still, Jude did not turn down the trips to Rich's or Davison's, did not turn down her mother's offers to buy any bright, shiny thing she saw. She knocked the teeth out of Jude's mouth once, sent blood and adult molars flying across the hardwood; in return, Jude got the closest thing to an admission of fault—a slice of warm pound cake drizzled with lemon glaze, permission to use the car, permission to be alone.

They meant nothing, Ma'am's apologies, and nothing changed. Sweets and treats were nice, but they wouldn't make her a woman in her mother's house, wouldn't make her anything more than a whipping girl. There was no future, only Jude and Ma'am graying and decaying, Ma'am's cane cracking her back and Jude standing there and taking it, smiling like an idiot even as she was mashed into a pulp.

Jude blinked slowly, froggily, and said, "Can we have beef stew?"

Ma'am left her then—pat on the hand, dry kiss to the bandaged head—and Jude waited until the door was fully closed and her mother's shuffling steps had receded to her own room before slipping out of bed. Carefully, mindful of her headache, Jude knelt and felt the floor for a loose board. She found it, lifted it and set it aside, and reached into the slot for her collection of secret things.

She was fourteen when she started helping with her aunt Phyllis's tailoring business. What little money she made—a nickel for buttons, a dime for every item mended, and a quarter for each choir robe she returned with a straight hem—went into Ma'am's pockets, for her upkeep, but what Jude kept for herself she hid under the floorboard in a tea tin alongside slim, well-used diaries, a tube of red lipstick, beads, costume bracelets, acorns, and other small treasures.

There was just a little over two hundred dollars in her tea tin in ones and fives and coins. Kneeling, Jude counted and recounted her stash, tucked it back into the tin, and dragged from beneath her bed a hefty quilted bag. This she filled with necessities—skirts and modest dresses she'd cut herself, plain starched shirts, a pair of slacks she'd purchased but never dared wear outside her bedroom, nightclothes, underthings, tights, a pair of flat black shoes, and her sewing kit. Of her contraband collection of pulpy fantasies and romances she kept in her closet, Jude packed only *Jane Eyre* and a newer Baldwin. For toiletries, she took her toothbrush, a washrag, and an unopened bar of soap.

She looked over her haul, her things packed tidily into her bag, and the sight of it was some relief. She could, if she was smart, get out of the house with this bag and a coat alone. Comforted by the thought, Jude slid the bag back beneath the bed, replaced the tin of money and her secrets beneath the floorboard, and crawled back into bed.

The sleeplessness didn't surprise her. Too much was on her mind, her plans and her injury, and Ma'am, mostly, what sort of woman she was. Her mother, a trinity unto herself—saintlike Ernestine, lover of the Gospel, believer of prayer, she served on the ushers' board at Mount Tabernacle Pentecostal, smiled without teeth and walked tightly, stiffly, so her hips wouldn't sway; Nessie, smiling toothily, giggling, played card games with her sisters and despised drunks but cheerfully took sips of gin, if Vivian or Phyllis was offering. And then Ma'am, who smiled rarely and hissed and snapped and could not be pleased. Nessie knew dances she'd made up back in Sparta, wore her hair in wild braids and bared her legs; Ma'am whupped Jude for being fresh, for listening to secular music, for the sliver of bare midriff accidentally exposed. You could meet Ernestine's gaze, could tell Nessie a story and have her throw back her head to laugh at it; when Jude looked Ma'am in the eye, all she got was a knock to the side of her head.

All three, at least, stank of jasmine.

Only after fitful sleep and changing her bandages did Jude stop to consider herself and what sort of woman she was. She was, at forty-one, a child still, slump shouldered and cowed. Where she came from, she did not know. There was a golden band on her mother's finger, but no one ever said anything to her about a father, and there were no pictures of Jude in the photo albums. It was pointless to ask Ma'am anything; the best she got from Ma'am were abbreviated anecdotes about the plantation in Sparta where she came up, sharecropping, or half stories about her aunties fussing over infant Jude, the sisters whispering to one another about Jude's muteness, how she never seemed to laugh or cry or make any of those charming noises babies were supposed to make.

"You was the quietest thing. Your auntie Vivian, she thought somethin' might've been wrong with you, considerin.'"

"Considerin' what, Ma'ammy?" Jude would ask, hopeful for a scrap of something from her mother's mind, some thread to connect them, but by then, Ma'am would be tired of talking about the past, done with all them questions, and didn't she learn Jude any better than to pry?

Her own memories of her childhood were spare, more sensation and sound than image: the whistle of a wooden hairbrush cutting through the air and landing *thwack!* against the meat of her thigh; her grandfather's gangrenous leg perched on an ottoman, pipe smoke obscuring his face as he whittled some small toy for her; sudden bursts of color and joy at Auntie Vivian's wedding, Auntie Phyllis's wedding, followed by the strained restraint of the parlor at Pappy's wake, the wake of her infant cousin.

There was school, briefly, but that was ruined soon enough by the taunting of her peers, the disdain of her teachers. Clearly, they saw something in her or they'd consulted with Ma'am beforehand, each of them having decided, independently, that Jude was too fat, too Black, too tall, and too damn ugly.

Jude thought it was true, then. In the dark of her bedroom, consulting her reflection in a hand mirror, she wasn't sure. In the glass: black eyes, mournful and barren; dark striped skin, mottled with scars, the mouth perpetually frowning. The mirror would not show the rest of her, how beneath the pressed hair and fractured skull there was a mind that spiraled and wandered and flashed, electric, with thoughts chthonic.

She did not see what her mother saw, could not understand what *thing* lived inside her that made Ma'am hate her so. Jude was her mother's child, Ernestine's match, and they shared everything from eyes to smile to singing voice, so what was it? Jude came to her mother innocent, curious, and watchful, and each trait was perverted; her curiosity into mere nosiness, her innocent silence into surliness.

Jude's head bandage oozed. She put a hand to it, saw her blood shining black on her fingers. She considered the state of her skull, the ease with which Ma'am hurt her. Did it cost so little, her blood, that her very own mother could spill it without blinking? Was her life so forfeit that saints, her aunts, could watch her bleed and feel for her no pity? The roach of violence twitched its legs, righted itself, and scuttled to the forefront of her brain.

Love was not enough. Sweet talk and sweet times, bowls of cabbage and slices of cake—they wouldn't mend what had been broken. If it was, all this time, love that had stilled Jude's hands and made her faithful to her mother, she would cut it from her chest. If the only way out was through, if it had to be red and terrible and violent, so be it.

For her freedom, for her life, Ma'am would have to die.

2

It happened in the kitchen. Very germane—butchery in the cooking place, the cleaver and carving knife bearing witness. The tile, slick, grouted, was receptive to the killing; it expected bloodiness.

That she was the one preparing her own special dinner of beef stew did not surprise Jude. Ma'am's peace offerings rarely kept their original shape, and over the course of the night and morning, the early afternoon, the promise to cook for Jude had changed into permission to do what she liked in the kitchen.

All the better. The kitchen was her place, and Jude liked the tenacity of the faint rays of sunlight that managed to break through the fence of trees to illuminate the brown-green wicker-weave tile, the matching green walls. The cabinetry was dated, faded yellow, complementary to the stark white of the fridge and range. Yolk-yellow curtains hung at the window positioned over the farmhouse sink, its drain ringed with rust. Whenever Jude washed dishes or filled pots, she looked out to the front of the house, to the green fence and the lawn, her mother's tidy garden.

Her cooking was, as always, attended to by angels. On the countertops and high on the shelves, scattered across the small, square table at the center of the kitchen, were her mother's glass angels. Every spare corner was occupied by ceramic cherubim, every nook and cranny christened with porcelain putti, all of them brown faced and beatific, praying and singing, heads bowed, on their rouged knees, coupled together with harps and halos, or set apart to smile their glazed smiles on their lonesome.

Sweat gathered on Jude's upper lip, dripped down the back of her neck. She panted through her mouth as she undressed onions, chopped celery and carrots into medallions. Tall, flaky biscuits cooled on the table, and on the stove a pot of stock bubbled. Jude licked her lips, her sweat, and used one of the sturdier angels to prop open the window.

Nina Simone on the radio, Billy Graham shouting hellfire from the television set upstairs. It was easy to lose Nina in the noise. *I'm just a soul whose intentions are good! Oh Lord, please don't let me be misunderstood!*

"Judith!"

At the moment, Jude felt— Well, if she were honest with herself, if she were frank, she'd say she felt like kin to the knife in her hand. It was nothing fancy, just a simple cleaver, but it was weighty with a sharp, clean blade. The wooden handle fit perfectly the curve of her palm, an easy extension of her arm. Whenever she honed it, she honed herself. Back and forth, back and forth, grinding down against the whetstone until both blade and woman were keen to cleave and slice.

"Judith!"

And she had been whetted all day, all week, all her life. Ma'am throwing her into the wall was only one in a series of humiliations. Earlier in the week, Jude had dropped one of Ma'am's angels, an honest mistake while cleaning; her punishment was almost two hours of derision, her aged mother winded yet determined to grind her down, down, repeating over and again how stupid Jude was, how useless, how clumsy. She had gnawed on the velvet of her inner cheek to still her mind. Still her hands.

"*Judith!*" Ma'am's voice carried through the near silence. "Girl, don't you hear me?"

"Ma'am?" Jude turned her head, listening to her mother's progress through the house, the thump and drag of her lame leg. There she was in the upstairs hall, now on the stairs, now in the dining room—Jude turned to her mother as she entered the kitchen. The woman wore a quilted robe over her nightclothes, house shoes, and her grayed, pressed hair was brushed back severely from her face.

Ma'am had been nineteen when Jude was born, a hale girl who spent the whole of her youth sharecropping with her sisters and parents on a plantation. Sixty should not have looked so poor on the woman, but the work of her youth, her years as a laundress, had exhausted her and illness had sapped what remained of her vitality. She squinted, she limped, and her hands, once as graceful as Jude's, were gnarled, the knuckles like stones. Even so, Ernestine was an imposing woman and within her diminishing form, she held reserves of violence, stored away like winter preserves.

"You ain't hear me calling you?" asked Ma'am.

Jude slid the vegetables from the cutting board into the pot, adjusted the heat. She opened her mouth to the scented steam, thyme and parsley, and exhaled flavor.

"I heard, Ma'am. Dinner's almost done, if you want to set down."

Ma'am groaned as she sat, and Jude returned to her work. There wasn't enough distance between them to dispel her mother's smell of camphor and shit. *She smells old*, thought Jude. *Old and sick.*

"These biscuits is falling," Ma'am said.

"Only settling. Here, I can get you a plate and some butter—"

Ma'am waved her off. "Don't worry yourself. You been doin' a lot today, even with that headache of yours. Living room, bathroom, the shopping, even." She stretched out her legs, hissed, and folded her hands over her stomach.

"It's nothing, Ma'ammy. Better to move with it than lay up in bed."

"That's right, uh-huh. And 'sides, you wouldn't want to muss up your bedroom. Not when you got it all neat and tidy."

Nina Simone begged to not be misunderstood, and Jude watched commas of onion bob in the stew like swimmers treading water. Sweat on her upper lip, sweat pouring down her back. She pushed her face closer to the open window.

Calmly, as plainly as she would discuss weather, Ma'am said, "I went in there lookin' for the sewing tin, and you know what I found in there instead? Can you guess it?"

"Ma'ammy, I didn't want to do it like this."

"A *bag*, Judith. Hidden under the bed and packed with clothes, clothes *I* bought you. And I was thinking, looking at all them things in there, tucked in your little secret bag, how much of it came from my money? How much of it came from my sweat? And *you*, hiding it away, trying to sneak out with it, like a thief."

Jude's nerves were being ground like herbs in a mortar. She was short of breath, short of patience. Wiping the damp from her face, she turned the flame off from under the pot, and then turned to her mother. "I ain't want it like this," Jude started. Her voice was quiet, even. "I wanted us to talk about it, civilly, over dinner, but . . . Well." She exhaled, the metal clasps of her brassiere and girdle digging into her skin. She had her hands up placatingly, spread them open.

"I'm leaving tonight, Ma'am. I'll finish dinner, we can eat, and then I'm going upstairs and I'm taking my bag and I'm leaving."

"You'd leave me here sick? Alone?"

"You won't be alone, Ma'ammy." Jude crossed over to her mother, extended a hand to touch the woman, and then thought better of it. "You have Auntie Vivian and Phyllis, and you can find a nurse to come mind you. It just can't be me."

Ma'am shook her head, incredulous, eyes wide. She whispered, "What kind of child are you? All I've done, all I've sacrificed, and you'd leave me here! *Abandon* me!"

"Ma'ammy, *please.*"

"You can't. You won't." More fiercely, Ma'am shook her head. Her face was pinched, pained, and she was hoarse when she said, "I won't let you."

"Let me?" Jude could not and did not disguise the exasperation in her tone, the exhaustion. She rubbed her hands into her eyes. "Ma'ammy, I'm not a child no more. Look at me," cried Jude, and she stood back, gestured to herself, tall and grown, a person complete. "I can't stay here and let you scream at me and rail at me and beat on me. *Yes*, Ma'ammy, beat on me, like I'm a slave, like I'm a dog to you."

There were tears in Jude's eyes, heat in her face and chest, sick rising in her throat. She said, voice catching, "You don't like me, Ma'am, so why keep me? Why hold me here?"

For a moment, mother and daughter only looked at each other, daughter crying silent tears and mother watching impassively, face like stone. Ma'am wobbled to her feet, stepped toward Jude with a hand outstretched, and Jude flinched away. Ma'am reached again, grabbed hold of Jude's upper arm, and this time Jude wrenched herself bodily from her mother's grasp.

Jude saw it happen in flashes—Ma'am's raised hand, the golden band winking in the light. And then sensation, the sting of the cut, the dribble of blood from high on her cheek, the pain of her head injury renewed, and then, finally, the shame, the mortifying shame of being so grown, taller than her mother, and to be slapped across the face like she was nothing more than a woman from off the street.

Jude staggered back, back to the counter, and threw out a hand to catch herself from falling. Cleaver and cutting board dropped, clattering, to the floor, vegetable scraps skating across the wicker weave. When she looked up at her mother, hand to her cheek, she saw nothing in Ma'am's eyes, not even hatred. Again, the apathy struck harder than the blow.

Body hot with humiliation and with wrath bucking in her like wild horses, Jude slapped her mother back. All her life, she thought striking back would be on par with murder, that every time she resisted the belt, the palm, all she bought herself was more grief, a weapon that promised more damage. But now Jude was the weapon; the whistling switch plucked of its leaves, the leather strop, the wire hanger, and the phone cord all in one, swinging wildly, catching without prejudice the breasts and genitalia, tearing up the back and buttocks and stomach, lashing arms and legs. Jude beat Ma'am nastily, ruthlessly. With one hand she clawed her mother's hand and with the other she pulled out clumps of heat-damaged hair. Old anger exhumed, past indignities remembered; the taste smacked out of her mouth and teeth on the hardwood, her head striking the wall. Jude gritted her teeth and did not stop.

It was not a fair fight, Ma'am being older, diminished, but it hadn't been fair back then either, when Jude was too small and afraid to flee the belt. Jude kicked her mother's leg out from underneath her, meaning for her to fall alone, but Ma'am grabbed hold of her as she fell, dragged Jude to the floor. The house shook as they landed, a bodily shudder that grounded cherubs, porcelain wings hissing across the tile like garden snakes, disappearing beneath the stove. Ma'am screamed at the loss of her angels, at landing hard and painfully on her hip.

They sat apart, Jude on her back and Ma'am on her side, panting, sweating. Jude was still catching her breath and plotting her next move when Ma'am scrabbled over, clambered on top of her, and wrapped her hands around Jude's neck.

It was slow going, quiet. The only noise was the radio, Jude's grunting and whimpering, the squeak of her feet against the floor. She scratched Ma'am's arms, tried prying off the iron vise from her throat, but her grip was too strong. The hands around her neck had hauled hundred-pound bags of cotton and laundry, had picked rice and cut down sugarcane, had hoed and tilled and dug for longer than Jude had been alive. Ma'am slammed her head against the floor (sparks, blackness and then sparks, explosions of light), glared down at Jude, cold and unfeeling, her eyes as empty as insect husks. Bloody drool plopped wetly onto Jude's cut cheek.

Urine cooling rapidly on her skin, cold tile on her back. With wide, bulging eyes, more bloodshot white than black iris, Jude stared up into her mother's face. Beautiful, beautiful! What a picture she made, and how honest she looked to Jude, snarling, nostrils flared, the facade of motherly love done away with at last. The frankness of it, the stench of her piss and fear, her mother's sweat, her anger, was all Jude had to hold on to. Her mind was slipping, loosening. Brain lacking for oxygen, vision dimming, the air flowed white, then red. She felt each and every one of her violent prayers as lightning behind her eyes, as an infestation of roaches skittering through her brain. Jude wanted death, wanted to be finished with this whole ugly affair, but her body, resolute in its determination to see Ma'am dead, wouldn't let her quit.

Jude flicked her eyes from side to side, searching the floor until she saw the gleaming, grimacing blade of the cleaver. She threw out her hand, fingers clawing the tile, and grabbed for the handle. She grabbed the blade instead, virgin blood like crushed cherries against the steel. Jude took hold of the knife, took hold of herself. The kitchen lights blinked above her like beacons.

Jude gripped the knife, raised it high, and sank it into her mother's face.

The knife lodged itself into her temple and sank down half an inch before Jude was able to adjust her grip and pull it farther, the movement of her hands purposeful if not steady. The blade cut through the eyelid, the cornea, split the iris, stuttered across the broad nose and sliced the lips into four distinct sections. Ma'am's face, Jude's first mirror, halved on the diagonal; it burst, split. Blood, hot and dark, poured over them both, Ma'am's hands and Jude's face, her neck, her chest.

With a sharp pull of breath, Ma'am released Jude, her unharmed eye spinning wildly in its socket. She felt her face, felt its ruined edges and struggled to her feet. Stumbling, slippers sliding through her own blood, Ma'am staggered over to the stewpot to see her reflection. Red fingers danced over the jellied eye, the shredded lips, the nose and its dangling nostril. She lowed, hands trembling, and soon her lowing became short, panicked screams. Again, she touched her ruined face, touched her reflection. Vomit poured awkwardly from her broken mouth, caught itself in the grooves of her lips, and splattered onto her robe, the floor. Reeling, Ma'am backed away from the pot, slipped in the mess of blood and vomit, and fell to the floor with a house-shaking thud.

Wheezing, panting, Jude touched her throat. The pain of swallowing was lost among other, grander pains, and the left side of her body tingled numbly. Her head was on fire; the lights were too bright, everything too sharp and clear, and in her ear, she heard buzzing, chirring, crashing. She rolled her eyes, breathed laboriously, coughed and spat up globs of blood. Her sounds were inhuman, bestial grunts and moans, and Jude clawed her way across the room, until she was at Ma'am's side.

Ma'am with her Picasso face looked up at Jude, whimpering, scanned her daughter's face for mercy. Jude barked out a laugh. How many times had she prayed, pleaded, and gone unheeded? And now it was her turn to play God, her turn to turn a deaf ear. She rose to her knees to get a better look at her mother. There was no way for Ma'am to survive her comeuppance; she'd either die then and there, quickly, or else later in the evening, gagging on her own sick. The wrothful portion of Jude thrilled at the thought of it, Ma'am prone and suffering, begging for a mercy that would never come. The rest of her, the portion that wept to think her mother didn't love her, swallowed her rising bile.

Jude met her mother's eye. She watched the eye widen, search, and then close before taking up the cleaver and drawing a line across Ma'am's throat. The blood of the lamb cleansed, restored, but Ma'am's blood only scorched and stained.

A minute Jude sat by her mother's side, then two, then ten. Blood and life left her, the singsong gasp of her final breath. Jude got to her feet, washed her hands in the sink. The clean skin was like long brown gloves compared to the rest of her, drenched in scarlet.

Back at her mother's side, Jude covered the woman's face with a dish towel, held and kissed her hand, slipped the golden band off her ring finger, and slid it onto her own.

Jude held her hand up to the light. The ring smiled, and Jude smiled back.

3

Now it was done. Now she was her own creature, no longer her mother's child, though she felt newly born, cast in red, her mother's fluids in her mouth, her hair. Jude blinked, and through a scrim of crimson saw the wicked works of her hands. Had she really done this? Had she really—

In all her forty-one years, she'd never been truly alone. Always, there was Ma'am just out of sight, in another room, always the promise of Ma'am returning. Dazedly, Jude walked the house. Hers was a tidy prison, all brick and odd-cut rooms, decades of amassed furniture, plastic-covered sofas. The walls were papered brightly, the windows were many, and yet the house was grim, lightless. Jude wondered how it was that a house could be so unfriendly, whether the menace was foundational or if it was something tracked in on somebody's shoe.

Unmoored from herself, Jude wandered upstairs and into her mother's en suite. She perched on the rim of the avocado-green tub and filled the basin with the hottest water she could stand, poured in scent from a vial of tuberose oil. She dipped a hand to test the heat, then a foot, another foot. Jude hissed as she settled into the bath. In the humid heat of the bathroom, she naturalized, hair frizzing, skin flushing dark. She was patient with herself, slow working the grime from her limbs and hair, scrubbing gently to lift the layers of blood. The water was brown when she left it, murky with dead skin.

Before the kitchen, the warped tile, and the world washed red, Jude was forbidden from going into her mother's room without express invitation. Dirty hands, dirty feet—Ma'am didn't want Jude's grubby fingers touching her bedroom set, the four-poster bed and white vanity with its large, glittering mirror. Fine for then, but now it was Jude who wore the golden band. Thus emboldened, she pored through Ma'am's little box of jewelry (string of off-white pearls, costume rings, a pretty pair of sapphire earrings Jude never remembered her mother wearing), her wardrobe, which housed Ma'am's sensible shoes and blouses, starched skirts and dresses, the bleach-white usher's uniform she wore to church each Sunday.

Bare skinned, Jude considered the bed. It was unmade; a faintly ammoniac scent puffed from the sheets, and Jude felt embarrassed for her prideful mother, who, even at her weakest, refused incontinence pads and scorned all references to chamber pots. *She'd sit in her own filth before admitting she needed me*, thought Jude, and the thinking of it made her sorry for what she'd done. Beyond the stink of the bed, the room smelled of her mother's cologne, the oil she daubed on her wrists. How long would the smell last? Jude wondered. If the bedroom door was never again opened, if no one bothered to see about the chifforobe, the purple-pink quilt folded at the end of the bed, it might go on stinking for years, the odors woven into the very fibers of the carpet.

Jude returned to her own bedroom to find it in chaos. All she owned was strewn around, ripped and torn. Her traveling bag sat on the bed like an accusation, her clothing removed and slashed. With the strained patience of one accustomed to destruction, Jude filed through the mess, sorting the salvageable from the ruined. She mourned the loss of her books, a favorite dress, and then repacked, rolling the gauze back into the first aid kit, finding and replacing each of her needles, pins.

From her hidden tin, she gathered her money, and then she went through the house in search of her mother's niches for hidden cash. Five dollars here, a couple of nickels there; in the sofa cushions, sewn into the stuffing, were twelve wadded bands—the whole of her mother's savings and the money left for her by Pappy. Jude took it all, stuffed it into her brassiere and the pockets of her skirt, sewed the rest of it into the lining of a coat, and left, at last, her mother's house.

Outside, her head began to clear. What now? What would she do now? Jude threw her bag into the back seat of her mother's sober burgundy Studebaker, hands trembling on the door's handle. *Sweet Lord*, she thought. *Jesus, what have I done?* Jesus did not answer, said nothing to help as Jude slid into the front seat and adjusted the mirrors, checked the seats and glove box for registration, maps. The two maps she found were outdated by a year, sticky, but seemingly reliable. It panicked her to look at them—her world was compact, insular. All she knew, really, were a handful of places, church and home and a couple of stores, homechurchstore, homechurchstore, homechurchstore, and sometimes, rarely, the park, or to Auntie Viv's house or Auntie Phil's house, but nowhere else, not even to the theater.

Jude started the car and peeled out of the long, winding driveway. She drove without direction, surprised by each turn she took. She was still within the city limits when she took her first break about an hour or so after she had left. There wasn't enough on her belly, and she was flagging, nauseated with hunger. At a diner friendly to Negroes, Jude ordered water and a plate of eggs. The waitress who served her was a young slip of a thing, chatty and brash with the few other customers, but when she came to Jude she looked solemnly and furtively at her parti-colored face and neck. To spare the waitress the embarrassment of questions, Jude asked her for the time ("Quarter after nine, Ma'am") and if the diner had a phone.

"There's a booth outside. You can't miss it."

Jude thanked her, paid the dollar she owed for her meal, and walked to the phone booth. Without quite registering the movement of her fingers, Jude dialed her aunt Phyllis's house. She hoped the woman wouldn't answer, hoped she would ignore the ringing, but she knew too that the noise would startle Phyllis from her sleep. In her mind's eye, she saw her aunt in her robe and slippers, bleary-eyed, grumbling down the hall to discover just who had the nerve to wake an old woman. She flexed her injured hand, resisted the urge to slam down the receiver before anyone picked up.

The line connected. Her aunt's voice, husky with sleep: "Hello?"

"Hello, Auntie Phil. It's Judith."

"Judith? Girl, don't you know what time it is? What is this?"

There was fear in her aunt's voice, despite her trying to suppress it. She thought of Phyllis clutching the receiver with her thin, bony seamstress's hands, and squeezed her eyes shut until the lights behind her eyes had blotted out the image.

"I need to . . . I need to talk to you about Ma'ammy, Auntie Phyllis."

Silence from the other side, a crackle of static and then a hissing, exasperated sigh. "Don't start this again, Judith. I can't hear it no more, I won't."

"You have to hear me," said Jude, firmly as she could manage. Her throat was tightening and her eyes burned with the start of tears. "Listen, Auntie, I wouldn't call if it wasn't important. I wouldn't . . ." Her voice caught and in a high, choked voice, she cried, "I don't . . . Auntie, just hear me—"

"No, sister, you listen to *me*." Phyllis's voice, usually honey-sweet and tempered, went as steely as her sister's. "I don't understand this, this constant whining about God knows what. And your mother, ill as she is, having to take your attitude, your complaining, after all she's done for you!"

Food in your belly and clothes on your back and shoes on your feet, and *I brought you into this world and I can take you out,* and on and on. Jude held her tongue. Phyllis could interrupt her, speak over her, but Jude couldn't do the same. She took her lashings in silence, trembling, inwardly scolding herself for having indulged the notion of sympathy. Hadn't she been shown, time and time again, that her aunts were not to be relied upon? Hadn't Phyllis watched her sister beat and berate her? Jude dug her teeth into the meat of her inner lips, scratched the booth's metal until silver paint flaked off in her hand. Ran her uninjured hand along a jagged edge, searching for something sturdy enough to cut herself on.

"—Selfish! Just selfish and ugly and ungrateful. Coming to me and Vivian cryin' about a little smack to the head! What is it you have to do in that house—where you live for free, mind you—that's so awful? The dishes? The *laundry*?"

Jude excused herself from the conversation and turned her attention to the metal biting into her skin, the pearl of scarlet that rolled down her palm and onto her wrist. She put her mouth to it. The night was loud around her; she gave the crickets her ear, Phyllis's voice fading to nothing as she soothed herself on her blood.

Phyllis asked again why Jude was calling and Jude snapped back to the present. Sense and impulse warred within her. *Ma'am's hurt, see Ma'am on the floor; she slapped me across the face like I was common, and I had to, I had to.*

"I had to do it, Auntie," said Jude. "I *had* to."

"Had to do what?" asked Phyllis. "What are you talkin' about?"

Jude closed her eyes, ran her bloodied hand across the booth's smudged window. "I don't think I'm sorry."

"Sorry about what?" There was a note of alarm in Phyllis's voice, and it gave Jude a sick twist of pleasure, the thought of Phyllis affected by something she said. "Not sorry for what, girl? What are you saying?"

She held her breath, held the feeling of blood drying on her palm and the music of the crickets, the coolness of the metal against her cheek. Without answering, Jude slammed down the receiver and exited the booth, clenching and releasing her hands.

Back on the road, Jude pointed the car southeast. It wasn't a conscious decision—she liked the names on the map, Macon and Perry and Valdosta. Down and down she went, farther into stands of trees and down narrower roads. She lost track of herself, hands and feet drifting off into space. Night and highway unspooled before her, weaving, curling, tangling into the dark canopies of the spruce pines, sweet gums.

Paranoid of violence, the meanness of white folk, Jude kept to herself, stopping only when she was desperate. City after city, Unadilla, Vienna. In Sibley, Jude was hungry enough to risk dinner. The people there weren't bloodthirsty, but they weren't kind either. The white woman who served her wouldn't let her sit inside to eat, so Jude sat in her car, forced herself through a mug of tarry coffee.

Deeper into Georgia she drove, through towns and unincorporated villages with names like fine ladies. Mind aflame with luminescent thoughts, body abuzz with the terror-awe of her violence, Jude wondered at the breadth of the world. For so long, there was only her mother's house on Westmoor, and now there was everything, too much. It was as if the earth, having sensed the boiling, bubbling energy jailed within Jude, was opening itself to her. Burning, Jude bore witness to the world's colorful insides, the greens and blacks streaking past her window like watercolors.

She crisscrossed county lines, the radio's signal scrambling. Soft, twanging country songs of wheat and long-lost somebodies bled into cheery pop ballads. Pentecostal pastors screeched about corrupting influences and called down mercy for the end of days, their high tinny voices struggling to be heard over the lonesome moaning of jazz and blues. *I go out walkin' after midnight, out in the moonlight, just like we used to do . . . Catch a falling star and put it in your pocket . . . Just sit there and count your fingers . . . In your towns, in your churches and schools, yes, even in the schools with your own little children,* yes, *criminals,* freaks, *niggers sitting in the seat beside your wife, sir, sharing water with your little daughter!*

Five, almost six hours later, somewhere between Folkston and Millard, she brought the car to a stop. The map informed her that she was somewhere near the Okefenokee and the Georgia–Florida line, but not much else. Jude pondered her options. The night was alive with noise, owls and frogs, nocturnal insects singing in chorus. Ahead of her, two signs; one sign warned travelers that they were approaching government-protected natural land, and the other, below it, pointed to the right and read, "Whitnee, Two Miles East."

Somewhere, a twig snapped, and elsewhere, a bird startled from a tree.

"Alright," said Jude. "Well, alright."

4

Phyllis didn't know which was worse, being woken up in the dead of night or having the phone slammed down on her. Ears ringing, off-kilter, Phyllis replaced the receiver. The nerve of that girl, ringing whenever she like, saying such crazy things! Her heart did a little two-step in her chest, and she made herself breathe slow to settle it.

She was never so cold to her niece as her sisters were. Too soft, she supposed, her heart worn tender by the longing she felt for her baby boy, Monrose. What Ernestine and Vivian took as purposeful acts of rebellion, Phyllis took as growing pains, and she often wondered if her sisters would be as rough with Monrose as they were with Judith. She was only a girl, Phyllis thought, and then only a woman, an overgrown child, all bent neck and distracted.

Now, though, Phyllis reconsidered her position. Maybe Ernestine was right about her. *Phyllis* would've never thought of talking to an elder the way Jude spoke to her. Wryly Phyllis smiled, recalling the first and only time she had mouthed off to her father's sister—something mumbled under the breath, something slick, no doubt, and quicker than she could prepare for *pow!* Right in the face, eleven-year-old Phyllis with a busted nose and black eye. Never had anything slick to say after that, that's for sure.

Phyllis glanced at the wall clock—nine twenty in the evening. Resolving to call Ernestine about her daughter at a more reasonable hour, she returned to her bed, slippers shuffling loudly against the wood. She removed her glasses, laid down her head. In her final moments of wakefulness, her niece's words echoed in her mind.

I had to do it, Auntie, I had to. I don't think I'm sorry.

Phyllis called Ernestine at their usual time, nine in the morning. It was a tradition of sorts, the sisters' daily calls, ever since the three managed to scrounge up the money to buy matching rotary phones. Once in the morning, once after work, and, occasionally, once more after dinner, the sisters called one and then the other, sharing their days, gossiping, complaining, offering and receiving prayer requests or advice, swapping details about church meetings and community goings-on, ideas they'd had for meals, blankets.

The phone rang on and on. *Must be asleep still*, thought Phyllis, though why the girl didn't just pick up the phone for her ailing mother, she didn't understand. Another tick against her. Phyllis clicked her tongue, tried again. After the third attempt, Phyllis called Vivian; the woman answered on the first ring.

"Viv? That you, girl?"

"Don't know who else would be in my house," replied Vivian dryly. Phyllis heard her cooking breakfast, eggs and bacon popping in the pan. "You hear from Nessie today?"

"That's what I'm calling you about. I tried her, but nobody answered."

"Might be she's still asleep. G'on and try her again."

Phyllis felt a bead of worry form in her throat and she rolled it around, pinched it to keep it small. "I did. Rang her two, three times and nothing." The bead of worry thickened. Phyllis swallowed around it, pushing out the words, "You don't think she's hurt, do you?"

Silence from Vivian's side, the sound of frying fat like a tap rushing in Phyllis's ear. At length, Vivian said, "I doubt it. Bet you anything she still in bed, though I wonder why that girl ain't answer. Thought she was raised better than that, at least."

Heat rose behind Phyllis's eyes, an unsteady thumping in her chest. She thought of Judith's call; it seemed so silly in daylight, the shadows cast by furtive night talking replaced by bemused unease.

Toying at the topic, Phyllis said, "Was funny—you know, Judith had the nerve to call me, round nine last night. I couldn't make head nor tails of what she was saying, some mess about *having* to do something and not being sorry, I don't know."

"I keep tellin' you, Philly, that girl ain't right."

Phyllis hummed. "Think I might go see about Nessie. Won't hurt none to put my eyes on her. Come along?"

Vivian sucked her teeth, sighed. "May as well. I'll walk down to yours and we can go together. Put your fool mind at ease, at least."

Half an hour later, Vivian trundled up the path to Phyllis's house, as steady and impervious as a steamboat cutting through water. Vivian had their mother's face, brown skin and a mean, narrow nose, dark squinting eyes that got lost in the fullness of her cheeks. The resemblance was made even truer by Vivian's getup, the ankle-length dress and scarf-covered head, the purse she held securely in front of her as she waited impatiently for Phyllis to lock her door. From the corner of her eye, Phyllis watched her sister's profile, her twitching mouth.

It was a twenty-five-minute walk from Thurmond Street to the house on Westmoor Drive. The sisters took their time, speaking little on their walk. Phyllis's worry was big enough to hold in two hands; she could no longer pinch it into shape.

They came upon the green wall that separated Ernestine's house from the street, a natural fence of princess trees and southern catalpa, thick vines of kudzu. Cloaking the brick house was a strange, undulating gray light. Like smog it sat low and heavy over the second story, blacking out the windows, and Phyllis knew, just from watching it move, that it was a physical thing, tangible. Knew crossing through it would be like crossing through cold grits.

"You see that?" asked Phyllis.

"I see it," said Vivian, and with a sharp inhale, she straightened her back and marched up the flagstone path to the front door, Phyllis close at her heels. Vivian knocked gently and then urgently. She peered in through the living room window, saw nothing, and gave the doorknob a turn. To their shared shock, the door swung open without protest.

"Viv..."

"I know."

The smell was the first thing to greet the sisters. Hot and rank, it coated their tongues, spilled down their throats. Images of decay flashed in Phyllis's mind—her father's necrotic foot, the gangrene eating his leg; her mother's barely cold body, never-breathing baby brother like a blood clot between her legs; her lynched uncle, her beaten husband, their faces bloated and tummies distended, and throughout each memory, the flies, the flies, the incessant drone of blackflies.

Neither sister met the other's eye as they followed the smell to its source. If they looked at each other, if they stopped for even a moment to consider what waited for them, a support beam would break in one sister or the other, and there'd be no recovering.

Vivian led the way, following the track of red footprints leading from the front room and down the hall, through the dining room, and, at last, into the kitchen.

Wind and silence, mourning doves singing counterpoint to the thrushes. The radio was playing a Sonny & Cher song—*Babe, I got you babe! I got you babe!*

There was too much blood. Oceans of it, rivers of it, inlets, enough to flood the grout. The odor was concentrated here, pure rot and heat, emptied bowels. In the center of the room, a body like an island surrounded by boats of porcelain shards.

For a good long while, neither Phyllis nor Vivian could move or speak. There was a shining behind Phyllis's eye, a migraine like a needle, radiating and burning with white light. If she could grab hold of it, she'd dig her fingers into her skull and pluck out the sight, the pain. *If thy right eye offend thee . . .*

She didn't know which of them made the first step. Only knew that one moment they were at the threshold of the room, mute and catatonic with shock, and in the next they were at Ernestine's side. There was a dish towel over her face. Vivian plucked it off, and Phyllis hated her for it. Beneath the towel was Ernestine, red red red, splayed and still, one eye blown wide and the other nothing but jelly. The mouth that had kissed them, sang with them, sassed them, was torn. Never again would she whistle a working song or whisper to them a story born out of her own mind. And her neck. My *Lord*, sit here Jesus, set *here*, her neck was cut clean across and deep, with barely any meat and skin connecting her head to her body.

Phyllis half screamed, half choked, and fell hard to her knees. The pain of landing on tile was faint compared to the horror that burned her. What prayers could she say? What hymns guarded a soul against such a sight?

"Her *eye*," moaned Phyllis. She touched Ernestine's face, stomach roiling at the shifting skin, the fat and sinew beneath it. "Oh, Vivian, her eye!"

Vivian's face was grim but motionless. *She's holding on to herself*, thought Phyllis. *Just like Nessie taught her. Get a grip of you, take your gallbladder, your intestines, your spleen, whatever, just have a hold of it, and don't let up for nothing.* It was what kept them standing throughout countless deaths, miseries. Phyllis fell too fast to catch herself in time, but Vivian was deep in that place, eyes distant as they welled with tears. Slower, Vivian knelt beside Phyllis. She clasped and unclasped her hands, moving to prayer and then suddenly catching herself, shocked from piety by the viscera at her feet.

"Poor gal," sighed Vivian. "Poor, poor gal."

Phyllis took her sister's cold hand in hers. They were calloused from working under Mr. Humphrey's whip, Daddy's belt. Scars and scabs from knife accidents, iron burns, an ugly blister from when she burned herself with lye. They weren't soft, but they could try at gentleness. She thought of Ernestine teaching her hand-games, braiding her hair. Phyllis ran her hand over the curled-in fingers and paused.

"Her band—they took the gold band."

Vivian raised her head and shook it. "Whoever did this to her must've took it. They take anything else?"

Phyllis glanced around the red and terrible room. The front door had been open and the windows were whole, but in the front room, the couch cushions had been torn. She said as much to Vivian and the woman frowned.

"This world, this wicked world," Vivian said. She turned away from Ernestine and Phyllis to weep, one hand over her mouth and the other clutching her heart. "Oh Jesus, my Lord, my Lord. Poor gal."

Phyllis settled onto her haunches. There was still lightning behind her eyes but she could direct it now, move it around her brain to light pathways, creases. She swept her eyes over the room, to the open window and broken glass babies. Phyllis cradled Nessie's head. There was no sound, only the groan of the house settling. Phyllis shone the blade of light and pain back to the nine o'clock phone call.

I had to do it. I had to. I don't think I'm sorry.

The blade of light plummeted from her mind, sliced through her lungs and heart, and landed, point first, into her belly. Nausea cut her like a gust of icy wind, sudden and startling, and she fought to hold on to her breakfast.

"Vivian. Where's Judith?"

5

Whitnee was like most of the towns Jude drove through—small, proud, and white as bone. It was nostalgic for its antebellum days, days of timber, bitter about broken promises to drain the swamps, and its mourning for the past was evident in the town's painted sign, the white faces haloed by cotton and rice, fish jumping from the water. It was all very charming, gas lamps and white clapboard, sturdy little buildings built up by granddaddies, great-granddaddies. Along the main street was a Pentecostal church, a decent-sized general store advertising the last sweet watermelon of the season, as well as a post office, a diner, and a butcher's shop, whole pigs with their meats spilling from them.

Jude found the inn farther up the road. Rustic, slapdash, the only proof of it being open was an orange light flickering in the window.

She hesitated. Hospitality, to Jude, was limited to the homes of distant relatives, bunking down with cousins on pallets and cots, breakfast in the morning. Her blood hummed and her lids felt weighted, but she could not afford to be a fool. What good would it do her, making it so far and escaping her mother, only to end up in meaner hands?

In the end, exhaustion and hunger won out, Jude telling herself that anything that wanted her neck could have it, so long as it gave her a drink of water and a pillow beforehand. She parked the car and entered the inn. It was pleasant inside if a little stale, like mildew and tobacco, and the carpet was gray-brown with grime. Some effort had been made to modernize the lobby, a few armchairs and a coffee table splayed with outdated newspapers, but the inn resisted time. In love with its glory days, the inn, much like the town it resided in, refused to submit to the reality of 1965.

Jude dinged the bell once, twice. On the third ding, a white girl cinched into a tatted bathrobe emerged from a back room. She squinted at Jude, frowned.

Hoarsely, Jude asked, "Y'all serve food, miss?"

"It's the offseason. 'Sides, we don't do handouts. You want something that bad, you can ask the colored church come morning."

She turned to leave, and Jude called out to her, saying, "I got money, miss." She dug into her pocket, pulled out a few bills, and showed them to the girl. "Whatever it is, I can pay."

The girl looked dubiously at the money and then at Jude. After a moment, she shrugged, put the money into her pocket, and gestured with her head for Jude to follow her.

In a kitchen no bigger than the lobby, the girl gave Jude her name—"Bette, like Davis"—and an unsteady wooden chair. Jude told Bette to call her Ness as she removed her coat, clutched it on her lap. With little conversation, Bette moved around Jude, pouring water and loading a plate with food from pots on the stove. It was meager fare, gray and flavorless, but Jude was too hungry to care. In between bites of boiled meat and dinner rolls stale enough to hammer nails with, she answered Bette's prying questions.

"You from round here, Ness?"

"No, miss. I'm from up north. Chicago."

"That so?" Bette hummed. "Guess you came down to see the forest. You ever been?"

Jude shook her head. "This'll be my first time. I don't think I ever been this far south before."

Whether or not Bette believed her stories, Jude didn't know and didn't care. It was three in the morning now—she hoped to be long gone by sunrise. After a second helping of food ("Lord but you sure can *eat*, Ness!"), Jude asked if there was anywhere she could stay for the night, an inn for colored people, or maybe someone's home.

"Maybe? I don't know much about that side of town," Bette confessed, shrugging.

"Is it very far?"

Another shrug. "You could walk it if you had to." She looked Jude up and down, eyes catching on her bandages and bruises. "Though I'm guessin' you might not want to."

"Any chance you let me take a room for the night, Miss Bette?"

The white girl scoffed and kissed her teeth as she rose from her seat, taking Jude's plate and cutlery and tossing them into the nearby garbage can. The waste of it annoyed Jude more than the insult, and she leaned up in her own chair, tone sharp as she spoke.

"Miss, I promise I don't like to be here no more than you do. If I had the strength in me, I'd go, but I'm tired, tired enough to fall right from this chair and die. Now, you can have a dead nigger in your kitchen, dirtying up your floor"—Jude gestured to the tacky, dust-covered linoleum—"or, you can rent me a room, and I'll be gone fore anybody ever knew you served me."

Bette narrowed her eyes, thin lips pressed thinner with thought. The gaze of white folk was dangerous, likely deadly, but Jude, full up on death and raw with fatigue, matched Bette's glare with her own blank, tired stare.

At length, the white girl hemmed and bade Jude follow her. Jude went, surprised, relieved, down a plain, unadorned hall to a tiny, bare room. In it was a narrow bed too short for Jude's height, a dust-gray nightstand, and a small, high window that let in a thin sliver of moonlight.

"You can have an hour," said Bette before leaving. Jude locked the door after her and took a seat on the bed. The trip her eyes took from the door to the opposite wall was laughably short. Ruefully, she thought of the bedroom she'd left behind, the white furniture that had been with her since childhood. When the moon came to her there, it was like the eye of God staring down at her, washing her in white.

Here there was only darkness, a sunken mattress stinking of mothballs. Jude kicked off her shoes, checked and replaced her head gauze, retied her scarf, and reclined on the bed, hands folded over her stomach. She was asleep almost immediately; she dreamed of glass cherubs.

Be it out of guilt or pity or kindness, Bette let Jude sleep another hour over the one she was promised. When she knocked at the door to the closet-sized room, it was five in the morning, dark, the sliver of moonlight that had crept along the wall earlier having moved out of sight.

Back in the kitchen, Bette provided Jude with bacon and toasted bread, a mug of weak and sugarless tea. Once Jude had eaten, Bette took the flatware, hesitating with it before taking it to the sink. Afterward, she leaned against the wall, arms folded across her flat chest, and asked, "Where'd you say you were comin' from again, Ness?"

"Chicago, miss."

"Oh? Round what part?"

Jude remained silent, focused entirely on her tea.

"Only, I don't think I've ever heard anybody with an accent like yours that came from up north." When Jude again did not respond, Bette came off the wall, shouting, "I *knew* it! Chicago, my ass! Farthest north you're from is Atlanta! Should've guessed it—them clothes, that car you got out front, all that money! Stolen, I bet anything!"

Jude blinked at the accusation, alarm rising in her like steam. Bette was right, but there was too much righteous indignation in her voice, too much joy at having correctly sniffed out her nature, of having ugly thoughts proved right. Her alarm morphed into annoyance, then anger. What did Bette know? She was just a girl, barely into her twenties. Her only authority came from her white skin. What did she know about running, about wicker weave washed in red, and the sound a skull made against plaster?

Jaw set, Jude spat, "What it matter to you? You took my money, didn't you?"

"I'll call the law," said Bette.

"Do it then. Call the law, wake the whole damn town. Just make sure you empty out your pockets when they come, Lord knows how much of my *stolen* money you stuffed in them!"

Bette drew back from the outburst. "You really not fraid of them coming to get you, are you?"

"Can't nothing be done to me that I haven't had worse."

The white girl nodded. She flicked her eyes to Jude's neck and hands, the gauze with its sunburst of blood tacked to her forehead. "I think I know where you can stay."

Bette went first and Jude trailed after, clutching her quilted bag.

"It's a ways from here—the walk's about an hour, if you stay on the path. There's a way to get it by car, I think, a little service road from when they were doing some logging out there, but it's useless at night."

"Begging your pardon, miss, but where you sending me?"

"There's a house in the woods. I never seen it myself, but you hear stories. Was a plantation at some point, and then there were two nigger girls up there, escaped or free or whatever." Bette tossed information over her shoulder as she led Jude into a storage closet. She clicked a string, revealed shelves of cans and linen. "Whoever they were, they were funny, with funny ways. Folks in town swore up and down that they were up to all sorts of evil, witchcraft and the like. Course, Whitnee being a godly town, they didn't take well to that so they got themselves a posse together and went out to see what could be done about them."

There was an excited edge to the white woman's voice, a cheeriness that belied the ugliness of her words. It surprised Jude when Bette told her not of lynchings, but of an empty farmhouse, meticulous save for a shrine in the cellar loaded with tokens, moldy plates of food, and the butts of melted candles. The bedroom was neat, the bed made and the floor swept.

"What happened to the women?" asked Jude.

Bette shrugged, threw batteries and a massive yellow flashlight into Jude's bag. "Nobody knows. Might've heard the posse was comin' and ran, or maybe they got ate up by something in the forest. We got bears round here, you know, and gators. Anyways, there wasn't so much as a shoe left behind. And some people . . ." She trailed off, hand hovering in the air.

"Miss?"

"Well, like I said, *I* never saw the place, all this having happened years fore I was born. I don't hold with spooks and the like, but *some* folk, they *think* something weird happened out there. They go up, looking to scare themselves, and come back with stories about footsteps and faces in the wall, furniture dancing all on its own. Some nigger," said Bette, glancing at Jude before clearing her throat. "Some *man*, he said the house tried to get inside him, eat him from the inside out. You believe in things like that?"

"A little," Jude admitted. Ma'am had dosed her with equal amounts of religion and superstition, the Bible balanced with tales of haints, the lingering dead. "Do you?"

Bette made a thoughtful noise and said, "I don't know. I reckon people will believe all sorts when they're in the middle of nowhere. Gators and ghosts and grizzlies—it don't do a mind good being that alone, especially when you got them fool stories in your head."

"And that's why you letting me have it, huh? 'Cause nobody else wants it?"

"Nobody but the ghosts." Bette smirked. "People have tried using it for hunting or camping, but nobody bothers with it no more. 'Sides, folks will be too scared to upset the spooks to come see another up in the woods. You'd be all alone." She nodded to the bruises circling Jude's neck. "Safe from whatever put that mean necklace on you, at least."

Jude touched a hand to her throat, thinking over the offer while Bette finished putting the last of the supplies into her bag. She didn't fear haints, or at least, she didn't think she did. So thin was the veil between life and death, faint as gossamer—the dead did not leave her family. They lived, in photo albums and locks of hair, in death stories retold ad nauseam, in the hearts of those who were hainted by them. Even now, Ma'am stood at her back, breathing, filling the storage closet with her rotten perfume.

"How much you want for it?"

"Take it," said Bette. "Like I said, nobody goes there and nobody wants it."

Bette handed Jude a brass ring of keys. "Front door, cellar, keys for the rooms upstairs. There's a generator, electric lights, but most likely, everything up there runs off wood or gas."

"Any plumbing?"

"Basic stuff, definitely a pump and a well. You'll be living off your wits out there."

Jude took her bag, slipped her keys into the pocket of her coat. She stood ready at the inn's door, and Bette gave her a final appraising look before saying, "Say . . . What did happen to your neck?"

"I got into a fight."

Bette kissed her teeth. "*Shoo*, whoever it was sure had one helluva grip! Hope you left 'em with something to match it."

Shards of porcelain, big body beached in a sea of scarlet. A dish towel over the face so she wouldn't have to see it. "Got her good enough," said Jude. She stepped outside and Bette led her down the street, across the little footbridge to the colored side of town and to an unpaved dirt path that disappeared in a tall, dark wall of trees.

"Right through there. There's a path, but not much of it. Gonna have to use your horse sense, but you'll know the place when you see it—big ol' overgrown field and then a farmhouse."

On a scrap of paper, Bette drew a crude map—a child's rendering of a house in the center of a circle, a winding line curving around swamps and ponds. Thus armed, Jude thanked Bette with a nod and went alone into the woods.

6

Jude entered the verdant maw of the woods, past its bark teeth and down its mossy throat, down into its humid green bowels. Surrounding her were bald cypress and swamp tupelo, their shapes made indistinct by thick blankets of kudzu. There were figures in the ivy, penitents bent in prayer, genuflecting on a periwinkle-and-bugleweed carpet. Fat mosquitoes circled Jude's head and gorged themselves on the blood of her neck, wrists, while fireflies danced before her, beckoning her farther.

Never before had Jude known a place so vast, so full. She was used to nature being contained—church picnics in secluded fields, the fence of green that fortressed the Westmoor house, her mother's tidy garden with its rosebushes, tomatoes big enough to eat like hand fruit.

Ma'am preferred nature small, tamable. She had had too much of it as a child. According to Ma'am, the whole of their family came from that plantation, four generations of Rices having slaved the land, even after emancipation.

"There wasn't nothing your pappy cared for save for working

and money," Ma'am said once. Jude had, somehow, caught her mother in a generous mood, and she listened with bald interest to stories about man-high stalks of sugar, the rows of cotton and scheming overseers, the tallyman with his hand on the scale. "The minute we girls was big enough to pick a boll, he had us out on the line with him and Momma. Never knew a day of settin' down till we came out to the city."

When asked what it was like, living on the plantation, Ma'am's eyes would fall and darken, and she'd say how green it was, how beautiful the trees were, even when strung with folks she knew. She asked her aunts too—Phyllis recalled Humphrey's son, their maybe cousin, the red-faced overseer with his hand on his whip; Vivian recalled its vastness, how no matter how far she ran, she could never reach the end of it.

"It was God's land if you owned it," said Ma'am. "Hell on earth if you worked it."

The moon abandoned her and Jude relied on the flashlight to guide her way. By stark white light, she navigated raised roots, fallen trunks, rocks, and patches of earth so eroded by streams and storms that the merest step collapsed them. The Okefenokee held its breath.

She touched little, but much touched Jude, branches carding like lover's fingers through her hair. Moths crowded the flashlight, cobwebs veiled her face. Jude breathed, and each inhale brought in spiders, spores, and the freshest air she'd ever tasted. She followed the path when she could, and where it had crumbled away, Jude followed her gut itself. The combination led her farther into the forest, through graveyards of thousand-ringed trees and past closets of jade, sealed from the world, and creeks and brooks and ponds, dilapidated lean-tos and fairy rings.

At the darkest hour, Jude found the swamp. It was a world unto itself, fragrant and warm, and secluded with trees. Cypress stood in, leaned over, or bowed to a pitch-black basin sheeted with moss and fallen leaves. One tree had fallen with its head on dry land, its roots in the swamp, and Jude climbed onto its trunk. She lay there catching her breath, watching the wind play over the water. Sleep had just about caught her when she heard a noise. She snapped to attention, heard again the cracking of branches, a rumbling so low it sounded as if it came from the earth itself. Jude grabbed for her flashlight and darted the light around. There was nothing there, only swamp and forest floor, the trees that penned her in.

She pressed on. For a time, it was quiet, the forest's noise at such a level that Jude could believe she'd imagined the sounds from before. But then, she heard it—its heavy, rumbling breath, its footsteps against the mulch. Fear made a steel rod of her spine, and Jude walked forward stiffly, staring straight ahead.

I'm only scarin' myself, thought Jude, yet even as she thought it, the creature was at her back, its breath moist and close on her nape. Hers was a rabbit's heart, pattering fast, straining in her chest as she stopped short. The creature stopped with her. A circle of white-yellow light was pointed at Jude's feet, and she willed herself to keep looking at her shoes, the flashlight's beam. It was pressed to her now, near enough to feel its coarse fur through her clothes. She shuddered, urine pouring down her legs, and the beast prodded her neck with its wet snout, scenting her.

All at once good sense and mobility returned to Jude. Screaming, her shrieks startling night birds, the creature, Jude ran. Blindly, she tore through the woods, uncaring of the branches that whipped at her face. There was a stitch in her side, hard to breathe through, and still she ran, screaming hoarsely, all the while sure that the beast was behind her. She could feel it on her, its fur, its breath, and Jude knew she wouldn't be safe until there was a door between her and the beast.

How long she ran, how far, and where her feet took her, Jude did not know. The woods were a blur of green, of wind, and when she came to the end of them, she allowed herself less than a minute to regain her breath and take in her surroundings. Above her hung canopies of Ogeechee tupelo, the fading moonlight making strange, human shapes of the branches and young limes. Ahead was the field, wild and overgrown, stalks of rice and sugar crowded out by English ivy. Wide and far it stretched, the long grasses interrupted only by tree stumps and, farther into the field, stark white against the black night, a farmhouse, two stories tall and watchful.

Jude glanced briefly behind herself—was that a glinting eye she saw? A yellow dagger of a tooth?—then rushed ahead. Her body throbbed with pain and still she pushed it, running, limping onto the land. Half blind, she crossed the lea, unsteady feet her only guide up the moss-eaten path to the sagging front porch. Jude put her back to the door of her new home, eyes darting across the field. She needed to be sure *it*, whatever it was that had chased her, hadn't followed her. So quietly it moved, so quickly... Movement in the field—Jude watched it wide-eyed and panting, but nothing came of it. It was only wind, some small critter making its way through the grass.

The house waited patiently for Jude to address it, and she turned to it slowly. It was a plain house, all splintered columns and discolored wood, its disorder like a caul over a newborn's face. Jude broke through it to enter her new home, and immediately, she knew that every story told about it was true. Yes, there were haints in the cellar, ghouls trapped up in the bricks and behind the wallpaper, stashed like jewels beneath the floorboards and crowded up the chimney. Yes, of course, there were spirits there, malignant and benign, festering in the well, clogging the pipes. The grounds, steeped with Black blood, released noxious gases; up, up they rose, through mud and rock, to squat over the house, to sicken it and its inhabitants. Malevolent and sticky, left too long to stew in its ugliness, the house churned as it adjusted to Jude's presence. Jude, nauseous and vertiginous, felt the house's discomfort as her own—together, woman and walls reeled with the sensation of invasion.

A shudder of movement—elsewhere, a door squealed open, slammed shut. Footsteps reached the top of the stairs but went no farther.

Simultaneously, Jude and the house explored each other. She felt it rifling through her as she walked the halls. There were nine rooms in total, each of varying size and shape, each leading to the other through a series of narrow paths and near-hidden doors. Downstairs was a screened-in parlor and a living room. A discreet wallpapered door connected the living room to the dining room, and then another connected the dining room to the galley kitchen. Upstairs: two rooms, one furnished and the other small, bare, and a bathroom with a very deep, very rusted tub on clawed feet. There was little furniture in the rooms, everything of value having been hauled off decades before. All that remained were castoffs, objects too big to justify lugging through the forest—a painted hutch and dining table, rugs and broken chairs, a wardrobe embossed with magnolia trees.

Jude saw the cellar last. The staircase down was steep and narrow, packed dirt fortified with slats of wood. The cellar sighed, a plume of warm, musky breath rising from the darkness. Dust bunnies and insect husks swarmed her ankles, whispering against the floors, *Skss-skss, skss-skss, come down, come down!*

So down Jude went, slowly, clutching at the rough walls to balance herself. There were wasps in her head, hornets in her chest; her body thrummed with a nervous excitement, an eagerness Jude could not parse. Spiderwebs fell over her face, adorning her with a veil of beetle legs and flies, the great mahogany wings of palmetto bugs. Jude grabbed at the darkness, and the darkness grabbed back, tugged her down, down.

Despite its sprawl, the cellar was a close space, tight and breathless. There were ghosts in the corners, furniture draped in white sheets, as well as a gas furnace, a generator, and two doors. One led to a cold little storeroom, the shelves empty save for the odd pickled vegetable, and the other led to a prayer closet. There was no other word for it in Jude's mind—it was small like a praying closet, and windowless. Not much was there: a woven rug for the packed dirt floor, a pillow for kneeling, and, shoved against the back wall opposite to the door, a walnut sideboard etched with curling, twining images of cotton and sugar, High John, robed figures holding wooden canes like scepters, baskets laden with crops. Atop the sideboard: a rainbow of melted wax, melted candles, china plates and wooden bowls, a sticky green glass full of caught flies, dishes of acorns, locks of braided hair, rusted nails, old coins, and a little box of matches decorated with a sly, smiling Sambo.

Light from the two small windows in the cellar disrupted the gloom of the closet, but Jude knew that if she closed the door, sealed herself in, the room would be as dark and noiseless as a grave. Even now, she felt buried, but the sensation was not unpleasant. It pressed at her, swaddled her, and Jude left the closet missing the heaviness the room provided.

Back on the second floor, the cellar door closed and locked behind her—she took her bag and tired body to her new bedroom, opened wide the two windows to dispel the room's staleness, crawled into bed, and promptly fell into a deep, dreamless sleep.

interlude: the house

There's something inside, something moving about and rifling through its rooms. It writhes, it ruins—an offensive taste on its tongue, parasite in its belly. It needs to be spat out. Shat out.

Haints swarm the intruder. Do they like her, or should they hate her? Is she one of us? *they ask one another.* Look at her wrists, her miserable neck, the dark of her skin! Sister? Sister? *they call but the she-thing, she sleeps, she don't hear.* Touch her face, open her eyes— ah, no dreams there, only red red red.

More are coming, slamming open doors and rattling windows, coming to see the intruder curled into herself. Chirren feet pounding on the steps, running down the halls, and still, the haints pouring in, blue-black shadows gathered round the bed. They put their heads together, whisper to one another. Should she stay? What do we do with her? Put her out, *says one, and,* Field her, *says another, and they agree, voices clamoring, to test her, tease her, roll her over, roll her out of bed.*

They take hold of the woman, entering her as smoothly as she entered the house—unlock, turn knob, open—and lead her down the stairs, out into the field. Usually, they wake, the intruders, and they panic and run and wonder, Oh where oh where did my body go without me, *but the she-thing, little sister, remains asleep. Where they plant her, she stays, sways.* Touch her, *says the house,* let her feel it. *And all at once, the field and the forest reach for her, the haints reach for her, and she is touched, filled. Grass sprouts from her arms, her legs. She opens her mouth and out pours black swamp water, pot liquor, newts and bullfrogs and bolls of cotton. She is colonized, chlorophyll in her veins and in her arteries, the very structure of her being transmogrified and yet, somehow, the same.*

One of us? *asks the forest.* Something like it, *says the house, but neither really knows.*

Formidable, *says the forest, and,* Familiar, *says the house. They let the woman go, let her go back to her bed. Hosts of haints guard her sleep. They call her Little Sister.*

7

Ernestine rotted, cooled.

Meanwhile, her sisters excused themselves to the living room to discuss her corpse. There were instructions, plans put in place, according to Vivian. After a brief search, Phyllis left to sit in the living room with her hands tacky with Ernestine's blood, Vivian produced a will.

"Is this it?" asked Phyllis. Ernestine's will was brief, scrawled on the back of a photograph of the sisters in their Sunday clothes. *To my daughter, Judith, the house, some money; to my sisters, Vivian and Phyllis, my quilts, my pearls . . .* "She ain't say nothing 'bout what she want done with her body?"

Vivian shrugged. "Don't think she saw much point in it. She always knew she was gon' do as Daddy told her."

Quiet spread between the sisters, their father's deathbed request lingering over them like a bad smell. Ernest Rice was a simple man; when he died, all he wanted was to be washed, shrouded, and buried on the land where he was born, next to his father and mother, his wife, and the couple hundred other Negroes who shared the misfortune of being owned by Cedric Humphrey. As for his daughters, all of them but namely Ernestine, they would be buried alongside him. Phyllis was not there when Daddy made his demands, but she saw the aftermath, Ernestine's stony face and the purple-black imprint of Daddy's hands on her wrist. He would not let her go, she'd said, wouldn't sign the deed over to her, unless she agreed.

Phyllis's lips worked, the words forming and unforming in her mouth, and after a beat, she said, "We don't have to bury her there, do we?"

"It's what Daddy wanted" was Vivian's whispered response. "And Nessie . . . Nessie agreed to it."

"Only 'cause he made her!" Even as she spoke the words, Phyllis shuddered. She felt her father's gaze on her like a brand, and she forced her head away so as not to look at him. "We can do things the right way. Reverend Matthews, he knows our family, and he'd let us bury her in the churchyard, no questions asked. And we can . . . We can see if someone at Tabernacle knows how to tend a body, if they can fix her face—"

"Fix her face!" Vivian's anger was much too big for the confines of the living room, and it seemed to Phyllis that her voice rattled the pictures, disturbed the curtains. She didn't mean to flinch but she did. Vivian caught the reaction, frowned, and said, quieter, "There ain't no fixing to be done, Philly. Her *eye*!" Vivian groaned, clapped a hand over her mouth. Shaking her head, she said, "No, no, we do this ourselves. All of it, the tending and washing and everything, it's ours. I can't . . . Phyllis, I won't let nobody see her like this."

"You not thinking straight. Vivian, *please*. What we know about cleaning a body?" Vivian interrupted, muttering about cleaning Daddy, but Phyllis ignored her, pressed forward. "And to take her back there! To that *hell*! It ain't right, you know it ain't right."

"What it matter if it's right or not! It just *is*, Philly. We have to put her somewhere, and if Nessie said she want to be laid next to Daddy, then that's what we do. It's what she would've wanted."

The lie was obvious, bold, and it lay between the sisters, an impassable bridge. Phyllis clenched and smoothed her hands on her skirt to give them anything better to do than beat on Vivian. How practical she was! How quickly she swallowed her bile and did what needed doing, be it advising Phyllis to bury and forget her baby boy as soon as possible or throwing their own sister into that cursed ground. *It just is*, she said. Phyllis curled her lip and thought, *Daddy's twin. Get a hold of yourself and don't think about what you're breaking.*

Phyllis flipped Ernestine's will in her hand. They were young in the photo, primly dressed and with Nessie in the center. She was the sole unsmiling face, and her grip on her sisters' hand and shoulder were firm, protective.

At length and with a sigh, Phyllis said, "Fine. Fine, Vivian, you're right." She threw up her hands, bowed out. Privately, she reminded herself to write out a will—a little money and her good church clothes to Vivian, the rest of the money in tithes to the church, and under no circumstances was anyone to put her body into the ground that broke their backs.

When Cephus died in '34 and Monrose went soon after, Phyllis had left the business of the funerals to her sisters. She couldn't bear it, had already worn herself out screaming and crying and carrying on, and so Vivian and Ernestine put her to bed, rousing her from her drugged slumber only to be cinched into mourning blacks and escorted to the church. It wasn't that she was calm at the joint funeral—only numbed, the miserable reality of a brutalized husband and small, cold son dampened by their clean, embalmed bodies and tidily folded hands, their starched Sunday suits.

There was no such luck for Phyllis, attending to the corpse of her sister. Vivian unearthed a bottle of dark liquor from the very back of under the sink, a leftover, no doubt, from their father, and bade Phyllis drink.

"For your nerves," Vivian said. She took her two slugs directly from the bottle, and Phyllis did the same, hands shaking and then stilling as the rum's heat washed her over.

Steeled, the sisters gathered Ernestine and carried the awkward load of her corpse upstairs to her private bathroom. They ignored the disarray—the open wardrobe, the carded-through jewelry box, and the bathtub ringed with red—and dabbed Vicks beneath their noses, made masks from their scarves, and carefully laid Ernestine out on her back. Together, they stripped her, peeling away the housecoat black and stiff with blood, the soiled undergarments. A hot, zinging flash of grief cut through Phyllis as she was confronted with the reality of Ernestine's body—her dainty toenails, the striped and stretched belly, the myriad scars along her trunk-like legs, the deflated breasts. *Poor thing*, she thought, and *how young!*

"Only sixty," sighed Phyllis.

Vivian hummed in agreement before having Phyllis help her move Ernestine to the tub. They cleaned her gently, gingerly, dried blood and dead skin floating like rose petals on the water's surface. How holy she seemed to Phyllis with her sisters' mingled tears anointing her face. How reverent their touch as they washed her loving hands, the soles of her feet.

Vivian sang as she worked, a hymn Ernestine loved, and Phyllis sang along with her:

> Glory, glory, hallelujah!
> Since I laid my burdens down!
> Friends don't treat me
> Like they used to
> Since I laid my burdens down!

Once Ernestine was washed and rubbed down with oil, Phyllis took on the task of mending her face. Vivian said it couldn't be done, but Phyllis tried, her steady seamstress's hand pulling together the torn lip and cheek, the dangling nose with neat, tight stitches. The ruined eye, jellied and dead as a fish's, she sewed shut.

"Should we dress her?" asked Vivian. She glanced at Ernestine's rifled-through closet, eyes no doubt on her usher's uniform.

Phyllis shook her head. "Let her go down bare, the way she came into the world. Besides," she said, smiling small, "she'd hate the waste."

In the end, they decided to wind her in a plain white sheet. It was a simple shroud, almost unworthy, but Vivian and Phyllis knew the worth of it, the decades of laundering it took to afford linen bought new from a department store.

Afterward, they brought Ernestine back down to the living room. Phyllis looked around herself at the mess of blood, and wondered aloud what they'd do about it and how they'd get Ernestine's body up to Sparta.

"We'll worry about the cleaning later, after we bury Nessie," said Vivian. She tore her scarf from her face and stuffed it into her pocket, hissed as she fell into an armchair. "Getting to Sparta's easy—we can borrow Deacon Yates's pickup."

"He won't ask questions?"

"Not of me," Vivian replied. She squirmed, dark cheeks flushing darker with embarrassment. Pointedly, she ignored Phyllis's curious look and wry half smile. "What time it is? Let's go over now, get it out the way."

Deacon Yates's house was only a bus ride away, and when they arrived, they were served coffee in mismatched cups. Phyllis peeked around; the house was neat but charmless, spartan in the way typical to the homes of widowers. She glanced at Vivian from the corner of her eye and wondered if she was doing the same, imagining curtains and rugs, pretty pieces of art to decorate the bare walls.

Vivian was different in the deacon's house, eyes all warm and acquiescent as she asked for the use of his truck. Subtly, she excluded information, dancing around questions about Ernestine with balletic grace.

"Sparta?" Yates whistled. "What you wanna go there for? It's bad country, even in the daytime."

"We know what it's like," said Vivian. "We grew up round there, see? Only . . . Well, Deacon, we goin' up to see about our daddy. He's buried there, on the land we used to work."

Yates nodded solemnly. He let the women finish their coffee before asking after Ernestine. "I thought Mrs. Rice had a car of her own. Nice one too. She won't let you make use of it?"

The sisters shared a glance, and Vivian cleared her throat, set down her cup. "Yes, you right, and any other time, we'd take Ernestine's car, but our niece, Judith—you remember Judith, don't you, Brother Yates?—went out of town with it." Yates started to ask more, but Vivian cut him off with a smile and a raised hand, and said, "Really, Brother, we'd like to get out there and see our father before it gets too late. Like you say, it's bad country."

If Yates had reservations about two aged, unmarried women taking off in his good truck or if he had any further questions regarding the nature of their journey, the suddenness of their departure, he thankfully kept them to himself. With a fond smile for Vivian and a strong, Christian squeeze of the hand for Phyllis, he handed over his keys.

※

It was a quiet drive up to Sparta. Two hours of silence with not even the radio to distract them, Vivian speaking only to ask about directions—Phyllis had not noticed, before, what little there was to say between her and Vivian. They'd always had Ernestine to act as a buffer and bon vivant, and without her, there was only static, the wind hissing through the cracked windows.

Some time along the drive, Phyllis half asleep, Vivian woke her, saying, "About Ernestine..."

"Yes?"

Her hands were clenched on the steering wheel, eyes fixed to the road. "Let's give it a few days, maybe a week, before telling people she passed. We don't say how, of course—just let 'em think she took a turn for the worse and say we handled everything real quiet-like, back home."

Phyllis said nothing, her face tight with dried tears. She tried to remember the dream she'd been falling into—something about Nessie, no doubt. "What about the girl?"

Too fast, Vivian answered, "What girl?" Shoulders drawn up to her ears, jaw working, she blinked, steadied herself. "What about her?"

"Don't you think we should try looking for her? It might not be what we think it is."

"What else could it be?" She shot Phyllis a disdainful look, scoffing, and said, "You saw the state of the house, what she did to Nessie. I ain't chasing her, Philly. Whatever she got on her, I don't want it round me."

Quiet retook the car. Three, four cities passed them before

Phyllis worked up the nerve to ask Vivian why she thought their niece had killed their sister. She had her own theories, ideas spawned in the hours between her and Judith's terse phone call and the discovery of Ernestine's body. Or were they older? Hadn't she doubts? Hadn't she questioned, inwardly, never aloud, Ernestine's methods? Surely, she wouldn't be so nasty to her own baby, had he lived long enough?

Or am I fooling myself? Phyllis thought. *Denying what I knew, what I'm like, so I can try to put my head down tonight.*

Vivian shrugged a shoulder and said, "Can't think of a single reason to cut your mother's face in two. Not a one."

"No?" Their own mother came to mind. Ruth Rice was a mean woman, ungentle, and she yanked and slapped and beat her daughters without reason, sometimes under her own steam but more often than not at the instruction of her husband. She was thirty-six when she died in 1919, shriveled, all the softness wrung from her. "You know, Ma'ammy, she beat me once for walking round the house with just my slip on. It was only us there, me and you and Nessie, her, of course, and Daddy. I was just crossing through, not hurting nobody, and she saw my legs, my bare legs, and she knocked me right to the ground." She chuckled. "Still don't like to show my legs, even now."

"You'd kill her for that?" asked Vivian.

"No," Phyllis admitted. "Or maybe, not for the slip thing, exactly, but for other things." The rough treatment, rough hands, the adult teeth she lost, the flash of evil in her eyes right before swinging a skillet. "For looking away, for ignoring when Daddy..." Her breath caught in her throat, and she exhaled slowly, shakily. "I wonder if that ain't what we've been doing. Looking away."

Vivian's eyes cut to her and she said, "I hope you don't mean to say Nessie was anything like Daddy."

Horrified, Phyllis cried, "No! God, no, never!"

"Then it can't be the same, can it?" Vivian pressed her lips tight, adjusted her grip on the steering wheel. "Kids get beat, Phyllis. *We* got beat, and far worse than she ever did. Anything Nessie might've done, it don't come close, it don't compare."

"It's not about comparing," said Phyllis softly. She shifted in her seat and looked out the window. She didn't want to look at Vivian as she said, "Only I wonder . . . What if it was my child? What if it was Monrose?"

"It's not."

"But what if it was?"

Vivian shook her head, huffed exasperatedly. "It wouldn't ever be. He was born good and he died good. Judith, there wasn't a chance in hell of her coming up right, not with . . ." She shook again, shook off the sympathy. "*No.* Nessie shouldn't have even bothered."

Incredulous, Phyllis whipped around to face Vivian. "You don't mean that, Vivian."

"What you know about what I mean? You didn't see how it was, really, when she was little. All you cared was that there was a baby in the house, something for you to play dress-up with, but the girl never smiled, never made any sort of noise. And the way she'd *look* at you, like she was digging inside of you, looking for something. Weird." Vivian shuddered. "Wicked."

"She weren't born that way, Vivian. Nobody is."

In the following silence, Vivian tight jawed and stony, Phyllis searched her heart, pressing at it to see if she meant what she'd said, and was surprised to find she did. Phyllis thought of Monrose, his tiny body growing frailer and frailer until it was nothing, only air, and then of her niece, small and watching. *That's right*, she thought. *There ain't no thing as a bad seed, only dry and unkind land.*

They found the Humphrey plantation the same as they'd left it—wide and endless, and with the prettiest trees they ever strung niggers from. Nobody was there to greet or stop them, so they drove the grounds in peace and arrived quickly at the Rices' plot of land.

The family graveyard was in the front of the house, two rows of corpses before the crops began. "Sure got a lot of dead," said Phyllis as she unpacked the shovels from the truck. Thirteen, she counted, and that excluding all those without crucifixes or markers.

"She'll have plenty of company," replied Vivian. "She never did like being alone."

It was thirsty work, digging a grave. When Daddy died, they had four men to help with the digging and hauling. Now, it was only the sisters, fifty-seven and fifty-one, hacking at the dirt and sweating out their pressed hair. They took breaks only for water and to relieve themselves, the routine of it as familiar to Phyllis as working a cotton line. Phyllis said as much to Vivian, and her sister laughed, said the only thing they were missing was Daddy at their back, hustling them to pick more, pick faster.

As she dug, Phyllis let her thoughts turn to Ernestine and to Judith. Back and forth, she vacilated, one moment red-hot with rage and the next only disappointed. Sorrow whipped her and then guilt, shame. Only a day ago, Phyllis had watched her sister knock her niece's head into the wall and what had she done? *Nothing*, Phyllis reminded herself. She saw and pursed her lips and she went back to sewing, her mind already on the next row of stitches before Judith had even gotten to her feet.

Another wave of rage, another crash of shame. She wanted to take the girl and shake her, for being so stupid, for killing her dearest friend, for not *speaking*. Wanted to shake herself too, shake and shake until she was boneless, thoughtless.

Phyllis looked up from her work, wanting to say some of what was on her mind, but Vivian was closed off, her cheeks puffed with exertion as she dug with single-minded purpose. That was the difference between the two of them. Whereas Phyllis had some give left to her, room to bend, Vivian was steel, inflexible, and she moved through life with the belief that tenderness was a luxury, joy short-lived and hard-earned. She moved as their parents had—always forward, every trial fortification against future tribulations.

She was right on that point, at least. If Ma'ammy hadn't gone and died in front of them, if Daddy hadn't clutched his heart and fell spasming to the kitchen floor, would either sister have been able to withstand the stink of Nessie's dead body? And if Daddy hadn't belted Phyllis's legs until they ran with blood, if Cephus's skull hadn't been crushed in by a white man's tire iron, if her little Monrose hadn't breathed his last breath in her arms, could Phyllis have ever survived the sight of her dear, sweet Ernestine mutilated, nearly decapitated?

It was midafternoon by the time the grave was dug, the sun high and concentrated on their backs. They were immodest in their labor, unbuttoned, wet down to their skin with sweat. Straining, the sisters considered the hole. It was no churchyard, no immaculate green plot, but it was family and it was theirs.

Vivian was right when she said Nessie wouldn't be lonely; Momma was there, to the left of her, and then Pappy and Ma'Dear, Uncle Mason and Auntie Caroline, all the children who came into the world more blood than shape and the others with features recognizable enough to mourn. Daddy was there too, of course, to the right of Nessie. Phyllis's throat itched, and she wondered if they shouldn't have buried Ernestine closer to their grandparents, their siblings.

"Should we say a li'l something?" asked Phyllis. "A song, maybe, or a prayer?"

"She made me a quilt as a wedding present. Sixty by eighty, rose triangles, or maybe it was brick top?" Vivian smiled remembering it, the pinks and purples, the delicate blue thread Ernestine used to spell out her nickname for Vivian on the back—Br'er Anne, for her mischief. "She spread it out on my wedding bed, and the two of us sat there giggling like girls over it, giddy about lilac stitches."

Phyllis, picking up the thread, said, "You know, I always liked the way Nessie made her collards. Just on this side of too spicy. You remember how she did 'em? Whole roasted peppers, and she'd thrown them in, seeds and pith and all. Nearly burn your lips to taste 'em, but *Lord*, were they good! And with the ham hocks?"

Vivian moaned, "Oh, *girl*, that ham! Just something 'bout the way she could handle a pig. That hog she cooked a few Christmases back? The glaze, them perfect thick slices. We was eating fried skins well into the near year."

Back and forth, the sisters went swapping stories, laughing, crying, moaning, snickering, one moment heavy with grief and the next raucous with memory. They remembered her mean, remembered her funny. Remembered her as the only one of them not afraid to climb trees, remembered her hemming their wedding dresses, embroidering the trousseaus; remembered her with Judith on her hip and Judith sulking at her side, Nessie aging and souring, sickening, but always with some measure of sweetness left for her sisters.

Sapped of memories, Vivian folded forward and bowed her head, clasped her hands.

"Ernestine, we know where your soul is, and we know where your body is too. You got your kin with you. You home." Vivian threw out her hand for Phyllis to hold, and she took it, squeezed it tightly. "The rest of you, your laugh and your smile, that gap in your teeth, the burn on your hand, well, Nessie, we gon' hold all that for you, till we see each other again."

Numbness swept over Phyllis, and exhaustion, but she held herself up, helped Vivian fill in and tamp down the grave. They made a crucifix with broken wood from the shotgun shack and scattered Ernestine's burial mound with a bouquet of toadflax, sedge. Phyllis found Spanish moss in the trees and she brought it over, spread it over Nessie like a blanket.

Wordlessly, dreading already the drive home, the inevitable return to the Westmoor house, Vivian and Phyllis packed their materials and left Humphrey's plantation.

8

For a month, Jude was confined to the farmhouse. She spent a week in bed, subsisting on soda crackers and tap water, her body fusing itself back together. The flesh healed, wounds scabbed over. Outside, autumn progressed, and her bruises changed color as the season did, black and blue to green, yellow. Inside, however, the hurt remained the same; Jude thought about what she'd done, and she bled and wept, the wound of missing Ma'am, hating Ma'am, burning through her system like sepsis.

When she was well enough, Jude walked back into Whitnee and retrieved her car. The Negroes she met were much like she expected, intrusive and curious or else dismissive. Wherever she was, they crowded her and questioned her. Who were her people and where was she from, what did she mean coming to a place like Whitnee, and what did she think she was doing, living out in the evil house in the woods?

Jude answered what she could, embellishing and demurring where the truth felt too dangerous. She sat on porches and in parlors, and played the role of the hapless, bemused traveler. Ma'am's ring helped—Whitnee's Negroes, piteous of the poor widow with no roots, no people, gathered her up. *Poor sister*, they said among themselves, and on subsequent visits, Jude was given plates of food, clothing, candles, and supplies for the house. Men hung around her while she shopped, offered to see about her roof or the plumbing, the state of her furnace, and Jude turned them down, asking instead for tools to do the mending herself. Sisters from the church pestered her about membership, ministry, and prayer circles until Jude, flustered and aggravated, told them she didn't hold with religion.

She wasn't normal, folks said, and Jude supposed they were right. There weren't many women, Black or white or otherwise, who drove, never mind went around asking after shotguns. The man that sold one to her—a Parker, smooth black barrel and a stock of lacquered walnut—was reluctant to hand it over, pestered her with questions about her proficiency.

"That's a serious weapon, sister," he said to her, patronizing, like he was talking to a child. "You sure you know how to use that thing?"

"Sure enough." Jude ran a hand over the stock, felt at the checkering and complex engraving. Her grandfather had something similar, though less ornate. "Granddaddy taught me how to shoot."

The man smiled, and Jude was sure he would've patted her head, if he could reach it. He told her there was a big difference between shooting pigeons and shooting buck as he handed over two boxes of shells. Jude hummed, kept to herself how she once shot a turkey clean through the eye, how big her granddaddy had smiled at her. Kept the rest of the story too, how Ma'am had slapped her when she saw Jude with her grandfather, hands covered with turkey blood. It wasn't ladylike, she said, and anyways, didn't she say not to be alone with Pappy?

Repairs for her new home were slow going. She mended the holes in the parlor's screens, oiled and tightened hinges, replaced rotted floorboards. For months on end, she scrubbed and swept and mopped, screwed and hammered and adjusted. The house, accustomed to its rot and dilapidation, wasn't exactly grateful for Jude's intervention. On all sides, she was beleaguered—taps and knobs turned of their own volition, filling the house with gas, water; windowsills dropped like guillotines onto her fingers, amputation avoided only by a matter of seconds. Doors slammed, invisible hands shredded the wallpaper, and all attempts to scale back the kudzu eating away at the house's exterior were thwarted by the plant's near-instantaneous growth, garden shears snipping at her heels like wild dogs.

There was never any peace in the house, her haints being needy and petulant as small children. The house worked itself up, building, building, and then, finally, cresting into a tantrum of items broken, items flung and shattered, dissonant voices shrieking and chanting and singing. Bone-tired, Jude listened and watched in horror as her house destroyed itself. Disembodied hands scrabbled down the walls and grabbed at her hair, her clothes. Cacophonous and absurd, the voices of hundreds fell upon her—she heard her mother in the din, her aunties, the booming shout of her grandfather tumbling out of pots and pans, from under the floors and behind the paneling, rising up and up from out of the cellar, all of them saying, *Little Sister! Little Sister! Look at your hands! See what you've done!*

Through bleary, bloodshot eyes, Jude looked at them and saw that they were red, dripping. She trembled, cowering in the living room with her arms thrown over her head to protect her from the flying vases, pots. Behind her eyelids, scotomata flickered and shifted, the pain in her right eye bright and hot. The chaos deadened her thoughts, and every brush of fabric, every minor sensation, was like an avalanche of feeling. Too much, too much! The haints called for her—*Judith! Judy! Jude!* and she opened her mouth and screamed.

What an exquisite emotion, rage. When she felt it, she turned it toward herself, gouged her arms and ruined her legs, plucked the hairs from her skin one by one, just to feel in control of something. She couldn't yell in her mother's house, couldn't yell in the city or in Whitnee, had always held her breath and held her tongue, let the anger boil her from the inside out. Hone the knife, whet the blade, but never wield it, never let loose the bubbling pitch that blackened her belly.

But what could stop her now? Guttural, piercing, Jude shrieked and unhinged herself. She felt hysterical, histrionic, the heat and curses and screams spilling out her mouth like vomit. She understood it now, why cats arched and hissed, why dogs mauled, why wasps stung, the frenzied droning of yellow jackets. Foaming and raving, eyes rolling madly, she sympathized with women whose only medicine was an ice pick to the brain. *A cleaver would do me*, thought Jude, and the idea of cracking open her skull and the vileness within her spilling out, pooling up to her ankles, her thighs, tickled Jude so much that her screams became laughs, became screams and laughter again.

Around her, the house stilled and fell silent. The haints watched her, murmuring, and returned to their hiding places, abashed. The furniture, cowed, righted itself, chairs and floorboards falling back into place. For a good, long moment, Jude stood in the quiet, nervous acquiescence of her scolded home. Her throat was hoarse, her head reeling—she ran out the house and into the field.

Out in the night, the biting, bracing air overwhelming her lungs. She took deep, gulping breaths, and as she staggered farther into the field, Jude's legs buckled beneath her and sent her sprawling onto the grass. Face down, arms pimpled with gooseflesh, her chest tight and hot, Jude buried her face in the dirt and sobbed. Oh, how long it'd been since she'd cried! She'd been fixing her face so long, she forgot what it was like, the relief of a dam breaking—how sweet it was to weep with abandon, to cry for her bruises and Ma'am's ruined face, for being too old and too young, for being Black and big-boned, for being strange and unlovely, for not belonging anywhere or to anybody.

She wept herself empty and heaving, hiccuping, dried her face on the grass. The coolness of the grass against her face, blades redolent with petrichor, was a comfort to her, and slowly, Jude pulled herself to a sitting position. Posed with her hands in front of her, her legs curled beneath her, she looked out across the field and to her house. It burned in the darkness, the windows glowing and light pulsating out from the panes like a heartbeat, like breathing. Jude breathed in time with it, in and out, and felt her rage, her sorrow, leach out through her hands and into the ground, dissipating into the roots.

Afterward, Jude called the house Candle. Like a mutt brought indoors, bathed and fed and collared, it came to heel. Naturally, it being a wild and possessed thing, it was not always obedient; it had its moments of pique, tantrums of cutlery and petulant furniture, but now when she called its name, it heeded her, and like its namesake, it burned in the dark.

Two winters into her stay in the woods, the beast returned. It came in the night, crept slowly through her door, up the stairs, and into her bedroom. Its growl announced it, shocking Jude out of sleep.

In the dark, she saw only its black eyes reflecting greenly. How had it come so close, Jude wondered, and she cowered from it, back pressed to her headboard as it crept nearer and nearer. Vertiginous, stomach clenching, she watched as the beast stalked forward, grumbling, growling. Fear pierced Jude at the navel, pinned her in place like a rabbit tacked for skinning. With a whimper, she dove under her sheets, blanket pulled up and over her head.

It's just a dream, she told herself. *Just a bad dream, and if I can't see it, it can't be real.* And yet, she smelled it, breath rank and rich and somehow sweet. It snuffled at her, nosed at her blanket, and she pulled herself in tighter, squeezing her eyes shut. How quicky could she leave? Jude wondered. How long would it take for her to pack her things and go tearing into the night, Whitnee and its beasts and wicked houses be damned? But then, what next? Another town, another hainted house, another horror to grind her down small until she up and ran again and again? Was that all life was, running and hiding, always at the mercy of somebody, something, anything?

Heat surged through her, the start of tears or a scream, and she threw off her bedclothes, ready to face, at last, the beast, but the room was empty, the door ajar and the heater purring.

The gifts of meat began the morning after, the mauled remains of animals thrown haphazardly onto her porch. Their bellies slit, deer and hare and waterfowl waited at her door, their innards spilled out from them like a cornucopia of meat. Occasionally, there were other gifts, colorful stones and bits of metal, flashy candy wrappers from the town, but death reigned supreme. Maybe it thought her a sorry, incompetent hunter; maybe it wanted her fat and juicy before it ate her.

Either way, the beast provided—turkey, pheasants, duck and chicken, wild hog, and other game that Jude couldn't know. When spring came next, there was a patch of wood on the porch stained red and warped from the beast's gifts, Jude's tacit acceptance of them.

The beast—*her* beast, her animal that stalked her and terrified her and fed her so well—kept no schedule. Sometimes, it came daily and sometimes, Jude wouldn't see it for weeks, months, and once, not for four lonely years. She missed it when it was gone for those long stretches, had longed miserably for the queasy pleasure of its company. When it returned—and it always did, her beast, return—Jude left gifts of her own: leftovers from her dinner, bone and gristle for it to chew on.

Set loose in the wild, a domesticated pig soon grew tusks and became indistinguishable from its feral cousins. So too changed Jude, a latent germ within sprouting, spreading. After two years in the woods, she was a completely different thing, inside and out, but she couldn't make sense of how her body betrayed her every night. She thought she had only dreamed her nighttime excursions in the woods—what else could it have been? She was, Jude thought, an ordinary woman placed in extraordinary circumstances, and she was only settling as a house settled, her body changing with age.

Still, she changed, and more and more, Jude craved the taste of salt and of kaolin, that bitter white clay her mother and aunts used to soothe stomach pains. By day, she overseasoned her food, took spoonful after spoonful of cornstarch. At night, however, Jude walked into the forest and ate her fill of dirt. Mud in her mouth, mud down her throat—she-beast, she-thing, she savored the crunch of beetles, ants. Come morning, there was grass in her hair and tiny legs between her teeth. She spat up silt and worried for the state of herself.

What was she becoming? Had it always been in her, waiting, or was it new, the precision and ease with which she shot and fleshed stags, hares? Snakes slithered through her garden and she cut off their scaled heads with the blade of her hoe. The first time she saw a wild boar, all bristles and mean, curved tusks, she thought she might've been looking into a mirror.

It shocked Jude, what she was capable of. Before killing Ma'am, she'd thought she was harmless, almost weak. But the woods opened her, and when she came across a nearly dead deer, heaving, struggling for breath, she knew, immediately, what she needed to do.

It couldn't live; torn neck, torn side. Jude recoiled, feeling the animal's agony as acutely as her own. Cautiously, she inched toward it, hands up in supplication. *There, there*, she thought to it, and she watched, nauseated, as blood pumped from its wounds. Jude's hand trembled as she felt along the blood-slicked pelt. She looked into its eyes—another mirror, another creature like her. The air it breathed was no less precious than her own, and just as she was the brutish, killing boar, she was the deer too, bleeding out slowly, waiting for something bigger to finish her off.

Jude searched the area for a large rock, her mind all the while thinking of her mother. Was this cruelty on her part, she wondered, or kindness, a mercy? When she found a rock big enough, she raised it high over her head and brought it down once, twice—*crack! Crack!*—on the deer's skull. Its blood and brain matter painted the forest floor, her bare legs. The deer twitched, spasmed, and with a final, almost relieved exhale, it died.

Blood drying on her legs, blood staining the leaves. She looked down at what she'd done, the blasted head, and bile rose in her throat. Jude turned, vomited in a bush.

"Oh!" she cried out, belly and throat burning. She spat out a mouthful of foul spit, grabbed at her stomach. *"Oh!"*

But even then, stomach aching, senses overwhelmed, Jude was calm. Her shoulders dropped and she breathed through the panic. Why fear? She knew what to do, inexplicable knowledge blooming in her head, and she let voices and thoughts unfamiliar to her guide her hands. They showed her the way, how to open the buck and reveal its glistening, steaming insides. They told her what cuts to take, what flavors she liked.

Liver, girl, you know how you like the liver. Dat's stew meat, right dere; always did like a little venison in my bowl. Chile, take that tongue and fry it up in lard, you can eat it with soup beans, collards.

Jude obeyed. By the time she was through, her basket overflowed with meat and pelt. At home, she wrapped the meat and set it into the icebox. Jude turned on the tap to clean up, but before she put her hands under the water, she brought the bloodied fingers to her mouth. On her tongue, iron and salt—she licked one hand clean, guiltily washed the other.

When Jude looked again at her spoils, the mass of red flesh streaked with fat, the still-bleeding heart and guts, her stomach clenched again, but this time she felt only hunger.

PART 2

Of course you're not. You're just becoming more of what you've always been. And I'm not changing, either. None of us are changing. Everything is fine. Let's have a picnic.
—JEFF VANDERMEER, *ANNIHILATION*

No live organism can continue for long to exist sanely under conditions of absolute reality; even larks and katydids are supposed, by some, to dream.
— SHIRLEY JACKSON,
THE HAUNTING OF HILL HOUSE

9

Summer
1978

Monday, she toiled; Wednesday, she sold; but on Sundays, clean and holy, Jude picked flowers.

Early morning, dandelion-yellow sun cresting the trees. The woods, her church, welcomed her, and she tipped her head to the oak-tree mothers with their veils of white moss, the deacons of pine and loblolly. Jude breathed, sighed. O holy incense of sedge and yeasty peat! O holy choir of loon and heron, frogs croaking scriptures while the mockingbirds sang devotion. Pitcher plants waited with open mouths for their communion of ants, flies. A gallant sweet gum tree offered Jude a fallen branch to negotiate the leaf litter, the gnarled roots and ivies underfoot.

Jude brought little with her into the woods—a blanket to lie on, a knitted bag holding her wrapped lunch and sewing supplies, and a wicker basket with all the sharp, precise tools needed for foraging. She walked the forest and she worked, kitchen scissors at the ready to clip and gather bluebell and teasel, heart-of-the-earth. Some plants she picked for medicine, others for aesthetics.

In either case, Jude was precise and mindful, her soil knife poised just so as she peeled the bark off trees. She took only what she needed, divided and replanted root systems or pocketed them for later use. All throughout the woods were sighs of her careful stewardship, her loving cultivation.

Jude was forty-one when she left her mother's house. Hunched and humbled, she did not think it possible for her to be in this world—to be at peace, to be alone, to exist for no other purpose than existence itself. Now she was fifty-four, and all that she was was of her own invention. In sunlight and solitude, she bloomed—she was tall in the forest, sturdy as an oak. Her skin was dark, and her features, the rounded cheeks and broad nose, were as pronounced and ornate as carvings in wood. Eyes like black chrysoberyl, chatoyant and flashing, watched and weighed the world. Silent, womanish, seldom she smiled, but oft she laughed.

She did not claim to know the woods like the palm of her hand. The lines of her hand were fixed, immutable; the woods changed constantly, always in flux, familiar paths having been warped by rain and rivers, the migration of animals. Even so, Jude knew her way to the cypress dome. It was high this time of year, black water littered with fallen leaves and circled with waterbirds, trees. Beneath the surface were cottonmouths and alligators, lizards darting and dashing, sunning themselves on cypress knees. The fallen tree, only bent when she met it thirteen years prior, was bowed, its bark worn smooth from years of Jude sitting and sleeping on its trunk.

Jude spread out her blanket, laid down her basket and bag, and toed off her shoes before wading into the swamp. The water body warm, comfortable as a bath, and she slid her feet through the mud and peat, tadpoles circling her ankles. From her shin-deep position, she picked purple loosestrife, swamp iris, cattail, water lily, and yarrow. She left the water stinking of summer, skin scented with the balsam-and-anise perfume of goldenrod, and laid her flowers out in the sun to dry before doing the same with herself.

Up on the cypress's bowed trunk she splayed herself, open legged and content as a house cat. The day was a good one, the humidity of the forest tempered by cool breezes. Others prayed by kneeling and bowing. Jude prayed through rest and through listening, ears perked to the chatter of songbirds. A long-legged ibis squawked a sermon between mouthfuls of fish and wild rice, and when a chorus of brown thrushes began to sing hymns, Jude whistled along with them.

It was a little after noon when she ate her lunch (butter and blackberry jam on brown bread, hard-boiled eggs, a thermos of tea) and emptied her knitted sack of her supplies, her needles and felt tomato. She unpacked her quilting project and let it lie unfurled on her lap; it was a relatively simply pattern, a housetop variation she meant to spruce up with cloth women and fabric trees. Jude gnawed her lip. Pondered texture and color, the inclusion of a shirt she'd burned over a delicate scrap of scarf.

Sewing was like breathing for Jude; she didn't need her whole mind to do it. Practiced fingers pierced and pulled, pierced and pulled, as Jude thought ahead to what chores needed doing about Candle, the balms and tisanes she had to prepare for Wednesday, to when it was best to start turning the garden over for fall. Pierce, pull, a tug here, tie and snap off there. Color spilled over her hands, calico and florals, gingham. She flowed unthinking, and, in her distraction, Jude drove the needle's tip deep into the fleshy pad of her thumb.

Flash of silver, flash of pain. Kissing her teeth, Jude removed the needle and examined the tiny wound. She gave her thumb a squeeze, and from the pinprick dewed a single ruby bead. She brought the bead to her mouth, sucked.

Deeper into the day, the sky apricot and blush, Jude packed her things, her tools and tin, the unfinished quilt. Shoes on, the blanket tucked around her like a shawl, she cradled her long-stemmed flowers and started home. She moved with purpose and speed, cutting through the darkening woods as silent and sure-footed as a fox. Her sisters ran alongside her, yipping, racing to their foxholes—none of them liked the woods at night, the watchfulness like fingertips on the nape.

Jude approached the tupelo tree arch, the edge of the field. Six hundred and seventy-six Sundays, countless journeys to and from the woods, and still it was bliss, returning home.

There was meat waiting for her on the porch. Liver, it looked like, and shank. Blood pooled under the meat, still warm, and she used her lunch's wax paper to gather the gifts before placing a bouquet of goldenrod and bluebell in the sagging red depression.

Jude entered and Candle greeted her, rumbling, rattling, dousing her with its scent.

"Hey now," she said as she came out of her blanket and shoes. She gave the house a once-over, checking the usual places for things gone awry while she was out. Candle was self-sufficient but it was old too, prone to sinking and leaking, the inevitable failings of a house more than a century old. There was, at least, little mischief from the haints; a broken vase, a raised baseboard. These Jude fixed easily, nailing the board back into place and shushing at a stair rail until it settled.

Afterward, in the kitchen, Jude prepared her remedies. All that she knew of herbal medicine came from her mother and her aunts, and from them she learned the many uses of calendula, black cohosh. She kept her pantry well stocked with salves, balms, and teas, and whatever Jude didn't need, she sold in town. More often than not, she returned from Whitnee on Wednesdays with seeds, fabric, produce, a little money, and, once, two surly laying hens.

Dinner, next. She unwrapped the gifted meat, washed it, and dusted the shank with salt, pepper, and ground rosemary. Balletic, Jude flitted from icebox to stove, lighting burners and cleaning her greens, pulling cookware from the haint-blue cabinets. On one burner, she seared her shank, and on another, she cooked down collard and mustard greens with a pinch of sugar, salt and pepper, vinegar for tenderness, and chicken stock for flavor. She cut the shank into thick slices, threw the slices in with the greens. The liver she dredged with flour and fried in butter before adding onions, herbs, and crushed garlic.

As the gravy thickened and the greens softened, Jude hummed, occasionally throwing in a stanza or two from a song off the radio. A little Al Green, a little Roberta Flack—eventually, she settled on a hymn she remembered Ma'am liking, and in her own house, cooking her own food, it felt like good thrift, mending a tear.

Jude was her own creation, yes, but she was a quilt, patchworked and pieced. The very best of her—the way she sang and the care she gave herself and her home, her garden and her lively kitchen, the patience with which she made a quilt—she prized like precious heirlooms. The rest of her, the wrath and violence simmering beneath her skin, the wasp-wing whispering at the back of her mind that lashed and shamed and compelled her into grander and grander acts of destruction—well, there was nothing to be done about that, was there?

She was a bit like her mother's house, tidy rooms and furniture, everything just so, but off-kilter in some indefinable way, her mind just as uneven, steep, and tilted as the halls and walls of the Westmoor house.

The greens were done, and the liver. Jude served herself in the dining room, the table set with a yellow plate and matching glass, a cloth napkin she'd embroidered with holly leaves. In a celadon vase streaked with white, Jude had garnished a bouquet of loosestrife and goldenrod with green fronds. By the light of the waning day, she dined and ate seconds, the contented rumble of Candle settling her only music.

After dinner came the altar. Jude gathered her offerings—tied bundle of High John root, dried sassafras, dimes, a plate of greens and liver—and went down into the cellar, into the prayer closet. As she descended, she felt within herself a narrowing. Felt like being taken over, and the same heaviness that made folks shout and run and speak in tongues laid over Jude's head, making her serene, focused. She lit two tall white candles, and the world cracked open, the thin gap between the seen and unseen widening.

It wasn't exactly praying, what she did in the cellar closet. It was more like a conversation, the house speaking and Jude receiving, listening. She spoke to the haints as if they were her aunties and uncles, curmudgeonly elders in need of young company; the candles bowed and sputtered, and when both parties had said their piece, Jude doled out the gifts, the High John and greens, and blew out the candles.

Sunday evening, belly sated and comfortably tired, Jude set her house alight. Her box of matches was unremarkable, its beauty coming solely from its use and the reverent touch she bestowed on it. When she held it in her hand, her right arm deadened, numbed, while the left arm tingled with anticipation.

Jude held with haints, held with roots and cords, book, bell, and candle. She had heard it said that the women who lived in Candle before her were witches—root women smeared with mud, stinking of herbs, incense—and she followed in their footsteps, head and hands primed for working mojo. Black magic, nigger magic; if Whitnee's whites ever guessed what sort of black business she got into each Sunday, they might've grown bold enough to storm the woods, the wicked house, and set it ablaze, doing, finally, what the posse couldn't all those years ago.

Luckily for Jude they were cowards, but if they did come, they'd be sore disappointed. There was no cauldron save for her stockpot, no naked sprints through the woods, no broomstick wetted with the blood of white infants. No baying at the moon, no flying, no pacts with red devils. God, *no*, not ever! Jude was only ever lighting lights.

She started in the cellar, two tea lights winking in the high windows, singing, *This little light of mine, I'm gon' let it shine!* Up to the living room, the parlor, the kitchen—where there was a window, there was a light. Strike match and glow, strike match and burn—now the bathroom, her bedroom, and her sewing room, until each windowpane was alight with red and yellow tulips.

Jude was still humming to herself when she went out to the field. She groaned as she lowered herself on the grass, aged bones sore with work and with cold. She looked to Candle. The light was good and she had made it, and the pale-green luminescence that emanated like moon haze from her land was inseparable from the warm, inviting glow of her home.

10

Candle slept and the field slept, and even the Okefenokee, writhing and alive with nocturnal creatures, slept, but Jude did not sleep.

Her mother was on her mind, the anniversary of death imminent and inevitable as the sunrise. All throughout the night, Jude dreamed of her: Ma'am as the rottweiler, foaming at the mouth and lunging as Jude failed to shoot her; Ma'am as a shadow at her bedroom door; Ma'am as a disembodied voice crying out, *What kind of child are you?* Jude woke shadowboxing and saw she'd injured herself in the night—scratches along her arms, ropy welts on her legs. Ma'am, persistent as a lover and smitten with revenge, came to her night after night, to claw and rend and mark Jude's guilty flesh.

It was three in the morning, the moon out of sight and the stars dimming. Jude considered the darkness of her room and the darkness of her thoughts. More sleep would be good, but it seemed unlikely, so she rolled out of bed and into her house shoes. She stripped the sheets from the bed, stripped out of her clothes;

laundry today, she told herself as she padded to the bathroom for a quick, cold wash in the sink. Jude dabbed her skin dry, dabbed witch hazel on the worst of her scratches. She wondered, not for the first time, if it was isolation that made getting rid of Ma'am's memory seem so hopeless, or if this was simply the weight of guilt, grief.

Dressed in loose clothing and not quite ready for the day, Jude yawned her way to her sewing room. Of all the rooms in the house, it was her favorite. She had dragged a table up from the cellar to cut on, and on its scratched surface there was muslin, paper patterns, a pedal-operated Singer, felt tomatoes stabbed with pins, sachets of needles, tins repurposed to hold beads, ribbons, buttons. A water-damaged Chippendale-esque highboy, its finials like a beetle's jaw, housed an array of fabrics, some wool and some linen, some cotton and a little colored velvet. There was just one window in the room, but it was wide and opened out in the French style, and in the summers, Jude put her wingback chair right under it to read and to sew.

Small and cluttered, the sewing room had all that she needed: a plush chair, a lamp for light, and, of course, her cedar chest of quilts.

All her life, for as far back as she could remember, there had always been quilts in a Rice's house. Her mother quilted and both her aunts, but of the three, Jude loved Ma'am's work the best. Mean ways be damned, the woman was a skilled and deft hand, and she could turn the merest of scraps of fabrics into masterpieces within months. Fondly, Jude recalled Ma'am and her aunties in the front room singing little play songs as they pieced together massive housetops and bricklayers. She thought of them with their heads together going, *Mama's li'l baby loves shortenin', shortenin', Mama's li'l baby loves shortenin' bread*, the usually austere and serious women transformed into little girls, laughing, trading this piece of old skirt for that bit of scarf.

The quilts of her youth—Granny's pink and purple, Aunt Vivian's wedding quilt, and Auntie Phyllis's pretty swaddling cloth, Ma'am's abstracted collage of work clothes and the countless others—were lovely, but they were plain compared to Jude's work. In Ma'am's house, she stuck to strict rules and followed set patterns, too nervous of Ma'am's ire to try anything new. Grown and alone, beholden to no one, Jude unleashed herself, her quilts expanding from basic stripes and triangles to complex, fantastical scenes. She had, so far, twelve quilts in total, one for each year in the woods.

Her earliest offerings were bleak affairs, blue and violent; indigo corpses, long brown throats necklaced by hands of ebony wool, checkered tiles interrupted by irregular splotches of cotton blood. Over the years her quilts became greener, softer; she put the uglier ones in the cedar chest, and used the pretty quilts for decoration—there was a twenty-four by thirty of the field in the throes of a storm pinned to her bedroom wall, and, at night, she slept beneath a blanket of moss and sky dotted with dainty purple irises.

Jude clicked on the lamp, brought her unfinished thirteenth-year quilt and her basket of sewn squares over to the table, and started where she'd left off on Sunday. She worked in near silence, stitching, restitching bad lines, flipping the quilt back and forth to check her work, and within moments, she was consumed. All of her was in the blanket, every fiber of her being, and she whistled to amuse herself, tsked at mistakes and laughed at private jokes. Jude sewed and the morning rose around her, early birds chirping at their worms and warm light pouring like egg yolks over the room's walls.

When she had a good fourth of the quilt done and she could no longer ignore her stomach's grouching, Jude ate a little breakfast, then did her chores. Houses, like children, were not independent creatures; they needed constant care and upkeep, and Jude went about tending hers with only the mildest of complaints. First was the kitchen, the floors and the pantry, and then she pruned back the ivy sneaking in through the parlor's screens, wiped down the bathroom, and swept the upstairs halls, her bedroom. With no small amount of grumbling, Jude lugged her laundry to the backyard, where she scrubbed and rinsed and hung up the linens, her sheets and shirts and dresses flapping like flags in the wind.

A break for lunch, and then back to it—Jude weeded and watered the garden, and fed it a compost of eggshells in rice water before moving to the wider field. Never did she feel closer to the former inhabitants of Candle than when she worked the field. She cut down overgrowth and uprooted bamboo and invasive ivies, and they moved alongside her, pointing out rabbit holes and pests. They said to her, *That's good sugar, Little Sister*, and Jude nodded and cut it down to snack on later.

As she moved farther into the field, Jude made note of what animals were living in it. There were rabbits, of course, and a warren of stoats not far away. An ibis's nest, a little hole that sometimes housed possums. There was something new too, something Jude couldn't place. She saw where it had flattened the grass and saw its claw marks on the trees, its scat riddled with small bones and seeds, grasses, a few undigested berries. A shiver went through her, and she sat back on her haunches, her smile irrepressible.

It could've been nothing—a black bear wandering too near, sniffing out the heat from her house and curious—or it could've been her beast. Even now, Jude didn't know what kind of animal it was, only knew that it was big and stank of rot, flowers. She remembered Sunday's dinner and Monday's leftovers, all the treats and tasty things that had been brought to her before, and wondered what her beast meant to bring her next. Duck? Hog? Her mouth watered, and she returned to the house whistling.

interlude: the beast

It flicks its round ears, excited, eager. With glee, the beast recalls the first time it entered the she-thing's home, how it had crept up the stairs and into her bedroom, gorged itself on air perfumed with sweat and fear. There had been so much frisson in the air, everything taut and trembling. The she-thing—its she-thing—peered into the darkness, right into its eyes, and the room was electric, fizzing, and if the she-thing hadn't burrowed herself in her sheets, the beast would've lost all control and eaten her there and then.

What a treat she would've been, how filling, but the beast had waited and waited, and years had gone by, the she-thing growing stronger, fuller. She's ripe now, fattened with the beast's kills, and when it eats her, the beast knows it will be full for weeks, months. The woman likes stewarding the woods? Good, she can be its fertilizer.

The beast pants. Drools. Its hunger is a bottomless chasm, a toothache. Move, it thinks. Move now, but it's pinned into place by the sensation of wanting. It needs her, this fine and strange thing who screams and tears through the woods like a wildfire, this thing *who speaks to the hainted house so sweet and kind, as if it is a pet and not a thing rotted with ghosts. Impossible creature, reckless and horrible, who each Sunday sets the house ablaze. Burning, burning red-orange-yellow in the night, but it, like the she-thing, remains standing, a sequoia budding only in the aftermath of fire.*

It can't last, this sick and all-consuming fascination. It gnaws at the beast's bones, drinks its blood. What irony! The devourer, devoured.

Unaccustomed to and dissatisfied with being anything's prey, the beast sheds its fur and rises to two feet.

11

The woman came in the dark of night, stock-still and incongruous to her surroundings, to herself. There was a hole in one of her black boots, but the heavy leather coat she wore, brown and supple, looked new in the foyer's limited light. Her voice was soft, almost too low to be heard over the din of frogs and owls, and Jude leaned in close to hear her say that she was lost and cold, that she was tired and needed somewhere to lay her head.

Jude hesitated. The woman had come so far—what stopped her from staying in Whitnee? Hand on the knob, Jude said, "You ain't wanna go into town?"

The woman shook her head. She stood out of the light, rare flashes of yellow illuminating a sliver of nose, half a dark eye. "I stop there, but nobody help me. White lady in a big house, she say go to the coloreds. Colored man, he say to me, go out there, see the woman in the white house."

"Folks told you to come *here*?" Incredulous, Jude furrowed her brows, opened the door an inch wider.

"Say there a woman in the wood, in the white house, can help me. You help me?"

Jude didn't want to, not really. She might've given the woman some matches or her flashlight, maybe a little food to last her while she took the long walk back into Whitnee, but she didn't like the thought of a stranger in her house. It didn't settle with her, the Black folk in town not taking her in and feeding her, and the unlikeness of it stilled Jude's hand.

But then the light changed, the moon discarding its robe of clothes, and Jude saw the woman's face, her glossy black eyes like stones washed in water. The woman matched Jude's gaze, unflinching. Familiar.

Like lookin' into the eyes of a near-dead buck, thought Jude. A pang of hunger struck her, and her mouth watered. Swallowing, Jude pulled the door open and said, "Might as well come in."

"I can stay?" asked the woman.

"For tonight, at least."

In the foyer, Jude saw her guest in totality, her long body all odd angles and bones. Her eyes roved wildly in their sockets, and she whipped her head round and round to see all that she could. She gawked without shame, blinking only when she caught Jude staring at her. Tall, the woman was, and awkward, and she stood in the hall as if new to her body, unaccustomed to skin and to limb. Her smell filled the space like a gas: stale sweat and jasmine, lichen, anise, and something sweetly rotten beneath it all.

"You called something?" asked Jude. She nodded toward the woman's coat and the woman shrugged it off, let Jude hang it on a hook.

Many emotions flicked across the woman's face as she considered the simple question. Jude wondered if she hadn't hit her head or something, the confused gloss of a head injury familiar to her. Eventually, the woman said, "Nemoira. I'm called Nemoira." The woman met Jude's gaze again, eyes wide, and canted her head. "What you called?"

"Judith, but you call me Jude."

"*Shoo*-death," said Nemoira. She pronounced the *J* as an *S*, and Jude found herself oddly charmed by the whistle it made against the woman's teeth. "Jude."

With a hum and an approving nod, Nemoira continued, asking, "I take these shoes off?" She didn't wait for a response, only knelt down to untie the tatty boots and left them standing by the front door. Nemoira pulled the scarf from off her head, letting loose a flow of black coils that fell past her shoulders. Then, as if sensing the heat emitting from the living room, she breezed past Jude and sat herself down in front of the hearth, bare feet pointed to the fire.

Jude frowned and followed the woman, annoyed by the presumptuousness but intrigued as well. She reminded Jude a little of herself, how she eschewed social mores for the sake of comfort. Simple but never simpleminded, she moved to what suited her with a bluntness easily mistaken for rudeness.

"Can't imagine there's much I can do for you," Jude started. She waited for a response from Nemoira, but she said nothing, kept her back toward Jude. "Folks don't usually come here. Too scared."

Nemoira turned so that a single black eye was visible over her shoulder. "Scared of what? The woods, the house? You?"

Jude shrugged, sat on the arm of the couch with her arms folded over her chest. "People rile themselves up with stories, but nobody's ever bold enough to see if they true. Better for me," she said. "No unexpected company."

Nemoira gave Jude more of her face, enough for Jude to see her small, yellowed teeth and brown, meaty gums. "You don't like people?"

"People don't like *me*."

"Shame," said Nemoira. "Your house is pretty. Strong too."

Candle rumbled, a cat's contented purr. Jude's face warmed, and her tongue swelled in her mouth, suddenly too cumbersome to speak with. She excused herself to the kitchen, considering cutting the embarrassment out of her, and decided against it. It was bad enough, the stranger seeing her flush from a little compliment. Returning to the woman with a palm full of blood, face hot, the woman's curious eyes on her hand—it was too mortifying to even consider.

Unable to set the feeling down and unwilling to carry it around with her, Jude cooked. She put all that ailed her up in her spice cabinet, and took down a cast-iron pan and a pot, pulled a couple of ham steaks out from the icebox. For her guest, Jude made a late dinner of ham glazed in brown sugar and mustard, soft-boiled eggs, and thick slices of brown bread smeared with butter. In lieu of coffee or tea, she poured them both mugs of hot milk flavored with cinnamon and cream. Jude returned to find Nemoira standing in front of one of her quilts—year nine, no real pattern, just squares of purple and blue, an emerald semicircle to represent the cypress swamp. Jude set the plate and cups down on the coffee table, cleared her throat. Nemoira turned slowly, eyes on Jude first and then the food.

She smiled. "This for me?"

Jude nodded, returned to her position on the couch.

"None for you?" Nemoira asked. She settled on the floor, pulled her plate near to her, and sniffed at her drink.

"I ate already. You g'on ahead, fore it gets cold."

The woman ate and Jude watched her with unmasked pleasure. She wasn't a dainty eater, Nemoira. She ignored the cutlery, preferring to eat with her fingers, tearing off chunks of ham and bread, sopping up egg yolk with her toast. There was syrup at the corners of her mouth, crumbs, and when she'd finished her milk, a sheen of sugar on her bottom lip.

Hungry girl, Jude thought. *Sweet, and sweet to look at*. Felt like lightning looking at Nemoira, her long and dark hands, her hooded eyes, her lips the color of a black lily. By firelight, her skin was black as the night, velvet indigo, and Jude fought valiantly the urge to reach out and touch her cheek, to run a hand over the long, coiled hair that swelled around her like a pelt.

She consumed—the room was hers and all the air in it, even the air from Jude's lungs. Again, she faced Jude, those impossibly deep eyes fastening onto her, seemingly more amused by Jude's attention than aggravated. Others would've turned from her by now, would've blinked or flinched, but not Nemoira; she held Jude in place, swaddled her in her gaze.

"The food good?" Jude asked, breaking the moment, the look. "You want more?"

Nemoira blinked at her empty plate, the smears of sugar and egg. "Very good. And no, no more for me."

The room fell silent, Jude at a loss for words and Nemoira inscrutable. After a while of watching wood crackling in the hearth, Nemoira asked, "You mind if I wash?"

"You want a bath?"

"You draw me one? Only if it ain't no trouble."

It was trouble. The house had, in theory, hot water, but the pipes were finicky, and on any given day, the water would come out boiling hot or freezing cold with little variation in between. Today was a tepid day, none of the taps getting any hotter than room temperature. To run the woman a bath meant having to boil and lug four or five miserably heavy pots of water upstairs. Nothing in her wanted to do it, not even for herself, and yet Jude sighed, rose to her feet, and bade Nemoira to follow her upstairs.

Jude kept the bathroom clean but not tidy, and even after the day's cleaning frenzy, the vanity was a mess of oils and soap, sachets of dried flowers, dried oats, a crow's hoard of earrings, necklaces, little baubles she found in the woods. She muttered an apology for the disarray and gestured for Nemoira to sit on the toilet's lid.

"It's gon' be a while, filling the tub," Jude warned. She turned on the tap, let the cold water flow into the tub. "You mind the wait?"

Nemoira shook her head and offered no assistance. She sat, legs splayed wide, and ogled at Jude's candles and vials of cologne, the carved wooden tray on which sat a much-eroded bar of jasmine soap.

Down in the kitchen, Jude filled her three tallest pots with water and set them to boiling. As steam rose and wetted her face, she thought about what clothes she had to give the woman, and when the first pots were done, Jude carried them upstairs, filled the tub, and went down again to boil more water.

Once she had the bath full, Jude poured in a little Epsom salt and camphor oil, and crushed some mint leaves into the water. Nemoira watched her work, rapt, and when she was through, Jude nodded at the tub and asked Nemoira to test the water's temperature.

"Too hot?"

"No, it's good. Perfect, actually."

Jude rose from the rim of the tub, started to turn to give Nemoira a modicum of privacy, but found herself unable to move a muscle once the woman started to disrobe. Lightheaded, prickling with sweat, Jude took her in—the hips and fatty thighs, the soft pouch of belly, the long and muscled legs. She felt her heartbeat low in her groin, hopelessly intrigued by the black, coiled mass of pubic hair, the breasts like anthills. Nemoira tied her hair in on itself, exposing the dark column of her nape, the feline curve of her back.

Glancing over her shoulder at Jude, she whispered, "Is it deep? You help me in?"

Jude grabbed uselessly for a response, but her tongue was glued fast to the roof of her mouth. With a sharp exhale, she snatched the empty pots from the floor and tore out of the bathroom. Outside, in cooler air, she leaned against the wall and put a hand to her heart. In the past, Jude would ogle a woman, envious and covetous of her dexterous hands and thighs, the roiling sway of her hips, but she was good, then, at taking hold of herself and at convincing herself that her interest was solely aesthetic. No such luck out here in the wilds. Hungry thoughts of Nemoira's legs and breasts, the sweat collecting in the subtle folds of her tummy, made her slaver, shiver.

In the kitchen, Jude set the pots in the sink to cool and then stood holding on to the counter, clenching and releasing her fists. The pent-up heat in her face, behind her eyes, burning through her chest, the throbbing in her stomach—Jude grabbed a knife and bored a hole into her hand, the bowl of her palm slowly filling with blood. As the heat in her head and between her legs subsided, Jude emptied her hand, rinsed it, and made her way back to the bathroom, stopping briefly to fetch a rag and a towel from the linen closet.

Steadier now and braced against the sight of a nude Nemoira, Jude reentered. The bathroom was a hothouse, tropically warm, the air sage green with the blended odors of grass, camphor, jasmine, and mint. Steam obscured her vision, and Jude was grateful for it, for any relief she could find from the woman in the water. She put the towel on the vanity, offered Nemoira the washcloth. Caught, trapped. With undisguised interest, Jude drew her eyes across Nemoira's wet face and black areolas, the dip of her belly, how it slanted oh so perfectly into the water, down into the nest of curls just out of sight.

Jude tore her gaze away, and Nemoira, unfazed by her nudity, took the washcloth from Jude's hand. Their fingers met, palm brushing against wounded palm, pinkie grazing thumb. Jude's body burned, a thousand Sunday candles burning like votives in the hollow of her chest. Though the smoke filled her mind and shaded her eyes, her thoughts were clear and focused. Nemoira, Nemoira, all maddening scent and dark eyes, the careful way she watched for Jude's reactions.

It was too much. Jude yanked her hand away and ran from the bathroom once more, door slamming behind her.

It took Jude the whole of Nemoira's bath to make the parlor presentable. She never used it for its intended purpose, preferring the living room to relax in, and over the years it had become a cluttered storage area. Jude dug through her mess, shifting miscellaneous pieces of furniture and scrap wood down into the cellar. There was a slightly musty sofa in the parlor, and she sprayed it down, dressed it with freshly laundered sheets and a couple of pillows, a simple yellow-blue quilt of stars. On a side table she usually used for Sunday's candles, Jude placed a lamp and another hot mug of milk.

She was in the process of tucking the sheets under the sofa cushion when Nemoira entered the parlor, hair dripping, steam rising from her naked skin. She blushed, bade the woman sit on the couch while she rummaged in her wardrobe for something for her to sleep in. Nemoira was a good three inches taller than Jude, and thinner, but an old nightdress would do fine. It hung loose on Nemoira as she settled into her makeshift bed, one shoulder bared as she reached for her cup.

"You'll be fine here for the night. If you get cold, there's a thicker quilt just there," Jude informed her, pointing to a wicker basket that held some of her smaller works. Her eyes kept dropping to the woman's shoulder, the goose-pimpled flesh, and it pained her to look away.

"What if I hear a noise?" So gently she spoke, her voice like the whisper of leaves.

Jude shook her head, reached out to put a reassuring hand on the woman's covered knee, and decided against it. She clasped her hands in her lap and said, "Won't nothing bother you. This late, it's only frogs and cicadas and the like. Scariest thing you'll hear is a loon."

Pleased with Jude's answer, Nemoira rested her head on the pillow and closed her eyes. Jude left the parlor quietly as she could, and when she slept that night, she slept fitfully, mind's thread caught on the nail of the stranger dozing in the room just below her.

12

On the anniversary of her mother's death, Jude dreamed that Ma'am shoved her clawed, wrinkled hand down her throat in search of her ruined eye. Jude tried to tell her, mouth full of arm, that she didn't have it, but Ma'am ignored her, determined. She rummaged through Jude's belly as if it were an overstuffed purse, shoving aside the intestines, the uterus, the kidneys, but there was nothing there, only carrot peels and celery fiber, jagged shards of beef bone. *Liar*, Ma'am called her. *Thief!*

She pulled Jude's stomach. Jude startled awake, threw herself over the side of the bed, and vomited. *See?* she told Ma'am. Porcelain angels with cracked faces and wings askew floated in her dinner and digestive bile, but no eye. She returned to her pillow, felt her chest caving in with invisible weight. It hurt to breathe, hurt to swallow, hurt to blink and to keep her eyes open, to move even an inch. Her eyes drooped closed, and Jude saw her mother's kitchen, the wallpaper inlaid with rolling, shaking jellied eyes. Glass cherubs strummed at golden harps as they fell from their perches, tinkling renditions of "Don't Let Me Be Misunderstood" that ended abruptly as each angel hit the floor and shattered.

"Jude?"

Through narrow slits, Jude regarded the figure at the door. She couldn't make sense of the face, but she moaned when a cool hand pressed itself to her dark, flushed cheek. Speaking was out of the question; a hoarse, aching throat stymied all attempts to communicate or to swallow even water.

In and out of consciousness, Jude drifted. She was Candle, sweating, and now she was in the house on Westmoor Drive, in her former bedroom. Everything was as she remembered it: the pink-and-white wallpaper and lace curtains, the furniture Pappy carved himself. On the dresser sat overdressed dolls, little bottles of scent, and a jewelry box. Inside the jewelry box were her knocked-out teeth, a baby's bracelet, her first pair of earrings, and Ma'am's eye. It scanned the room from its cushioned position and settled on Jude, who promptly threw the box closed.

Awake, the vomit and the swimming angels were gone, and a ceramic heater droned in the corner. A mountain of blankets crushed her, cloth bears and sheep, women climbing off their quilts and scrabbling over her body. Fevered, Jude hacked and wheezed, and Nemoira brought her things up from the parlor to sleep close to her. By day, Jude fought her bedding, fought for breath, and at night, she was as still as death, insensible. Ma'am, the loudest voice in her mind save for her own, said to Jude, *Just when you mean to come home? Ain't you sorry? What sort of thing did I raise that would bleed its mother and steal my ring, leave me cold and spilling red on the tiles my daddy laid?*

Choked by memory, choking on her sick, Jude tried to explain herself. Didn't Ma'am understand that that house on Westmoor was poison? Couldn't she see that there was no such thing as home, only miserable rooms and walls and halls that hated?

Ma'ammy asked her how could she do it, how could she dare, but what other choice was there? Violence was her birthright, anger her first gift—*I only did what you taught me, Ma'ammy*, thought Jude. *Ain't this what you taught me?*

Nemoira dragged a cool cloth over her forehead. Jude rolled over in bed and woke in a vermillion hell stinking of meat, ammonia. She rolled again, and her mother was laid out to the right of her, her death rattle overwhelming the heater's incessant hum. To her left, her grandfather slept on his cooling board, arms folded over his barrel chest, and Ma'am hunched over his corpse, screaming, *Don't! Oh, Daddy, don't, don't! You can't!*

On the ninth day, pearls of sweat beaded on Jude's collarbone, the fever broken. She had Nemoira help her as far as the cellar door, and then left the woman at the top of the stairs so she could give her thanks in private. The sideboard groaned under the weight of her retroactive offerings, a week's worth of roots and rum and prayers.

Jude prayed and wondered over the significance of this year's terrors. There had been bad anniversaries before, years where the house was raucous and her bed trembled beneath her, but never were her visions so real or the destruction to her body so complete. Scars ruptured open and out flowed the old blood, brown and thick and clumping. What could be done for it? Prayer helped, sometimes, and looking too closely at the past, the foul works of her hands, only served to hurt her. Fingering a wound only irritated it—what could Jude do, really, other than pack the gaping hole with gauze and with good food, sew it shut, and leave it be?

When Jude was well enough to walk, she made up her mind to go to Whitnee. She wanted to give the woman something for having nursed her, so in town she bought catfish and grits, all the while fielding questions about where she'd been, the strange woman that'd been calling herself a friend of Jude's.

"She been looking after me while I've been ill," Jude said. People clicked their tongues and nodded, muttered axioms about the turning weather. A granny wife she often supplied with herbs gave her a sachet of sassafras and a recipe using bone broth.

Jude was slow coming home. She had missed her time in the woods, though the woods showed no sign of missing her. She ambled along, clean morning sunlight warming her head and shoulders. Jude ran her hands through the hanging moss, picked up and discarded shiny rocks, seedpods, unconsciously tucking a few into her pocket to show to Nemoira.

When she returned to Candle, the house was seething. She put a hand to a wall and shushed it.

"What's gotten into you?" Jude asked. The sideboard scraped across the floor, and Jude grabbed it, held it in place. She waited until the piece was still before she entered the kitchen. For her guest, she prepared a breakfast of flaky biscuits, hot fried fish, buttery grits, and a pot of sassafras tea. She thought of Nemoira as she cooked, and what was to be done about her.

Jude liked to be alone, liked her solitude and her freedom, but she was lonely too. She felt it like a hole in her stomach, gaping and growing with each year, and every second she went without another voice, another body, without anyone to *know* her and need her, the hole spread. She didn't intend to call Nemoira her friend when she was in Whitnee, but the more she thought about the woman, the more appropriate the title felt. That they'd only spoken a handful of times, their time together focused solely on Jude's health, was irrelevant; there was a warmth between them now, Nemoira touching her forehead and Jude leaning into the coolness of her fingers, Jude alert and listening as Nemoira hummed little nonsense songs. She couldn't think when someone had last looked at her with such tenderness. She didn't want it to end.

Jude plated their food. The dining room, neglected, rattled as Jude entered, and Jude clicked her tongue at it.

"Don't start," Jude warned. She draped the table in a pink cloth, filled a cornflower-blue jug with dried verbena. "I won't have you kicking up jus' 'cause you got an audience. You hear?"

The hutch rocked, thumped two legs in its best approximation of a stomp.

Jude and Nemoira collided as Jude went to fetch her from the parlor, the woman on her way in as Jude was on her way out. Exhaustion drained the vitality from her movements, but not from her eyes, which still shone like lacquered stones. She took in the table Jude had set, the food, and when she met Jude's gaze, she smiled.

"For me?" asked Nemoira. Jude pulled out the chair across from her own and bade Nemoira sit.

"Thought you might like to eat something heavier than soup."

It wasn't nervousness that darted between them, nor was either woman abashed at the frank intimacy Jude's sickness had thrust them into. Jude served, doling out food and tea to Nemoira first and then herself, and found that she liked the joy it gave her handing things to Nemoira.

They spoke over breakfast, wordlessly and with gesture. Jude chose a language of clicks, clinks; her spoon scraping the curve of the bowl, her teeth catching on the lip of her mug. Nemoira, breathier, more air than metal, sighed and hummed and crunched delicate catfish bones between her molars.

When the last spoon of grits had been savored and digested, Nemoira stood and began to gather the dirty plates.

"Oh, don't do that," said Jude. She rose, tried taking the plates from Nemoira, but she twisted out of Jude's reach. Jude huffed, put her hands to her hips.

Nemoira shook her head, gathered more of the dishes, stacking bowls onto plates, cutlery into cups. "You been in bed for two weeks, you need rest. Let me help, huh? You cook, I clean. Fair?"

Understanding from the sternness of her tone that there'd be no further argument, Jude retook her seat as Nemoira crossed into the kitchen. She fiddled with her hands, uneasy at having somebody cleaning up after her, and she kept her ear perked to disaster. Some small part of her wanted one, for a glass to explode in Nemoira's hand, for the cabinets to disgorge their contents, but Candle was still, waiting, it seemed, for Jude's final verdict.

Jude gnawed her lip, started to tell herself she didn't know what she wanted, but she knew she did. No one else intrigued her like Nemoira did, but then again, nobody else bothered. The townspeople were plain, decent—they offered iced tea and church sermons, advice on cooking greens. Nemoira came to her empty-handed and needy, wriggled wasplike into the fig flesh of Jude's house and mind. Jude didn't know just then if they'd rot or bloom together, but she was curious to see what the woman did next. What havoc or happiness Nemoira would wreak on her innards remained to be seen, and Jude, curious, wanted to see what she did next.

So, Nemoira would have to stay, would have to sleep in the parlor and eat Jude's food and flash her black eyes over every lovely little thing in Jude's house. Time, conversation, sprays of flower, cups of tea, plates of food, peeled fruit; for as long as Nemoira was willing to hold out her hand, Jude was willing to put something in it.

There were no disasters, nothing broken, and when Nemoira was finished with the dishes, she excused herself back to the parlor. Jude followed on the pretense of needing to return her bedding, and if Nemoira doubted her motives, she said nothing, only smiled and took back her sheets, pillows.

"Your house missed you," said Nemoira. "It fussed the whole time you were out."

"Hope it didn't upset you. It hardly ever acts up like that. I used to . . ." The story of her first year in Candle came to her unbidden, and Jude swallowed it, unwilling to share what she feared might make her sound ridiculous. "I meant to ask you . . . Begging your pardon, but where did you mean to go, when you came here that night?"

"Go?" Nemoira canted her head, considering Jude's question. "I don't know. Don't remember."

"Were you fixing to stay in Whitnee?"

"*No-oo* . . . You think I should go there?"

"No," Jude said with a tone of finality. "Whitnee ain't friendly, not really, and the rest of the state ain't much better. I think you should stay here, in the parlor." She did not add the words *with me*, but they hung in the air. Nemoira's lips twitched into a smile, and in the dining room, the hutch shook and thumped.

Later, as she replaced forks and spoons and knives, Jude heard singing from the parlor, a song she knew the tune to but not the lyrics.

13

Everything in Candle had a name, a purpose, but after two months of sharing Jude's home, Nemoira was still unquantifiable. Nebulously, she hovered between kingdoms and genera, too warm to be reptilian and too cold and aloof to be entirely mammal. Like a rabbit, she was alert to noise and sudden movement, but her similarities with prey animals stopped there. Her perked ear, her watchful eyes; Jude saw within them the cool, measured confidence of alligators—what she wanted, she'd have.

Unable and increasingly unwilling to taxonomize her, Jude gave Nemoira a place of her own, a spot fit for women who laughed loudly and killed garden snakes and ate with their hands, chins shiny with grease. She thought about everything, about nothing; she couldn't care less for Jude's collection of books, showed no interest in reading anything on her own, but Nemoira liked to hear Jude read. Like cogongrass, dry and green and greedy, she sucked up Jude's oxygen, uprooted her, siphoned off her time.

Nothing bored Nemoira, and she was eager to help with any task, big or small. She was a deft hand at gardening, resourceful and thrifty, and over the course of Jude's convalescence, she managed to turn Jude's respectably lush home garden into a veritable Eden. Never before had the soil been so rich and richly scented; never had there ever been such variety and color, fennel and garlic and mint growing sister close alongside broccoli, hyacinth, and tomatoes.

Tuesdays, Jude prepared remedies, as Nemoira chopped and ground herbs, suggested new combinations, and on Wednesdays, she came along to trade and run errands. She was a natural, Nemoira, reserved with the customers at first and then bursting in animation when given the opportunity to expound on the healing qualities of this or that tincture. They made an odd pair, talking and giggling like overgrown girls. Jude leaned into Nemoira to whisper, Nemoira excitedly took her hand and squeezed it. She kissed Jude, once, on the cheek, just an innocent smear of lips on flesh, and Jude, flushing, felt the whole of the town turn to them.

Mrs. Meyers, a Black woman Jude had been supplying with ginger salves since '68, held Jude back as she and Nemoira exited her house, burdened with a small basket of string beans. Nemoira stood in the yard, watched a dog work himself into a lather over a passing car, and Mrs. Meyers asked, "Who'd you say that woman was to you, Mrs. Rice?"

Even now, being called a missus startled Jude. She tucked her ringed hand into her pocket and shrugged. "Just a friend, Mrs. Meyers."

The woman clucked her tongue and said, "And how long is this *friend* of yours planning on stayin'?"

Another shrug. "Until she move on, I suppose. She with me, for now, and I don't mind the company. Now, look here, you got to remember to put the ginger on as often as you ache—it won't work if you ain't consistent."

"I only ask, you know, 'cause folks have been wonderin' about the two a you, up there in that funny house with no men." Mrs.

Meyers crossed her arms and her sweater against the chill, her face and voice betraying nothing.

Jude laughed her short, joyless laugh, her grin like a grimace. She felt where Meyers was pressing, had felt the press for years every time she denied a man or resisted courtship. Unnatural, they called her. Jude's grimace broadened into a snarl, and she wished Mrs. Meyers a good day before stepping off her porch and returning to Nemoira.

In the notions shop, Jude tried and failed to suppress her aggravation as Nemoira darted around the store, ogling at the rainbow of threads, fabrics. *Folks have been wonderin'? Let 'em wonder*, thought Jude, but the pinch of shame, sharp as a side stitch, couldn't be worked loose. She rubbed her thumb along her nearly healed palm and pressed at the wound until it bled.

Meanwhile, Nemoira gasped and sighed, fascinated by every button, bow, and ribbon she laid her eyes on. She presented Jude with treasures and Jude grunted, distracted with her thoughts. After the fifth time she came to Jude, she glanced down at Jude's hand, saw the smear of blood, took Jude's hand in her own, and said, "Will you make me a dress?"

Jude looked at their clasped hands, her blood on Nemoira's skin. "What for?"

"Does there have to be a reason? Can't I jus' have it for being pretty in the house?"

Jude gave Nemoira a little smile and led Nemoira to a rack of fabrics. Her face was cooling, relaxing. She filed through the jacquard and wool and polyester with her undamaged hand, and asked, "You got a color in mind?"

"*Ummm*. Purple, maybe?" Nemoira scanned the rack as well, her stained fingers daubing red on blue crepe and brown satin. "Pink, like a sunset or like an azalea."

Jude searched the fabrics, discarding colors too drab or pale. She didn't want Nemoira in a pattern, nothing checked or striped, nothing floral to distract from her blue-black skin. It was only after she made several laps around the store that she found a long bolt of fuchsia cotton. Jude brought it up to Nemoira's arm. "How about this?"

"Oh yes, Judy! And with pretty buttons down the front! And pockets! You make it for me?"

Jude's smile broadened at the nickname, at the whistling susurrus of her name in Nemoira's mouth. "Of course. You can have anything you like."

The sewing room wouldn't let Jude in—at least, not with Nemoira behind her. If she approached the door, the room sealed itself, the knob and frame disappearing into the wallpaper.

"See!" laughed Nemoira. "I told you your house don't like me."

"My house don't know what it likes," said Jude.

She led Nemoira to the dining room, and by waning daylight, Jude wound a tape measure around Nemoira's breasts, her waist, her hips, mouth decidedly dry as she measured the woman's calves and thighs, bare save for her thin underthings. The smell of her jasmine soap on Nemoira's skin was dizzying, heady as summer wine.

It took Jude four days to make Nemoira's dress. She had constant company, Nemoira at Jude's elbow with a hundred questions. She asked Jude about her sewing, about Candle, about Whitnee, about herself. Why this and who that? Where did you come from? Don't you have people?

"My folks is dead," said Jude flatly. She stuck a pin in at Nemoira's waist where she wanted the dress to sit tighter. "And I'm from upstate, Atlanta."

"I never been," admitted Nemoira. She held the felt tomato in her hand and was playing with the pins, passing them along to Jude as needed. "You like it there?"

"Not really. I never saw much of it, tell you the truth—I didn't get out the house much." Red tiles and steel flickered in Jude's mind. She felt hands around her throat, felt her body start to go slack with memory. Discreetly, Jude jabbed a pin into the meat of her thigh. "It's better here, alone. I tell you, I don't care much for being around other people. I don't fit with 'em."

"I don't think I fitted either. Like a stoat among rabbits, I was."

"Different?"

"Dangerous," answered Nemoira.

Days later, Candle appeased with rum and pound cake, Nemoira entered the sewing room. Jude shuddered. She felt broken into, opened, a thumb pressed to the yielding skin of a peach. Breathless, Jude watched Nemoira explore. Her eyes were wide and bright with curiosity, and everything she touched—the patterns, the quilting squares, clothes half finished, notebooks of calculations and measurements—she touched with a reverence that reverberated through Jude like the thrum of a harp.

Nemoira, drifting, came to a quilt Jude had tacked to the wall beside the window. She fingered the fabric, mouth parted in wonder, and Jude tried looking at the quilt through her eyes. It wasn't her finest—too mean and too messy, an orange corduroy fox with a black felt rabbit in its teeth, gingham droplets of blood spilling from the wound. If she made it now, she'd be more judicious with her choice of color and pattern, disliking immediately the clash of stripes and plaids and dots.

At least, Nemoira seemed to like it. She exclaimed, clapped her hands together, and said, "Oh, Judy, it's just . . . Oh! Look at how it feels! The plaid!"

"It ain't too much?"

"How could it be!" She felt the rabbit's flocking, the ribbed pelt of the fox. "You never said you was a root woman, making dead things alive."

Jude gave Nemoira little grin, a nudge with her shoulder. She regarded the tapestry and tried to imagine the mood she'd been in when she'd sewed it, but found she couldn't. The moment was so light and so sweet, and Jude was too pleased with her company, pleased at having made Nemoira fall silent with awe. How odd that woman seemed to her now, that grim creature who stitched lacy gore into fox fur.

"It's savage," sighed Nemoira, wistful. "Ugly as sin, but good. Lookahere, the most basic of lessons, animal eating and animal being eaten. The rabbit know his neck belongs to the fox's mouth, same as the fox know he belong to the bear or the vulture, the gator sneaking out the water..."

"You really think like that?"

Nemoira shrugged, a single blasé shoulder, and hummed. "Why not? You can't deny nature."

Jude's fixed smile waned. Nemoira couldn't have known what she was saying, not really, but it pinched at Jude nonetheless. She tried at nonchalance, made her own humming noise, but to her ears it sounded forced, strained. Jude said, "Maybe not. But sometimes what you are isn't what you *are*. Bigger and meaner things get knocked down by small ones every day."

Nemoira glanced at her, lips twitching and eyes flashing with mischief. She turned, put her hands on Jude's hips, squeezed, and asked, "Sweet Judy, Br'er Judy! You think if you was the rabbit you could outrun the fox?"

"Br'er did it, didn't he?" She met Nemoira's gaze, the look in her eyes more cutting than she intended. "If he could do it, why not me?"

After dinner, any dinner, Jude took their dishes, scraped the bones and scraps into the compost, and then prepared another bowl—potatoes, leeks, chicken in brown gravy. Nemoira watched her and asked, teasing, if Jude was so hungry as to want seconds.

To Nemoira, she said, "It's not for me."

"For your pet, then?"

"My pet?" Jude replied, voice hitching. She turned to Nemoira, who smiled coyly, shrugged her shoulders.

"Whatever thing it is you feed out there. Seems like food goin' to waste to me, it don't hardly eat much of anything you leave it."

Jude regarded Nemoira head-on. Like with many things she considered hers and therefore private, she didn't speak about the beast. To do so would feel like a betrayal, like the bond she shared with that sun-eyed animal would somehow be broken by testing it. Already, things had changed between Jude and the beast, the creature being scarce ever since Nemoira came to live with her.

Jude carried the bowl outside, set it on the porch in the soft red depression. The food was for the beast, kindness returned for the years it fed her, the gifts of wrappers and stones and nuts, but it was for herself as well. Just as the altar was a whetstone for her to sharpen and hone herself on, so was this small act. She lit the candles, the world narrowed and widened, the beast brought her hare and buck—so it was, so it would be, and Jude would do it all, the not-praying and the offerings, even if the beast never returned, even if it had left her for good.

Nemoira stood with Jude on the porch, hands clasped behind her back. "Might be something else eatin' your food. Possums, raccoons, foxes . . ."

It was Jude's turn to shrug. She hummed, nonchalant, and told Nemoira that it didn't matter to her if it was her *pet* that ate or any of the forest's many critters. It was true. The beast would leave, like summer into fall, like fall freezing into winter, and just as the frosts melted to reveal new buds and blooms, so too would the beast return. It'd be hungry, whenever it came back.

August became September became October. Jude swallowed indigestible memories, and they burned through her organs like acid. This year was a mean one, uglier than the ones before, though why Jude couldn't begin to fathom. Her mind was unusually cruel to her and it reminded Jude as often as it could of Ma'am's dangling nostril, rooms washed in red, rooms queasy with new death. Sights and actions benign upset her—Nemoira gently brushed hair from Jude's nape, and Jude nearly hit her. She caught herself with her hand in the air, Nemoira staring unflinchingly at her, waiting, looking to Jude as if to say, *Well?*

Jude excused herself to her bedroom, closed and locked the door behind her. She put a hand over her mouth, put her back to the door. What was she *doing*? Did she really mean to hit Nemoira, or was it only a reflex? And if it was a reflex, what kind of person did that make her, if her first reaction to touch was violence?

Her mother's hit-first-ask-later anger simmered in her blood, and Jude's mind twisted and knotted itself on every one of her flaws, perceived and real. She wondered if Nemoira would leave now, wondered if, in that brief lapse of control, she'd managed to peek into Jude's macabre mind. Was it ruined now? Now that she knew that Jude was broken, now that Jude had proved herself to be like her mother, worse than her mother, was it over? Was she hopeless, was she like her mother like her mother like her mother, was she irredeemable, was she—

Nemoira knocked on the bedroom door, calling for her. Jude remained where she was on the floor, shoulders tensed. The itching voice in her head said, *If you bite long enough, she'll go away*, and in the fog of mania, the idea made perfect sense. Her blood was a comfort to her, her wrist a useful muzzle against the vile, bilious words burning holes into her tongue.

For hours, Jude's thoughts were like thread, spinning out, looping, spiraling down and down, until it hurt to think, until all she heard and saw was blackness. Her black hands, her bloodied palms, the evil grin she shared with the blade she dragged along her mother's throat. Jude whined, itched her face and legs. Her pillow was wet from crying, from saliva where she had bitten into the down and screamed.

Later in the night, Jude heard her bedroom door creak open. She peered into the darkness, hackles raised in alarm. *I locked it*, she thought. *I locked the door, didn't I lock it?* After a moment, she heard Nemoira say, "It's only me, Judy."

By the moon's thin light, Jude saw Nemoira's eyes, black and flashing. She followed the woman's steps with her ear, body still tense, clenching as she listened to near-silent feet pad across the room.

The lamp's string jangled, and Jude shot out her hand to catch Nemoira's wrist. She hadn't the strength to let Nemoira see what she'd done to herself.

"Don't," whispered Jude. "No light, Nemoira. Please?"

A beat of silence, Jude's staggered breathing and Nemoira's soft exhales. At length, Nemoira said, "That's alright, Judy."

The sheets were drawn back and the bed dipped, creaking, as Nemoira slid in beside Jude. Paralyzed, uncertain of her hands and the closeness of Nemoira's fragrant skin, Jude hesitated before making room. Nemoira's thigh against her own, her cheek dangerously close to Jude's shoulder. Heat built in her face, excitement and mortification, and she turned her head away as tears began to well. She wanted a reason to move her leg, for Nemoira to roll them closer, for the bed to read her mind and tilt them into each other, but everything and everyone, she included, was stiff and still and waiting.

14

Like Ruth trailing Naomi, taking on her land and her people, wherever Jude went Nemoira went as well. Blithely, Jude wondered if Naomi ever wished Ruth had stayed behind. The breathing room would've been nice, and there wouldn't have been someone at her heels all day, eating her food, begging for her time and patience.

How quickly her moods changed! One moment, Jude craved Nemoira's company, sought it out, even, and in the next, she was resentful, exhausted by even the minutest of Nemoira's actions. She was always *there*, over Jude's shoulder, in Jude's way, except for when she wasn't—whenever Jude wanted her most, when she needed an ear or a shoulder or just another body beside her, Nemoira was out of reach, off on one of her adventures. Was it the inconsistency that rankled at her, the unpredictability? She wanted Nemoira in her hand. Wanted Nemoira to leave her the hell alone, to let her breathe for a moment, just a single damn moment. Of course, it didn't make sense—Jude crowed about loneliness, she longed, she needed to be held and spoken to, and yet the chafing, the claustrophobia.

If Nemoira felt some kind of way about Jude's caginess, she kept it to herself. Still, Jude was aware of being watched, studied, and still, Nemoira pressed and pressed, ignorant to or uncaring of Jude's growing discomfort. When Nemoira asked, for the hundredth time, if she could come along with Jude and see what she did in the woods, in the cellar, Jude told her flat out and frankly to leave her the hell alone.

"It's got nothing to do with you," she said. Already, she was grabbing her things, angrily packing her basket with her foraging tools. That chittering, itching voice in her mind suggested nasty, biting words to say, and Jude silenced it with a hiss. "It's *mine*. I don't go askin' after you, do I, when you out doing God knows what, so leave me *be*."

Nemoira did not flinch from her as Jude thought she would. Coolly, she regarded Jude and responded, "You could ask. I'd tell you."

"*I* don't want to know."

"You not even the littlest bit curious 'bout me? Where I come from? What I do, what I *can* do?"

Unease rolled through Jude's body like a wave of nausea. Candle rolled with her, the light fixtures swaying above her head. Both she and Nemoira glanced up to watch the fixtures dance, yellow light moving back and forth, back and forth over their upturned faces.

They didn't talk about it again, the not-talking. Jude went on her way and Nemoira went on hers, their paths crossing but never meeting directly. For three days, they were at silent war with each other. Jude remained in her bedroom or in the woods or in the cellar. Nemoira, for her part, kept to the sunroom and her parlor bedroom. What she ate in that time, Jude didn't know. She didn't cook for her in those days and there was never any mess in the kitchen, and yet she remained full and flush with life.

The impasse broke on a Sunday morning. Jude, on her way out to the woods, hovered by the door to the parlor. Nemoira was singing in there, a song Jude had taught her and that she had modified with runs and twists and lyrics of her own. For a minute or so, Jude listened, tension in her chest lightening as Nemoira teased out funny notes, funny sounds. She blew laughter through her nose and knocked.

"Nemoira?" she called. "Can I come in?"

There was no answer for a while, only the shuffling of things being adjusted and moved, of someone approaching the door, and then Nemoira, greeting Jude in her bonnet and nightgown. Jude saw, over Nemoira's shoulder, the state of the woman's bedroom. Her bed (a real daybed, now, instead of the couch) was unmade, strewn with dresses, jeans, and a pair of tights hung over an armchair. All her surfaces, the nightstand and the repurposed coffee table and her dresser, were covered with her curios and oddities from the forest floor, bird skulls and insect husks, buttons and seedpods, pots of herbs and flowering plants. Nemoira shifted her weight, blocked Jude's view.

"What is it?"

"I wanted to know if you wanted to come to the woods with me," said Jude. It was no real apology, she knew, and more akin to something Ma'am might've given her, but she didn't know what else to do. Gestures, if they were grand enough or thoughtful enough, could hold a wound tight until better work could be done.

"The woods?" Nemoira hummed, canted her hip and her head. "Thought it was none of my business."

Jude bit her inner cheek. Avoiding Nemoira's eyes, she said, "I shouldn't've said that. It wasn't . . ." She shook her head, shook off the discomfort of an apology. "Come to the woods with me?"

A moment of silence became two moments, three, four, and

after an interminable amount of staring down at her bare feet, Nemoira said, "Let me dress."

It was chilly now, the days shortening and cooling. The trees wore their new colors, and Nemoira wore her fuchsia dress, walking alongside Jude with near-silent footsteps. They did not speak much as Jude led them through the woods. Jude had her own thoughts to contend with, and Nemoira had hers, but occasionally, Jude would glance in Nemoira's direction and find that the woman was looking back at her, an odd, contemplative look on her face.

Jude asked her what was on her mind and Nemoira answered, "You, mostly."

When they arrived at the cypress swamp, Jude spread out her blanket and made her usual preparations. She watched from the corner of her eye as Nemoira explored the space, gawping, staring at the woven net of gold and ruby that covered them. The morning sun, mild and strained through the dome's leafy ceiling, painted their skin yellow, orange, warm.

Nemoira approached the swamp, and before Jude could ask if she'd like to wet her feet, the woman kicked off her shoes and waded ankle-deep into the water, mossy scum at her shins, tights clutched in one hand and the bottom of her dress bunched in the other. The spell of pensiveness broken, Nemoira laughed, kicked her muddy feet, and splashed. She teased Jude with water, flicking it and throwing it at Jude until she joined her, and together, they giggled and pushed, shoved. They squealed at the feel of little insect legs running over their toes, tadpoles and minnows circling their ankles, captured and released frogs, chased lizards, and chased each other. They were girls together, mud daubed and cackling, playing games Jude hadn't played even as a child.

At lunch, Jude and Nemoira ignored the blanket Jude had brought along and chose instead to climb onto the bowed tree to eat their sandwiches. Their feet, dangling, grazed the grass, and they talked idly, saying for the first time things they'd forgotten to mention, origins and favorites. From Nemoira: her favorite color, the emerald green of pond moss; that she never knew her parents, but she came from a place like this, secluded and barren of company; a cheeky admission to preferring soft, chewy caramels over the chocolates they sometimes bought in Whitnee. In return, Jude told her that her own favorite color was black (black, like Nemoira's skin; black like the night sky in winter), how she loved singing gospel in the morning and blues in the evening, and how every minute she spent in Nemoira's company as her friend made each day molasses-sweet and each year before she had known her all the sadder.

"Was you lonely before me, Judy?" asked Nemoira.

"I think I was, even if I didn't say it, not even to myself. I thought if I kept it quiet and didn't let myself feel it, it wouldn't be true." She reclined against the cypress, supine, hands folded comfortably over her belly. "You?"

"Hmm, I think so. Thought it was jus' part of being alone, being one instead of more, but it wasn't. It was missing. Longing."

Their gazes caught, tangled. Jude's face burned and she turned away, twisted her fingers into strands of Spanish moss.

There was nothing sweet for the women to eat, so Nemoira took it upon herself to search the area for berries. She returned with two handfuls of fat, black muscadine grapes, damp with dew. From her periphery, Jude saw Nemoira peel back the black skin with her teeth, saw the hot pink of her tongue swipe juice from her dark lips. Warmth pooled in her belly, and again, she wrenched her eyes away.

"I'm surprised these is still here," said Jude. She peeled a grape to give her hands something to do. "Usually, they gone this time of year, ate up by the bears."

"You see many bears round here?"

"Black bears, mostly, and a few of them li'l Florida bears. There's one . . . Well, I don't know if it was a bear exactly, but it used to come here, big and scary as anything."

"You never seen it head-on?" asked Nemoira.

Jude thought of it in her house, its dark eyes watching her, and twitched. "Only once, and I reckon I don't ever wanna do it again."

Nemoira bit a muscadine, made a little contemplative noise. "Why come you never kill it? I seen you shoot, you could fell jus' 'bout anything, big or small."

Softly, Jude said, "I don't want it to leave me. It scares me, but it excites me too, the feeling of something so . . ." Here, Jude stretched out her arms, spread wide her fingers. "So *massive* caring enough to stalk me and come into my house, to leave deer on my porch. It's like having a god that looks only at you."

Later, Jude invited Nemoira down to the cellar. Nemoira trailed after, her hands weighted with offerings, dried peaches and crumpled dollar bills, half a bottle of rum. Whatever questions Nemoira had, for once she kept them to herself, and Jude was grateful for the silence. She needed time in her own mind to consider what to say to the haints and to the house, how she could best explain to Nemoira her need to convene with the living dead, the spirits that dwelled in and around her.

Jude came down the steps, felt the world stretch thin and then expand. In the altar room, she showed Nemoira the proper way to fill the bowls, plates, and cups. She lit the candles, and around them, the dead leaned in.

It was a tight squeeze in the closest with the two of them. Their shoulders bumped and their hips collided as Jude bowed her head, silently and then softly making her requests, introducing, finally, Nemoira to Candle. She peeked at Nemoira; the woman was twitchy here, eyes alert and darting.

She put a hand to Nemoira's elbow and said, "Be calm, girl."

"How you like it here, being so under?" hissed Nemoira. She looked at the roots, the candles, and the candles bowed away from her, the china plates trembling. "Being *buried*."

Jude leaped to protect the flame, the dishes from falling and breaking, and sighed. "It's different for me, I guess. It don't feel like being buried to me, more like, being close to the source. Being grounded."

Nemoira looked to her, expecting more, and Jude tried to find more words for her. She said how she always liked the feeling of dirt beneath her feet, how when she walked barefoot in the field she felt as if she were one with everything in the grass and in the forest, a minor part in the grand tapestry that was the Okefenokee. She told Nemoira that all of it, being in the altar room, feeling the heaviness of spirits, holy or hainted, brought her closer to those who went before her.

"Dead things," said Nemoira.

"My mother," explained Jude. She ran her palm over the twin flames, to distract herself from what her mouth was doing. "I go under, I come here where the veil is thin enough to pass through, and I feel like I can touch her."

Nemoira asked, "Was she very mean, your mother?"

Jude's mouth twitched, smiling-snarling. In her mind, her mother's throat opened like lips parting—Nemoira's lips parting around a muscadine, Nemoira's tongue wetting her lips. Jude snatched her hand back from the flame and blew out the candles. In the darkness, her and Nemoira's eyes the only points of light, she told Nemoira pieces of it; Ma'am armed with a belt, a shoe, how as a child she learned to differentiate the seasons by the feel of the switch—sharp and stinging in spring, brittle and aching in fall.

"She wasn't meant to be a mother, or she wasn't meant to be *my* mother," Jude said. "The day before I left, she slammed my head into the wall. I was on the floor, bleeding, and she stepped right over me, like I was nothing."

Her mind looped the sound of her skull against brick, the inane chatter of her mother's friends, her aunts. Ma'am's mangled face was a flash-bang in her mind, too loud and too bright to think around, and Jude blinked away the burning start of tears, nudged past Nemoira into the open cellar.

Next were the lights. Jude sang her little Sunday school hymn and Nemoira sang it with her. Together, they went from room to room, lighting candles, lighting Candle, and once they were through, Jude brought Nemoira out to the field, bare legged and shivering.

Nemoira wrapped her arms around herself and asked, "Will you come back out later?"

"How you mean?"

"You here now, yes, but sometimes you come later in the night. I see you from the parlor window, stood there like a scarecrow with all the field come to greet you. You glow green, like a firefly."

Jude stopped short, body tingling, and Nemoira turned to her, face bright with amusement and then confused. She said to Jude, "You didn't know?"

Jude forced a smile, but it was a grim one. She dropped it, let out a bark of laughter, and said, "My body, she never stay where I want her to stay. I always thought I was dreaming, even when I woke with my mouth tasting like dirt, clay in my teeth." Another bark of laughter bubbled out, this one tinged with hysteria. She kept her face out of the light of the house, corners of her mouth twitching, twitching. *Hold on now, girl,* she said to herself. *Now, you just hold on.* "Hope I didn't scare you."

Nemoira rounded her and put herself directly in Jude's line of sight. She stood and waited until Jude brought her eyes to meet her own, and when they found each other, Nemoira said softly, "Nothing you do could ever scare me."

Such sincerity there was in her voice, such meaning. Mouth still fighting between a rictus and a deep frown, Jude went farther into the field. She planted herself, sedge and purple panic grass, myriad oats and wild rices tickling her legs. The dead plantation rested at her feet, and its dead workers milled around her, their touches like wind against her skin. Ahead of her, Candle, luminous and all-consuming, and for the first time, she saw it through the eyes of another, its terrible brilliance, how it lit the field and the woods like wildfire. She glanced at Nemoira; washed in Candle's glow, she was resplendent as she was dark, and even still, she was the brightest thing burning.

Together, mossy bioluminescence and steady, golden radiance—small fingers brushed, an index finger crossed a scarred palm. Panting softly, skin alive with sensation, Jude grabbed hold of Nemoira's hand and was consumed with heat.

Eleven in the evening, the house black and silent save for the sounds of settling; Jude was awake. Restless, sweating, she stripped off her blanket and counted sheep, counted combinations of herbs and of fungi, the teas and blends she could make to settle her mind. Her hands itched, jerked. Twice, she shoved them under the sheets, fingertips grazing her hips and upper thighs, inching farther down, and twice, she snatched them back up, face alight with embarrassment.

It wasn't the touching that shamed her. She was too grown for it and too accustomed to the pleasure it gave her. Even in Ma'am's house, Jude treated herself, biting down on her pillow or her wrist to muffle her joy, the guilt and horror bested only by the hot, white shock of pleasure as she reached her peak. She had lost that guilt living in the woods, lost the need to muffle and to atone, but now it was back, the shame, the act harmless but the face that came to her as her hand wandered very dangerous indeed.

Jude wasn't ignorant. She'd known even as a young and sheltered thing that there were folks bent like that, folks pushed to the outer edges of the world. Her mother had names for them that Jude loathed to think even now, and her fear of being like *that*—bent, discarded—taught her to temper her passions. If her eyes lingered a little too long on a sister's thick brown legs or watched too closely the sway of an ample bottom, then surely, she had punished herself enough with cuts and flagellation. She thought of Mrs. Meyers, the knowing glances of strangers. Funny, they called her. Unnatural and confused, inverted, queer. Dyke. Bulldagger.

Her hands turned to claws on her thighs, and she stopped them, curled them into fists. She wouldn't do that, not here, not in her sacred and special house, not when Nemoira—Nemoira, *Nemoira!* Doused in the turpentine of desire, lit with a match of lust, Jude burned. She slipped her hand under. Pulled it back up. With a frustrated huff, Jude rolled out of bed, stepped into her slippers, and left her room.

Nemoira was coming up the stairs as she was coming down them, and for a moment, the women stared at each other, blinking, blushing. There was no light here, and in the dark, Nemoira was a streak of indigo and electric white eyes. Jude opened her mouth to speak but nothing left it.

Dizzy with choices, body raw with wanting, Jude took the half step to stand just over Nemoira, tilted back the woman's scarfed head, and kissed her brown mouth.

Sunday after Sunday of candles blazed in Jude's chest, her belly, her hands. Nemoira surged into her, all lip and motion, a small whimper as Jude took her into her arms. Being eaten alive would've been less consuming; Nemoira kissed as if starving, biting and lapping and nipping at Jude's jaw.

Jude broke away from Nemoira, panting. She held the woman's face in her hands, lifted her head so that they could look at each other. Nemoira's pupils were blown, and her breath was warm and sweet as it puffed up into Jude's face.

"Is this what you want?" asked Jude. She didn't know who the question was meant for, her or Nemoira. Her hands shook. She thumbed Nemoira's blue cheek. "You tell me now, Nemoira. Tell me this is what you want, that I'm not bending you or chasing you or—"

Nemoira grabbed Jude's hands, turned her face deeper into her palm. She kissed the thumb, the lines, flicked her pink tongue across the map of scars. "There ain't nothing in me that you can bend that I hadn't already broken."

In Jude's bedroom, darkness and heavy breath—Jude clicked on the bedside lamp, flaying herself in the lamplight. She revealed to Nemoira the crosshatched skin of her arms and legs, her buttocks rippling with scar tissue. Her scourged back was a mountain range, all ridges and deep valleys, the flesh mottled and puckered. Nemoira's hands, cool as water against the shamed, inflamed fire of her body, traced a knotted keloid that started at Jude's shoulder and ran down to her hip.

Jude tensed, back flexing and flying away from the touch. She felt Nemoira pull away and willed herself to relax. "My grandfather's whip," Jude explained of the raised scar.

Nemoira said nothing in response, gave no sign of disgust nor pity. She only clicked off the light, and in the darkness, her hand against Jude's collarbone, cupping her breast, was a balm. It soothed and it cooled, every swamp and river overflowing, soaking the soil and roots. Nemoira touched her, and her body burst into spring, iris and jasmine and hyacinth blooming wherever her fingers landed. Nemoira bloomed as well, her scent fragrant and intoxicating as Jude tangled her fingers into the pelt of her pubic hair, as Jude sealed her mouth around her clitoris, dark pistil flush with blood, and drank moans from her like a woman parched.

Once they were done, once Jude had wrung from Nemoira every groan and orgasm, once Nemoira had left Jude's skin raw with bites and scratches, Jude fell flat, her head on Nemoira's stomach, Nemoira drawing lazy circles on her back with her fingertips.

15

Meanwhile, Candle decayed. Vapors rose from the cellar, warping wood and peeling back the wallpaper. There were odd smells in the kitchen, in the bathroom, like mold or gas, and Jude propped the windows open against them. The windows, oddly resistant, refused to budge, and when they were opened, they threw themselves shut soon after. Rot ate the floors, the hardwood soft and caving in in the parlor, the dining room, the kitchen.

When a chair fell through the parlor floor and smashed itself to pieces in the cellar beneath it, Jude moved Nemoira upstairs into her own bedroom. It was where Nemoira belonged, her shoes under her bed and her clothes hanging in her wardrobe, her cache of trinkets lined up on the window.

Jude wrapped herself around Nemoira, buried her bleak memories in the graceful column of her neck, and around her, the house crumbled. Shingles flew from the roof, the pipes stopped carrying hot water. Coming up the path to the house one day, Jude saw the degradation in full—the sinking foundations and jaundiced siding, the kudzu that had all but devoured the exterior—and felt nothing but mild disappointment. What a shame, of course, her beautiful sanctuary going to pieces, but it was only a house. She and Nemoira could build another one, or they could find one in Whitnee proper, or maybe they'd leave the woods altogether one day, make a new life for themselves in a new town, a new state.

Either way, Jude would be housed, sheltered in Nemoira's ever-loving arms.

༄

Jude shot a goose down out of the sky, and it fell into her waiting hands like a woman fainting. A funny blend of breeds, it had a brown-and-gray chest and black feet, a pronounced and decidedly regal knob on its forehead—Jude twisted its neck, killing it.

At Candle, Jude entered with a shout, calling, "Nemoira? C'mere, come see this thing I'mma cook us!"

No response, no footsteps came running from the parlor or upstairs. Jude checked the parlor and living room, the bathroom, her own bedroom, the backyard where Nemoira sometimes liked to sit and laze in the grass. Out on another adventure, then; Jude sucked her teeth and took the bird into the kitchen, where she plucked, cleaned, and stuffed it before putting it into the oven for dinner.

She read and ate her dinner, minded the altar. Refused to worry. Too well she knew how Nemoira liked the attention that Jude's anxieties afforded her, those days of coddling and cooing, Jude scolding her for her recklessness but never meaning it. Any minute now, any second, Nemoira would stroll through the door grinning like a fool, heedless to the panic that'd been building inside of her lover. And, like a fool, Jude would go to her and click her tongue and take her coat, give her dinner, run her a bath.

Not me, Jude said. *Not this time.*

But then two hours went, then three, and still no Nemoira.

Jude glanced at the clock, glanced outside. There wasn't even a moon in the sky, no stars, only black night and clouds promising rain. *Fool*, she said to herself, but Jude grabbed her coat anyway, her flashlight—jolt of terror, Nemoira out there in the dark, Nemoira cold and lost—and her gun, and went into the woods.

It had been over a decade since Jude last needed to cross the Okefenokee at night. Returning to it, she wished she were anywhere but. She had forgotten it, how witched the woods were by dark, how strange, even the smallest of sounds, scents, and sensations elevated. Clutching at her flashlight, Jude pointed it here and there, illuminating bushes, patches of grass, but no footprints, no body. Unbidden, her mind provided her with images of Nemoira fallen, broken leg, broken arm, cracked skull; Nemoira slipped, drowned in black water and peat, lungs mossy; Nemoira attacked, beaten, her long neck stretched on a length of rope, her body dangling from an oak tree like moss. Jude shook out the thoughts and still they came, meaner, viler. She grunted. Stomped deeper into the woods.

It was past midnight when Jude quit searching. Her eyes and feet were tired, voice hoarse from calling the woman's name. Several times, she considered marching into Whitnee and banging on doors; even if Whitnee's whites wouldn't speak to her, she could try to rally its Negroes, all those patronizing men looking for a chance to play hero. Oh, but she didn't want them to see her afraid, didn't want anyone to look at her with sweat on her face and her hands shaking, the terror moving through her body like lightning through a tree.

Day after day, Jude returned to the woods to look for Nemoira. After a week, she entertained the idea of Nemoira having run off, but scrapped it almost immediately—if she had run, if she had decided she wanted no more of Jude and her greedy, hungry loving, she would've taken her fuchsia dress with her and her snail shells, her favorite blanket. Two weeks, three; Jude swallowed her pride and asked the pastor at the colored church to see what could be done, and for a little while, a week, at least, there was the promise of maybe, but in the end, people got bored or they remembered that Jude and Nemoira weren't like them. The pastor, when Jude asked again, only shrugged at her, said something about God's timing and what was proper and maybe would Jude like to join the church now, make a decent woman of herself? She wanted to say to him, what good was being decent if all it bought you was the same dirt and worms that a sinner got, but the words tangled in her mouth. He closed the doors of the church on her and Jude spat on them, her disgust with him, with God, oozing wetly down the wood.

After a month, Jude accepted that only death could've parted them and returned to her private search. Now, she looked for scraps of clothes, for hair. She used long sticks to stir up the bottoms of swamps, ponds, rivers, and brought up clumps of moss, the desiccated and decayed remains of animals mummified in peat. Something jammed itself out of the water, a hand pleading for rescue, but it was only a branch, mocking her. Vultures circled and dove, screeching, and Jude's stomach dove with them.

Two months, and Jude could no longer delude herself. No one was listening to her prayers, not God or the haints or even her wicked mother, who Jude, in her most desperate hour, had pleaded to for help. She was gone, Nemoira was gone and missing or dead. Stunned by the depth of her misery, Jude stumbled through the house, collecting Nemoira's things, and brought them all down to the parlor. She couldn't bury any of it, couldn't burn it either, so instead she put each of Nemoira's treasures back where they belonged and sealed off the parlor.

Grief deadened Jude, whole body numb and tingling. She moved as if through sludge, shuffling through the rooms dazed. Had she really spent four, almost five months, infatuated, reeling like a drunk through this very house? Had it really only been two months ago that she put her tired head on a woman's belly, her sounds of digestion a lullaby to her lovesick ear? And how had she managed it before, the loneliness, the emptiness of the rooms, how the hours went on and on without end, with no one to break them with song or laughter?

On Sundays, Jude did nothing, resentful of the woods and disinterested in the altar room. If Candle and its haints were dissatisfied with Jude's treatment of them, they didn't take it out on her. In fact, the house was gentle, swaddling her in silence, dampening the sounds of outside so completely it was like Jude's ears were stuffed with cotton. The haints let her body be, let her sleep through the night with no dreams, no terror. *She dead, I'm dead*, thought Jude, and Candle, the haints, didn't disagree.

Autumn's humidity faded into winter's biting cold, the weather temperate and comfortable until it wasn't. Jude woke one morning to frost on her windows and her lips trembling, blue, and forced herself out of bed. *Take hold of yourself*, her mother would say. *Stop lying there sorry! Fix your face!* So, Jude fixed hers, made herself bathe and eat, and shored up Candle for the winter. She hauled in vegetables from the garden, canned and preserved, stockpiled wood, insulated doors and windows, fussed at and reasoned with the boiler until the water ran hot again, winterized the pipes, grief rising and falling within her like mercury in a thermometer.

One day, sorrow scabbing over and healing slow, Jude looked up from harvesting the last of the sweet potatoes and saw Nemoira, plain as day, walking out of the woods. She looked hale, healthy—better, even, than when Jude had last put eyes on her. There was a fullness to her cheeks and her arms, and she trotted up to Jude smiling, all teeth and flashing eyes.

She stood at the edge of the plot of potatoes and said, "Hi, Judy!"

Jude didn't mean to punch Nemoira, but it was the only thing she could think to do. Wrath subsumed her, reddened her vision, her months of worry and prayer and terror building, building, and when Jude returned to her body, to her senses, Nemoira was sprawled out on the ground with a hand over her nose and mouth. Blood on her lips, blood on Jude's fist. Jude glared down at her, wanting nothing more than to sit on the woman's chest and to punch and punch until she blacked out those glittering eyes, that coy smile. Wanted nothing more too than to tumble down with her, fall into her arms, and kiss her and kiss her.

Nemoira looked up, red streaming through her fingers. "Not a very nice hello."

"I thought you was *dead*!" Jude screamed, balled her hands into fists and released them, balled them again. She stepped toward Nemoira, and the woman crawled back—nasty zip of satisfaction, glee. *Good*, thought Jude. *You betta be scared of me.*

"I wasn't," said Nemoira flatly. Her voice was nasal, her nose undoubtably broken. She lapped at the blood on her lips, looked Jude in the face, and said, "See here, Judy. I wanted to come back. I really did, but—"

Jude cut her off and in a low, serious voice that brooked no argument, she said, "You think *real* careful 'bout what you say to me now, woman. Months, I looked for you. Searched the swamps, the rivers, kept looking up into trees thinking I'd see your shoes dangling above me. *Months*, all I dreamed about was you bloodied up, eaten at, eyes picked out. I beat vultures off bones thinkin' they were yours."

There was nothing Jude could do to stop her voice from quavering and cracking, nothing that could prevent her body from trembling with rage. She wanted to fall to her knees, to bury her face in the dirt and scream till she shredded her cords, but she held fast to herself, kept herself standing tall and cold over Nemoira.

Nemoira's eyes softened, the glitter in them dampening. Softly, she breathed, "If I could only explain it to you . . . If I could only have you see it, Judy, without you hating me." She struggled to her feet, flicked her eyes to Candle. "Can I come home?"

You don't have one, Jude wanted to say. *Go back to where you came from, scurry off to whatever hole you crawled out of,* but instead she took her sweet potatoes and stomped into the house without another word.

What was there that Jude could say to Nemoira that wouldn't end in blood? She felt like her mother, wrothful and deadly and liable to strike out at anything. If Nemoira came too close to her now, if she even dared to give some fool's excuse, Jude was sure she'd wring Nemoira's neck as cleanly as she would a chicken's.

Bitch, thought Jude. *Miserable, lying bitch!* And even as she thought her ugly thoughts, she regretted them just as she regretted her vengeful prayers against Ma'am. She didn't mean it, she meant worse; she hated her, she loved her, she wished she'd never met her, never opened her door, and yet all of her, every part of Jude that had wept at the thought of Nemoira's bleached bones, wanted to reach out and touch her, make sure she was real and there, alive.

They ate goose for dinner—a different one from the one Jude had shot the day Nemoira disappeared—and didn't speak. Jude listened to Nemoira move around the parlor, adjusting her things, and when the woman came to the base of the stairs dressed for bed, eyes expectant, Jude threw her head back and laughed.

"You think you gon' sleep with me?"

"Please, Judy. I been away from my bed for two months. You'd deny me rest?"

The gall of it made Jude laugh again. "You ain't gotta remind me how long you been gone, first of all, and second—it's *my* bed and *my* house. I'll deny you anything I want." Gesturing with her chin to the open parlor door, Jude spat, "*You?* You sleep there. You wanna act like a stray, you can sleep like a stray."

"A stray?" Nemoira's eyes narrowed into slits, predatory and dark. She flared her nostrils, the effect strange beneath the bandage she'd fashioned. "Is that how it is, Judy?"

"That's how it is, till you tell me the truth. Till you say where you've been."

The first time they had argued, Jude went for only three days without speaking to Nemoira. This time around, she could've doubled the time or tripled it, the bubbling tension between the women like mud. Nemoira tried striking up conversation, chattering endlessly, but Jude ignored her; if she couldn't have the truth, she didn't want anything from the woman. She ate her meals away from Nemoira, avoided her entirely. When Nemoira wandered into the living room to warm herself by the hearth (never mind there was a fireplace in the parlor), Jude snatched up her sewing, her book, and absconded to her bedroom, doors slamming shut behind her.

Alone, her mind twisted toward violence—*pummel her face in, choke her, slash her, cut up that stupid smile, look you already have the knife in your hand, you did it so easily before*—and she wrenched it back. She thought she knew, before, the difference between her voice and the voice of her mother, but they sang in harmony now. Mean songs, bleak songs—whether the music came from within her, from Candle, or from her mother's restless spirit, Jude couldn't say, but she heard it, all day and all night, in her nightmares and in the small hours, her mind a symphony of rage.

On the ninth day of their silent war, Nemoira stood at the threshold of the sewing room and asked Jude if she'd like to join her for a walk.

"It's late," Jude grunted, and it was, a quarter past five in the evening, light leaching from the sky as they spoke.

"I know. Still, I want you to come with me. I reckon we got a couple'a hours fore the sun sets. We could make a picnic of it?"

Jude hummed a little nothing noise, aggravation and anxiety ratcheting higher. Inside, the wasp whispering told her to push Nemoira out, push her down, and Jude stabbed at her sewing to resist the urge to stab Nemoira. She heard the hutch downstairs topple over, cutlery spraying across the floor, and above her, the chintz lamp burst, glass falling like rain on her lap.

"No," said Jude. "And don't ask me again."

Nemoira sighed and said, "What are you afraid of, Judy? It's only trees there."

She raised her head, fixed Nemoira with a cold, mean look. She started to say to her how it was to feel the beast at her back, how when she closed her eyes now all she saw was the black of the woods, imagined shapes of the dead. Nemoira ignored the look, came into the sewing room—intrusion, invasion, Jude reeling back—and knelt in front of Jude. Her hand hovered over Jude's knee, cautious, and eventually, she let the hand fall to her own lap.

"Can't you see I'm tryna apologize to you?"

"Then say it!" snapped Jude. It was, perhaps, hypocritical of her, to ask for what she was previously unable to give, but it was what she wanted. What she needed. For once, at last, she wanted for someone to say sorry to her and to mean it, to grant her the remorse that Ma'am never did and now never would. "*Say* you are sorry for leaving me, for making me think you was dead and that I'd never see you again. Say you're sorry for . . ." Her voice caught and Jude blinked back her eyes. "For making me lonely."

Nemoira leaned back at that, stared up at Jude, then lowered her eyes and said, softly, "I am sorry, Judy. It weren't . . ." She reached for Jude's hand, and when Jude didn't immediately snatch it away from her, she took it in her own. "It weren't out of cruelty or to hurt you or, no, nothing like that. I swear to you. Swear it on my own life. And I want you to have the truth, but you gon' have to trust me and to come to the woods with me. Tonight."

"Just *tell* me," pleaded Jude.

"I can't. It's too big to say. I can only show you."

At length, Jude studied Nemoira, the graceful hand she held in hers, the open and beseeching look she wore on her face. How she had missed her, the texture of her skin, the smell of her cologne. It was almost enough to make Jude forget and forgive.

It wasn't forgiveness on her mind as Jude followed Nemoira into the woods that night, but dread. Only a handful of weeks ago had she walked those dark woods in search of Nemoira's corpse; that Nemoira walked with her now, burdened with a basket of food and their flashlight, did little to assuage her fears. Jude looked back over her shoulder, to Candle, its windows alight, and the windows winked back.

Snaking through the Okefenokee, Nemoira led Jude deep into unfamiliar land, dirt trails and copses Jude had never seen. They crossed lush fields of wildflower and marsh, the land shifting precariously underfoot. Deeper and deeper, they traveled, through a tunnel of pine and loblolly, the trees' knotted canopies blanketed with green. There was no natural light in the tunnel, only the fluorescent glare of the flashlight against the shrubs, the long waxy leaves like fingers, picking at her hair.

"I don't think I ever been this far in," said Jude. "You been this deep before?"

"Once or twice."

Irritated with Nemoira's closed-handedness, lightheaded with the scent of petrichor and of myrrh as Nemoira brought her even farther into the forest, Jude focused her attention on her footsteps, on keeping her feet moving one in front of the other. She swayed drunkenly, reached forward to grab onto Nemoira's coat, but the woman was out ahead of her, dashing to a gash of pink light in the otherwise green dark.

At the end of the tunnel, there was a glade in bloom, the tall grass and rolling hills awash in blush-and-apricot sunset. Edenic, it sprawled, a mishmash of fronds and flowering plants, little streams of clear water crisscrossing the vale. There was no sense of season there, no rhyme or reason; ornamental pepper grew alongside burning bush and wisteria, bleeding heart poppies and strawberry growing in the shadow of a fig tree. Jude's nose brought her to a tangled patch of wild peppermint, the menthol-scented carpet positioned beneath a massive weeping willow, its leaves a shower of creams and yellows.

Nemoira approached her wearing a small, coy smile, and Jude shot her a dubious look, asking, "This is what you were hiding from me?"

"Among other things."

"I guess you mean to tell me the other things later?"

Nemoira nodded, eased herself to sitting at the base of the willow tree. "I will, I promise. I don't want to hold things from you."

Jude peeked at Nemoira, her crooked nose, and said, "Sorry for punching you." She started to speak again, to maybe say something about her mother and the seeds Ma'am had planted inside of her, but it didn't seem the time for it. She only said, "Too much of Ma'am in me."

"I wish you would say more about her," replied Nemoira. "You still call out for her, in the night."

Jude chuckled, echoed Nemoira's earlier words. "If I could only have you see it without you hating me."

"What could make me hate you?"

Jude's mouth twitched, dropped. Jude reached for the picnic basket, unpacked their cold turkey sandwiches, their slices of sweet potato pie. Nemoira, for once, did not press, and they ate with little chatter, Nemoira asking after all the things she'd missed in the house and Jude answering in short, clipped sentences.

After dinner, the women walked and explored the field, Jude to one side and Nemoira to the other and Ma'am in between them. Thinking around her mother was difficult; she swallowed Jude's mind, made her distant and distracted, her senses blunted even as she knelt down to smell roses. Nemoira invited her to climb the willow tree and Jude sat on the bough, trying to predict how Nemoira would respond if she told her about Ma'am and what she had done. Sweat engulfed her, and she popped and flexed her fingers.

Nemoira nudged her with her shoe. "Judy? You think you 'bout ready to go home?"

They came out of the tree and started home. Nemoira led the way with the flashlight, Jude hurrying to keep up with her long, purposeful strides. She was, somehow, always ten paces ahead of Jude, never to be caught. Each time Jude tried, she lost sight of Nemoira, the woman disappearing into the night.

"Nemoira?" Jude called out. "Nemoira!"

Frogs and owls and cicadas answered, but no Nemoira. Jude stepped forward and a twig snapped underfoot, leaves rustling and crunching as she tried to get her bearings. Her foot connected with something on the forest floor; Jude bent and felt for it, found Nemoira's flashlight flickering, its glass cracked but still functional. She clicked it on and off, pointed the light to the shrubbery in front of her, the ground. There, newly imprinted in red mud, were paw prints, and from the shape of the pads, the distinct curve of the claws, Jude knew it was a bear's print. Alarm zipped through Jude fast enough to make her head spin, and with a sickening lurch, she realized she had nothing to protect her, no gun or bear spray, not even a blade.

Panic rising, Jude hissed, "*Nemoira!* This ain't funny!"

The nocturnal choir played on, deafeningly loud, and in the midst of the noise, the whirs and chirps and whoops indigenous to the forest, came another sound, a low and rolling growl. Next came its smell, cologne of rot and magnolia, a verdant belch of fern, peat. Fear pinned her, made her legs too heavy to move, and it took every ounce of bravery for Jude to point the flashlight ahead.

At first, all Jude saw was its long and sinuous back, its fur black and shining. Though the animal was massive, all fat and meat and rolling muscle, it walked with a balletic regality, the look of its shoulders and near-silent paws padding at the leaf litter knocking the very breath out of Jude. It paused and, as if sensing Jude's eyes on it, turned to her, revealing for the first time its face. It *was* a bear, the beast, a grotesque mutt of a creature too big to be a black bear but too far southeast to be a grizzly. The animal regarded Jude with intelligent black eyes, the dilated pupils like river rocks.

For a long moment, Jude and the bear studied each other. Steeling herself, Jude approached it, its eyes flashing with green as the flashlight bobbed in its face. Steady handed, terror and confusion warring within her, Jude stretched out her free hand and ran it along the bear's pelt, felt its hump and its head, fingers teasing over its snout. The bear nipped at her hand, gentle as a puppy, and nosed at her palm.

She knew those eyes, so clever and so human, and so Jude called the bear by her name.

"Nemoira?"

16

Jude didn't see Nemoira transform from beast back to woman (or was the bear what was natural to her, the soft indigo skin the illusion?), only saw her rising up from the ground and walking the rest of the field on two feet. Reeling, brain dulled with shock, Jude entered Candle and walked right into Nemoira's parlor, collapsing onto the daybed. Nemoira was at her heels, dropping their outerwear onto a chair before building a fire and seating herself at Jude's feet, legs crossed beneath her.

She couldn't stand to look at Nemoira. To look at her would make it true, and Jude kept asking herself if it was real, if she had seen what she saw. "What is this? What are you?"

"I'm Nemoira," she said with a shrug, as if the answer was obvious.

"That ain't what I mean and you know it. What are you? Really?"

"I don't know how else to say. I am Nemoira, and Nemoira is me, and sometimes I'm in a different skin." Jude asked how Nemoira did it, changed her shape, and the woman shrugged again, hands falling to her knees with the palms facing upward. "I can't say—it's so in me, like breathing. It'd be like if I ask you how are you human, how are you Judy. It just is and I just am."

"You tricked me," whispered Jude.

"Did I?" She lifted her head, met Jude's accusatory glare with cool, unblinking eyes. "I never said what I was. I kept saying for you to ask me, ask me, but you never did."

"That's not fair, Nemoira, and you know it. You *know* that if I told you to tell me the truth and you gave it to me, I wouldn't have been so quick to let you in. I wouldn't have let you into my bed, my arms, and *you* lied." Nausea roiled through Jude, and she closed her eyes against it, breathed slowly out of her mouth. "Why? Why'd you come, why'd you stay?"

Intently, Nemoira studied Jude, eyes shifting in thought. Crackling firewood, the ambient noise of Candle creaking as it settled, leaning in to listen. Nemoira spoke, finally, her voice all but deadened by the sound of the fire. "I was hungry, just hungry, and then it was a different kind of hunger altogether." She spoke each word as if she were discovering it for the first time, as if she were surprising even herself. "I wanted you dead, wanted to eat you whole, wanted to spend every hour of every day watching the lights in your window. I wanted to tear your flesh and to lap at every scar. Bring you meat. Make you into meat.

"I meant to kill you that first night. I should've done it." Nemoira chuckled, showed Jude her yellowed teeth. "Should've taken out your throat when I had the chance, but I left it too long, and now I couldn't."

"You could. Any wild animal could."

"But I *can't*, don't you see that? I been here for months and every time I stretch my jaw to bite you, all I can think about is the kiss I want to place there right after. You do something to me. Make me tame and stupid and—" Nemoira groaned and curled into herself, clutching at her stomach as if in pain, and then, snapping her head up, she said, "You killed me."

"Killed you? I never did."

"Oh, yes, *yes*, you did. Over and over and over. I was a snake, and you chopped my head off with a gardening hoe, scattered my parts throughout the field. When I was a buck and near dying, you smashed my skull in with a rock." Nemoira sighed wistfully. "*Oh*, my blood on your big brown legs. The way you gutted and fleshed me, ate me. I always liked that about you, Judy, how you never let a single part of me go to waste, even if it made it all the harder to come back."

"Is it that why you were gone?" asked Jude. "Because I killed you?"

"You really are one hell of a shot. Got me right in the chest and I fell into your arms. Last thing I remembered was your steady hands round my neck."

Jude felt her gorge rising. It unsettled her, the coolness with which Nemoira discussed both her own death and Jude's, but she was intrigued as well, the thought of Nemoira, the beast, living in her stomach, sustaining Jude even when she was gone.

"I can't put my head around it, Judy, what it is that you do to me. I look at you and my mind goes quiet, and I know I'd die a thousand times by your hand if only for the joy of coming back to you and being killed again."

Jude's stomach knotted, but whether it was from terror or titillation, she could not say. So closely entwined were love and fear that to separate them was impossible. She held Nemoira's gaze, remembered how very scared she'd been when the bear was watching her in her bedroom and the thrill she'd felt each time it had left some new gutted creature at her door. Nemoira's hand, the bear's paw crushing the skulls of lesser animals; that terrible, snarling mouth transformed into teeth that nipped only playfully, marked her neck, her thighs.

"I left you flowers," whispered Jude.

"And I loved them. Imagine me, a mean ol' bear with blue irises in my mouth!" Nemoira giggled, surged toward Jude to take her hand, to caress her face.

Jude laughed, laughed and sobbed out, "You horrible thing! You horrible, lying thing, I cared for you!"

Nemoira dropped her hands to her side and stood, rising to her full height. She was a little over six feet, a good three inches taller than Jude, but she stretched even longer as she straightened her back, to seven feet and then to eight. Her nose and mouth fell into each other and elongated into a black snout with flat nostrils, a wide mouth. Nemoira's bones cracked and shifted beneath her skin, and she fell to the floor with a pained grunt, her spine lengthening, back hunching with the grizzly bear's telltale hump. Her hands extended into paws, the claws as long as human fingers. Tufts of deep brown-black hair swallowed the dark skin until nothing was left of the woman save for her black, watchful eyes.

Transformed, Nemoira padded over to Jude, rumbling and purring. With a gentleness befitting a sheepdog laying down its head at the hoof of the lamb it kills for, Nemoira laid her head on Jude's lap.

To be loved by Nemoira, by the bear, was to be watched constantly and eaten daily. Her devotion consumed; Jude said once, before she knew who she was talking to, that having the beast's attention was like having a god that looked only at you. Flayed beneath the gaze of that furred and hungry god, Jude wondered if wasn't the other way around, if maybe *she* were the god and Nemoira the sole member of her cult.

Certainly, her sacrifices were grand enough. Nemoira said to Jude, "I love you, I love you," and threw at her feet game meats, portions of cow and hog and lamb. Offhandedly, Jude mentioned wanting rabbit, and Nemoira left, returned hours later with two rabbits in her teeth, their pelts ruined with blood. Jude patted Nemoira's gory muzzle, lust rising in her like dew. She felt the bear's round ears, ran a finger over its long, curved teeth, and thought of Nemoira's coiling hair, how her mouth curled just so when she was happy or on the brink of release.

Sighing, Jude took the rabbits from Nemoira and brought them into the kitchen. The bear followed her, positioned itself at the entrance to the dining room with its chin on its paws. Jude scrubbed her hands, laid the rabbits out on the counter, and then pinched one rabbit by its scruff, made a small incision on its back, and, using two fingers and a great deal of strength, stripped the rabbit from its coat. With quick, practiced movements, Jude removed the heart, intestines, liver, and kidneys. She tossed the offal to Nemoira and stored the remaining organs before repeating the skin-and-dress routine on the second rabbit.

The bear snuffling behind her, Jude rinsed the rabbits of blood and debris, skinned the meat from the fat. She cracked the rabbits' hip bones and thought about Nemoira's hands on her waist, feeling at her hips. She bit, sometimes, the tender-raw flesh of Jude's inner thighs, and Jude wondered if she hadn't been training Nemoira to eat her. Some animals did—hogs, grizzly bears—and you couldn't take it away from them, once they got the taste for long pig.

After dinner, Nemoira spread Jude out on the parlor floor and ran her hand along her neck, down her chest. Between the fire in the hearth and the fire of Nemoira's glare, Jude felt hot enough to steam. She opened her legs, let Nemoira feel at her ridges and folds, let her rock, moaning and hissing, against her heat.

Pleasure lifted Jude out of her body. She was air, breath, heat. Nemoira brought their bodies together, and Jude imagined the bear stalking the woods, sniffing out berries and fish (Nemoira hunting for muscadines, Nemoira triumphantly hauling catfish out of the water with a bare hand), the bear sniffing out their dinner. Her Nemoira, sharp of tooth and bright of eye, running, pouncing, climbing—the bear snatching rabbits by their necks, clawing at trees, clawing at its kills.

Nemoira's hand at her breast, at her collarbone. Jude threw back her head, revealing her neck, and Nemoira wrapped a hand around it. Jude plummeted back down to her body. With a jerk and an alarmed grunt, Jude gripped Nemoira's wrist, unsure if she meant to throw her off or hold her there. Her mind was a screaming, howling riot, every inch of her body calling out in alarm, and still, Jude moved against Nemoira, faster, faster, bringing her mortar to Nemoira's pestle. The hand tightened. Jude met Nemoira's black, thirsty stare. The need to finish hit Jude like a migraine, searing pain building and whiting out her vision, her thoughts. The bear with its belly exposed, Nemoira grinding with gritted teeth and choking her, claws digging into her throat—coagulated blood, the sudden burst of juice as teeth halved a muscadine.

Jude whimpered. She thought, *Don't, don't, don't,* and her rebellious, untamable body contracted, released.

17

It was a long and arduous winter. Punxsutawney Phil saw his shadow and fled back underground, leaving them an additional six weeks of ice and biting cold. Short days and long nights drained Jude, and she spent her time in bed mulling over the past and things she could not change. Around her, Candle suffered, sagged; a pipe burst in the cellar around Christmas, flooding it up to ankle height. Despite the women's best efforts to drain it, the stagnant water stayed for two weeks, the spores and microbes that floated in the black water the only new life in Candle for ages.

In late January, the furnace died, and the generator went a month later. They'd been in the middle of dinner when the lights went out, the subtle hum of electricity that suffused the house coming to an abrupt, deafening stop. Panic surged through Jude, then faded. She had, all along, been preparing herself for this; she groped in the dark for candles, her book of matches. By candlelight, Nemoira's face was lovely and tender, and Jude wished the lights would stay off forever, that there would only be she and

Nemoira with flames between them, their serrated edges softened, glowing.

There was a world outside of Candle, but Jude didn't want it anymore. She thought of getting into her car and crossing the woods, of going into Whitnee, and her mind was flooded by memories of fear, of the dismissiveness and scorn on the townspeople's faces when she came to them for help. She sent Nemoira to town in her stead, and the woman brought back paper-wrapped packages of meat (pork, most often, but also venison, sides of beef), headscarves, handkerchiefs, cheap and gaudy earrings, bangles, cuffs, costume rings, library books and brand-new paperbacks, bottles of expensive perfume, vials of oil, tailored dresses and flowing caftans, a record player and a stack of vinyl. In the cold dark, swaddled by quilts and surrounded by tokens of her affection, Nemoira murmured in Jude's ear—how she hunted and how she hungered, the people in town asking after her and their unkind words, rumors, gossip, stories. Jude turned her head from it, buried her face in the bear's fur until she saw nothing, heard nothing.

"They found hikers in the woods. Dead," whispered Nemoira. Jude tried closing her ears to the story, but Nemoira told it anyway—the young couple in pieces, a half-clothed leg left of the man; the woman was mauled, her face a mash of red, her back slashed to shreds. Her lungs, said Nemoira, were exposed and riddled with bites.

Jude's guts churned. She asked Nemoira why she'd told her that, why scare her, but she knew, of course she knew, that the fear was the point.

Voice buried in Nemoira's chest, she said, "Bears don't eat people, do they?"

Nemoira scratched her scalp, gently tugged Jude's tight-coiled hair, and responded, "Only when we're very, *very* hungry."

Seemed to Jude like Nemoira got hungrier by the day, her passions growing wilder, more brutal. With all the prey tucked safely into their warrens and holes, there was only Jude to sup on, and she made a ruin of Jude, old scars and bruises overlaid with love bites, gouging wounds from where Nemoira's claws stuck her. "You make me tame," Nemoira said, and Jude supposed it was true insofar as a well-chewed bone kept a rabid dog from barking.

Nemoira grabbed and bit, choked and gripped, and Jude threw back her head to give her more neck to destroy. She drove her crazy, brought out of Jude boar's tusks and meanness, a sort of nastiness she didn't think herself capable of inflicting on the woman she loved. Loving Jude made Nemoira into a penitent, head bowed at the altar of her cunt, and loving Nemoira made Jude senseless. She came to Jude with her breath stinking of carrion, and the taste of blood, the dregs of her latest kill on her tongue, was to Jude like Pavlov's bell; it rang and she drooled.

Springtime brought Jude out of her stupor, and she rose from her bed as sleepily as the rabbits emerging from their warrens. Choirs of songbirds sang arias they'd rehearsed all winter, and butterflies flitted through the mimosa bushes. Even the wasps were a pleasant sight, the maligned lovers of orchids and figs droning cheerfully through the grasses.

When she woke, Nemoira was gone, most likely hunting, and so quickly she bathed, threw on warm clothes, and drove the car into town. She was a minor spectacle, the wounded hermit coming out of the woods and sitting down at the drugstore counter, asking for coffee. Jude drank it black and bitter, and listened distractedly to people's talk. So-and-so's getting married, having babies, there's riots in the cities, folks burning things in New York and Chicago and Detroit. Someone mentioned seeing an oversize bear in the woods, a bear wandering near town. Jude laughed joylessly, paid her tab, and went home.

Candle, disintegrating, welcomed her warmly with a show of bangs and thumps in the parlor. Jude peeked in, saw Nemoira's dresser gearing up for a tantrum, and she let it be, reasoning that if it wanted to stomp through the floor and join the chair in the cellar, it had the right. Out in the garden, Jude raked away dead leaves and dug up dried foliage, preparing the garden for that spring's crop. She knelt in the dirt, grounded herself with handfuls of soil. Spade in, spade out, clang of metal against stone, a brief tug-of-war as she dragged out a tangled root system. Jude swiped the sweat from her forehead, stabbed her spade in again—another clang, this one vibrating through the metal and up her arm.

With a huff, Jude threw aside the spade and thrust her hands into the soil, feeling for the obstruction. She felt insects wriggling, skittering over her fingers, slimy and warm dirt, something hard and smooth. She scrabbled at the ground, unearthed handfuls of packed earthworms, and writhing maggots—some animal, Jude thought, something she killed or something Nemoira killed. Grunting, she forced her fingers under the solid mass and hauled it up.

A femur bone, long and yellow and unmistakably human, landed by her knee. She blinked, felt her gorge rising. She put her hands back into the dirt and pulled up more—finger bones, half a pelvis, a quarter of a spine, a big toe stilled clothed in its rotting skin. Jude dug and she dug, and into her hands fell molars, canine teeth, the degraded teeth of elders, and new milk teeth, bicuspids rotted with cavities, teeth so new they were soft.

Jude got to her feet, beat her hands against her pants. Roughly, she panted and she batted, but the slime and the blood and the dirt remained.

Look at your hands!

She didn't dare. Jude reentered the house, Nemoira's parlor. She inched around the gaping hole in the floor and approached the dresser, still raging. It rocked back and forth, back and forth, its brass handles clanging against the mahogany drawers. Nemoira's trinkets fell to the floor, and a lamp lay shattered on the ground. The drawers opened and closed, each slam and petulant stop of the dresser's carved feet sounding to her ears like, *op-en, op-en, op-en.*

"Please. *Please,*" Jude begged the dresser, the house, the haints.

Nothing and no one responded to her prayers. Jude drew open the first drawer, and saw within it Nemoira's collection. Nemoira, her morbid crow, had brought home, it seemed, more than jazz records and clothes. In all four drawers, there were ringed fingers, polished fingers, sets of ears and earrings, gold- and silver-capped teeth, brooches and pins and pearls daubed with blood. There were onesies for infants and well-worn dungarees crusted with dried viscera; a stiff, brown christening dress, a baptismal robe splashed with crimson. In between the layers of funereal garments and Sunday suits, ties and garters and laddered pantyhose, Jude found flesh: clumps and bundles of stringy hair, coiled hair, an entire skullcap upended like a bowl to hold loose rings, earring backs. Dried tongues lolled on breasts, buttocks, an orgy of genitalia in brown and purple and blushing pink.

With a lurch, Jude recalled Nemoira's story about the hikers, the bitten lungs. Her mouth filled with saliva as she dashed to the kitchen and threw open the icebox. She sorted through the wax paper packages, each labeled plainly with *lung* and *heart* and *kidney* but nothing of the animal it came from. *Breathe now, girl. Just you breathe a moment,* but it was hard to breathe when each inhale filled her nostrils with the smell of ice and of meat, when each whiff of meat and congealed blood reminded her of her own blood, her own pumping, wriggling organs.

Jude made it to the sink in time to void the contents of her stomach. Breakfast sausages ground from the meat Nemoira brought to her, that afternoon's liver-and-onions lunch—she gagged and heaved, the exertion aggravating her ribs, but she couldn't stop until all of it was out of her. Jude clutched the sides of the sink, trembling, and she watched as her tears fell into the ceramic bowl, swirling with her sick. Silently, she admonished herself—she should've known, she should've guessed, but she was too wrapped up in Nemoira. The smell of blood on her breath should've alarmed Jude, but it only inspired lust. Even now, she was hungry.

She rinsed her mouth and the sink, scrubbed dirt and blood from beneath her nails. Jude took the scarf off her head and made from it a bundle of small bones and gore, the fleshy trophies from Nemoira's collection. She left Nemoira's room untidied, but she reburied the larger bones. In the cellar, Jude got her gun and her bullets. She whistled as she loaded her weapon, a song she remembered from her youth about a wily rabbit, fast feet and an even faster mind.

In the altar room, Jude lit the two long-neglected candles. With nothing else to give the haints, she slipped her mother's ring off her finger and dropped it into a bowl, dropped her head. Months ago, she stood in this same space spilling her guts to Nemoira, and now, Jude could only be sorry. She said to the listening dark, "Beg your pardon, for letting her in. You been showing me this whole time, but I couldn't see it." Her lips twitched, a mirthless half smile. "Lovesick I was, but now I'm better. I'll bring bear stew when I'm done."

The candles bowed to her. Jude didn't know if the clamor in her ears was the wind whistling, the haints, or her own buzzing wasp brain roaring, screaming for her to *kill it, kill it now, the only way out is through.*

Up in the parlor, shotgun in her lap and the bundle of gore sitting on the dresser, Jude waited. Nemoira returned near five in the afternoon, singing out her name.

"Shoo-*death*! Jooo-dee!"

"I'm here," Jude responded. "In the parlor."

She heard Nemoira come out of her shoes, heard her stockinged feet pad from the hall. Nemoira entered her bedroom grinning, cheeks flushed with cold. She studied Jude's face, the rictus plastered to her face, and asked, "What you doing here sitting in the dark for?"

She drew back the curtains, sunset falling on the bundle, the shotgun. Her smile dropped as she took these things in, eyes dull. Nemoira licked her lips and said, "Well, baby. What now?"

18

Nothing in the parlor moved as woman and beast regarded each other, Jude on the bed and Nemoira leaned against the hearth. She scratched at the wooden mantel, the sound itching Jude's brain and rousing the hair at her nape.

Nemoira's face had changed, bestial with scant traces of humanity. The elongated chin, the canines long enough to disrupt the lips, the distinct lack of care in those black stone eyes; how Jude could have ever mistaken the creature in front of her as human was beyond her. *Lovesick and blind*, she thought as she watched Nemoira coolly. Inside, bitter thoughts bored holes in her brain, her tongue.

Jude did not bother asking how long Nemoira had been killing people; she assumed it was something natural to her, a disconnect between what was human in her and what was animal. Instead, she asked, "How long you been eating people?"

"Long as I've been me, I reckon."

"And how long have you been bringing it to me?"

Nemoira said, "For as long as I've loved you. So, I guess since that second winter, when I came into your room."

Jude scoffed. She said, "Don't say *love* to me. Not when you been feeding me human flesh."

"It's only meat, Judy. One stands on two feet and the others on four. Anyways, you never turned down anything I fed you."

"I didn't know what you were giving me. If you had told me—"

"What? You wouldn't've eaten it?" Nemoira laughed, interrupting. She said to Jude, "Careful, Judy, fore lightning strikes your lying ass."

Jude recoiled, shame and frustration heating her face. Blood on the breath, the bell ringing and ringing—whatever Nemoira killed, Jude ate with gusto. Jude steeled herself and said, "I need you to get out of my house."

Nemoira's brows rose and her eyes widened. "You don't mean that, Judy." Upon looking at Jude's firm, unflinching face, her steady grip on her gun, Nemoira gave her a soft, mocking smile. "Oh, what *is* this, baby? Almost a year you been laying down with me, not caring about what I was and what I do. And I been telling you the truth—*ask me and I'll say*, and haven't I been saying the whole time what I was and what I could do?"

"Silly me for not guessing what you meant, huh? Silly me expecting a tiger to change its stripes," said Jude flatly.

"Well, yes! Baby, I said my truth and you liked it. Loved it, even, if the scratches on my back are anything to go by." Nemoira pushed off from the hearth, crossed the space so that she stood near the hole in the floor. "Let this go."

"I won't, and I won't have you in my house." Jude swallowed, fixed her hold on the gun. "I'll say it once more time, Nemoira—get out my house."

Nemoira laughed, clapped her hands together. Giggling, she said, "For how long? Four days? A week? Should I pretend to sleep in the parlor tonight, or can we skip ahead to after you've clawed and burned yourself, when you decide none of this matters, and that all you *really* want is to be laid out and—"

"Only thing I'm laying out tonight is your dead body."

"With what?" Nemoira nodded to Jude's gun, smile broadening. "That? Oh, baby, you won't. You can't!"

Undoubtedly, Nemoira was thinking of Jude's scars, her stories of her mother beating and mortifying her flesh. No doubt, she was imagining Jude as she had been thirteen years prior, a scared and humbled thing, unable to lift her head, never mind strike back against the woman who had scarred her.

"You got no clue what I'm capable of," said Jude, and she granted Nemoira a coy half smile of her own. *Fool,* she wanted to say. *Arrogant, ridiculous beast.* Nemoira had built in her head a version of Jude that didn't exist, a woman unhinged enough to lie down with a monster, but too scared of her own shadow to kill of her own accord.

Nemoira rounded the hole, extended a clawed hand, and Jude kicked herself back, the metal scraping uglily against the hardwood as she scooted the daybed away from Nemoira. She cocked the shotgun and aimed it squarely at Nemoira's head. "Don't come near me," she warned.

"Did you forget you kill me before? I'll die and I'll come back. You die and... What? You rot? Turn to bile and shit in my belly?"

"*If* I die," said Jude, black eyes flashing with intent. "I won't go down easy. I swear to you, I'll be the meanest, toughest bit of meat you ever ate."

Nemoira's face bones cracked and fell outward, the snout jutting violently from the nose. Part smiling mouth and part grimacing maw, Nemoira snarled, "That's my Judy."

She morphed in a flash, the slow shift and flex of muscles under skin replaced by a rapid crunching, grinding transformation of bones, flesh. Terror held Jude in place as Nemoira's body distorted and became monstrous, the bear dropping to all fours and roaring. Jude aimed her gun at the bear's head, fired, missed, and the bear swatted her with a large paw. Jude decocked the gun and swatted back, swinging the shotgun at the beast's head, its grotesque face.

She hopped up on the daybed, and the bear rose to its full and terrible height, exposing its belly long enough for Jude to jab it with the butt of the gun. The bear roared, knocked her into the cold hearth with a single massive paw. Her skull rang against the stone—darkness, blinding light. Blinking back the pain, Jude felt at the back of her head, looked up in time to see the claws right before they slashed at her face. Jude howled in pain and in anger as daggerlike claws tore through the flesh of her cheek and mouth, her left eye. Stumbling back, blinded with blood, Jude rolled out of the way of the bear's next swipe and half ran, half fell from the parlor into the living room, the dining room, and then, at last, the kitchen.

She slammed the doors behind her as she entered each room, blocking the door to the living room with the couch and the door into the dining room with the hutch, the table. There was nothing to block the door with in the kitchen, and Jude listened as the bear smashed and broke its way through her barricades. She dug through the drawers for a knife, found her foraging blade, tucked it into her back pocket, and then backed herself up against the far wall, one hand on the gun and the other holding her face together. It was coming apart regardless, each breath forcing blood from her wounds, and the world was crimson and blurred.

If she got a shot lined up, Jude could blow a hole right through the bear's head or its stomach. She knew it wouldn't be like killing a deer—to fell a bear, one had to be exact and resolute, fearless. No more meek rabbit, no more tender woman; it was time for Br'er Jude to knock down big ol' Br'er Bear, even if it meant her life.

Outside the kitchen there were footsteps, not the heavy padding of paws but of human feet. Nemoira called out to her, "Judy! Come out now, love!" Jude heard the exhaustion in the woman's voice, how she panted as she taunted. *I winded her at least. Now, I just need one shot, just one shot to the gut and I got her.*

"Come on, baby. You know I love to chase you, woman, but *whew*, we getting too old for these games."

"You maybe," huffed Jude. She darted to the right side of the door, blinked blood out of her eyes. "Me, I'm spry as ever. Won't be nothing to cut you down."

"Is that so?"

"Oh, *yes*. I already know what I'll do with you. Bear stew, lots of rice and veggies, heaps and heaps of pepper, cayenne and chilis. I'mma put you head up on the wall—skin you, wear you as a coat."

No response. Jude licked her lips, inched to her door to hear better, and was slammed back as Nemoira, once more the bear, threw her weight against the door. *Boom! Boom! Boom!* Each bang shook Jude to the core, and she prayed as she'd never prayed before for the house to stand strong, for Candle and all its haints to sustain itself against the creature that dared to level it. The door began to splinter and cave. Jude stepped back, cocked the gun, priming herself for attack.

The bear crashed in growling, clattering over the now-ruined door. Jude lunged at the beast, got a swat to the side for her trouble, but the stabbing pain was worth it when the bear stood tall and exposed its brown belly. Jude gritted her teeth and pulled the trigger, blowing shots through the bear's center. It screamed, a horrible half-animal and half-human wail. Jude dashed to the left, toward the door that led back into the dining room, but the bear was ready for her, running her down and throwing itself bodily at Jude. The bear, five hundred pounds of muscle and of fat, knocked the breath out of Jude as they landed in the dining room, the soft and rotted wood creaking beneath their shared weight. Jude wiggled her hand beneath her, grabbed the knife, and slashed and cut at the bear's face, its belly, jabbing and stabbing without finesse. The floor groaned as they struggled, Jude kicking and scrambling for purchase beneath Nemoira's slashing, suffocating body, and then the world fell out from beneath them.

Tumbling, tumbling, slats of wood and nails raining down as Jude and Nemoira crashed through the dining room floor. They turned, flipping head over heels, bear over human and then human over bear, a confused mass of growls, screams, and gasps. Jude landed with an *oof*, the waterlogged packed dirt doing nothing to soften the blow. Her body roared, everything raw and aching and bleeding. Beside her, Nemoira writhed as she shook off the bear, her human form a column of red, buckshot holes all through her stomach.

The women glanced at each other, panting, and Nemoira surged forward, grabbing at Jude as Jude leaped to her feet. Her nails scraped down Jude's legs, leaving trails of torn flesh, blood. On hands and knees, Jude scurried for the steps, the first dirt stair almost in reach, a mere fingertip away, but then Nemoira took hold of her ankle and yanked her down to the ground hard enough for Jude to bite her tongue, for her teeth to rattle in her pounding head.

Mouth pouring blood, Jude regained herself and tried once more for the stairs. If she could get up, if she could only get her gun . . . Nemoira threw Jude onto her back by her shoulders, Jude staring up and out to freedom and to safety as Nemoira straddled her hips and wrapped her hands around Jude's neck. Jude's good eye blew wide-open, the other rolling in its damaged socket. She flailed, sick twinge of arousal uncoiling in her belly even as

Nemoira's grip tightened. *Don't*, her mind screamed. *Don't you dare!* She grabbed Nemoira's wrists, her arms. Above her, the gaping hole into the dining room pulsed with color, white and yellow, the broken wood becoming hazy as her vision darkened. Jude's mind unraveled, and she heard roaring in her ears, blood rushing, the haints screaming, her own wicked-waspish brain shrieking.

Wordlessly, Nemoira choked her. Jude looked into the woman's eyes, expecting to see there remorse or maybe even hate, but there was nothing. Apathetic and with an animal's hungry focus, she was killing Jude, who was, in this moment, only writhing, resistant meat.

If Jude had the breath or the tongue to do it, she'd tell Nemoira that she'd lied to her, that she never was, as she imagined, so helpless. She'd say that though she was often afraid, the terror so much that it paralyzed her and overheated her mind, that same fear was like a friend to her, a weapon she honed and sharpened with each indignity, each insult. If she could breathe, she'd use her final breath to tell Nemoira about the wasps and roaches in her fetid little head that guided a blade across her mother's throat. On limited time and with waning strength, Jude instead drove her knee up and into Nemoira's bullet-ridden stomach.

Drilling, digging, Jude bored a new hole through Nemoira, one she fucked open with her kneecap until Nemoira, jerking and spewing blood, dropped her hands and fell onto her. Jude shoved her off and searched through a screen of red and darkness for her foraging blade. Hand scrabbling over the dank ground, she found it, the handle curving perfectly in the palm of her hand. She saw her reflection in its blade, her crazed eye and snarling mouth, brown skin black with blood. Jude splashed back over to Nemoira, glaring down at her face bloated with bruises. One dark eye was swollen shut, the other fixed upon Jude with something akin to pride.

Her stomach was an oozing crater, and Jude blinked away the burning start of tears. Words blunted with blood, Jude said, "I told you to leave. Why didn't you *leave*?"

Nemoira turned her head away, tilting it higher so that the whole of the brown neck was visible. Jude huffed—only Nemoira could pervert death so completely, could make this moment be for Jude one of trepidation and horror, lust so strong that it threatened to break her.

"Say *something*," Jude hissed. The blade's handle was slick in her hands, and as she brought it nearer to Nemoira's throat, she trembled. "Say anything, just don't . . ." Tears coursed down her cheek and off her chin, onto Nemoira's face. "Don't let the last thing you do to me be unkind."

Nemoira caught and held Jude's gaze. She put her big hand over Jude's to steady it, to keep the knife level. "Use all of me, Judy. Don't you waste a single drop."

Then, slowly and with great effort, Nemoira transformed into the bear a final time, body stretching and cracking in the shallow water, pained features hardening into that of the animal's. As Nemoira fell away and the bear overcame her, Jude dragged her knife across its throat. Bear's blood glugged out over her hands, her legs, her clothes. The eyes she had feared and then loved dimmed then darkened entirely, and inside, deep in the pit of herself, Jude felt something essential break.

19

Jude came out of her stupor tacky with blood and with a bear's corpse beneath her. She ran a hand over its matted fur, its teeth, and though she saw her fingers moving over the creature, she felt no sensation, her body as dead to her as the animal she petted. She started to say, *Nemoira, help me move this thing*, but there was no one, so she drew her hand away. Got to her feet.

She took a bath, cataloged her injuries to see which ones she could handle then and which ones she'd let work themselves out. She washed the gore off her skin and from her hair, scrubbed her face, and fished broken teeth out of her mouth, let them sink to the bottom of her cold bath. Jude shoved aside her tinctures and healing salves for her stash of muscle relaxants, codeine; she took one of each, grimaced at the pain from her side, and took another one from each bottle.

Afterward, Jude returned to the cellar. She needed to dress the bear as soon as possible, lest she lose any more of the pelt and the organs. With adrenaline and a simple pulley system, Jude hauled the bear's deadweight up the cellar stairs, through the hall, and into the kitchen, straining and grunting. In the kitchen, she put down a sheet, senses still numb as she assembled a row of fleshing knives and rope.

Both Candle and Jude were oddly serene as Jude undressed Nemoira. She made two cuts with the smallest of her knives, one going longways from paw to paw, and the second going from Nemoira's neck all the way down to her groin. She made slits on each of the paws, slipping each digit from the fur as if she were degloving a hand. Jude was delicate with the bear, gingerly skating the blade and her hand along the plush, dark skin, peeling away layer after layer until nothing was left save for skinless flesh and bone.

It took Jude two days to flesh, salt, and tan the bear hide. In the meantime, in between salting and salt baths, soaking the hide in a tanning solution of Nemoira's brains (that wicked and clever mind swirling grayly in salt water, every joke and tease and story melting into a slime), Jude dealt with the corpse. Nemoira had died on her back, and all Jude had to do was separate her legs, taking the rope and binding each to the legs of two separate chairs she set apart at equal distance. Squatting between the bear's legs felt familiar, and Jude snorted as she made the hygienic cuts and ties, securing the anus so as not to spoil the rest of the meat. The numbness a comfort, Jude cut upward through the muscle and fat, moved aside the peritoneum, and sliced open the abdominal cavity.

Nemoira spilled into her hands, organs pink and fatty and steaming. Jude heaved the bear to one side to remove the liver and stomach, then cut the diaphragm from the breast- and backbone before letting her fall flat. Her hands were deep within Nemoira as she caressed the heart and lungs, the esophagus, the ridged trachea. Carefully, she slid her knife and free hand along the bundle of tubes and slick shapes, and with quick, decisive strokes cut through the tubes. Easing out her knife hand, Jude slowly slid the bundle from the chest cavity, a line of blood drooling, dribbling out of Nemoira as she did so. Just like that, she held Nemoira's tender heart in her hand.

Emptying the bear of its innards took time, Jude requiring frequent breaks to eat and to rest between rolling Nemoira from side to side, slipping her knife along the bone inside to sever the remaining diaphragm. She was relieved when the mess of intestines finally hung loose in the abdominal cavity, the tenderloins mercifully spared from her tired sawing. Once the bear was empty, Jude freed it from its ropes and hauled the corpse out to the backyard to drain it. Whatever blood was left in Nemoira rolled down the hilled backyard, forming rivulets and trickling streams of scarlet.

The hide was all but done by the time Jude was ready to handle the meat. She regarded the stretch of bear skin, the familiar fur that she had buried her nose in and toyed with as if Nemoira were only an oversize dog, and decided she'd sleep under it. A quilt using the hide wouldn't be difficult, and whatever she couldn't use there she'd use as a rug or another, smaller blanket.

Jude spread Nemoira's organs out on the counter and considered recipes. Stew, obviously, with the shoulder and the stew meats. The rest of her—the tenderloin, the flesh of her arms and legs and belly, her stomach and heart and kidneys and lungs—Jude would fricassee, fry, boil, braise, bake into hand pies, and sprinkle in her greens.

Jude wrapped and stored the meat, everything labeled *bear*, and cooked for herself, for Nemoira, liver and onions. She picked through the destruction of the parlor for their collection of vinyl, and, finding it, chose an Ella Fitzgerald record. As the First Lady crooned and cried about angel eyes and finis romance, Jude seared thick slices of Nemoira's liver in her congealed fat, sprinkled her lover with salt and pepper, sprigs of thyme. Nemoira liked her gravy thick, so Jude added twice the usual amount of flour and butter, threw in the rough-chopped onions, and let them all simmer together.

Jude made one plate for herself and one plate for the altar room. The final plate she brought to the front porch and placed on the sodden, sunken spot where she knew, in time, the bear would be expecting its dinner.

And suddenly—nothingness. She knew what it was to lose Nemoira, had experienced it all before, but that brief two-month disappearance was nothing compared to now. The knowledge that she was gone, killed by Jude's own hand, unmoored her. The world spun on, the sun rising and setting and rising again. Nemoira's garden bloomed and rotted away, the high rice and flowers and luscious fruits, vegetables rotting within moments of bloom. Candle raged where she could not, thrashing and seething as it hadn't in years, and Jude did not care. The haints came to her, showed their miserable shadowed faces, and Jude merely looked at them, unblinking, until they left her. Honey turned to ash on her tongue; Jude could no longer feel the warmth of the sun.

Sapped of vitality and drained of color, joy, Jude confined herself to her bedroom. Nemoira's smell was still there, trapped in the sheets, and she hid herself in them. Her sleep was dreamless, just long and empty hours of darkness that split the days into manageable chunks. Even awake, she was sleeping, and time became a jellied thing too thick to move through. She closed her eyes on herself making tea in the kitchen and woke in the altar room, hands poised over the altar. She closed her eyes again, found herself in the forest jamming mud into her mouth.

It was as if Jude were cleaved in two, one part of her buried beneath her Nemoira-scented blankets and the other half left to wander. The cognizant part of her walked out into the field and let her body grow roots, let the arms and legs be tied with kudzu. Woodpeckers roosted in her matted hair, and rabbits made burrows out of her stomach. When her injured eye liquefied and trickled down her face, a destruction of wasps built their nest in the socket. Furry moths were her only clothes as Jude was overtaken, eaten.

Jude kept hoping for madness to come, but it never did. There was only boredom, loneliness. She'd told Nemoira, once, that she'd never felt the force of her isolation until Nemoira came to fill it, and without that stopper, without the reprieve of Nemoira's voice, Jude was struck head-on with a wanting so bottomless it nauseated her. She hated Nemoira. Hated the bear for being a bear, hated Nemoira for lying and for forcing her hand, but she hated herself more for having that ugliness within her, for being in possession of a mind that knew the utility of violence, the usefulness of a blade.

The day the roof caved in was the day Jude decided to leave Candle. The house had had enough of her, and she enough of it—she hadn't the energy to mend herself, never mind a ruined roof and rotted floors, so she unearthed her quilted bag from the mess of shingles and wood, filled it with clothes and toiletries, her sewing tin and money, a well-worn copy of an older Baldwin novel. She recovered her mother's ring from the altar room and placed it back on her hand. Everything else, the destruction and squalor, the grime accumulated after a month of grieving, Jude left as it was.

When Jude closed the front door behind her, she locked it.

Outside of Whitnee, the world had changed beyond all recognition. New roads led to new highways, and towns that once stood proud and solitary were absorbed into sprawling cities. Attitudes were different as well; where once Jude couldn't so much as park her car on the side of the road to get a couple hours of sleep, there were now motels and inns friendly enough to let her stay the night so long as she had the money to pay. Cautiously but curiously, Jude emerged from her learned fears. She drank too-sweet coffee in a café in Sibley, bought a patch for her empty eye in Vienna, and spent half a day in Macon just admiring the city, marveling at the sheer number of Black folk she saw out and about.

At some point, her car began to point northwest. Her mother's house called to her, and like a moth drawn to flame, she went to it. It called to her over the radio, the chanting of her name drowning out the wail of electric guitars, of disco and rock and gospel.

Judith! it called. *Judith! Judy! Jude!*

PART 3

You said I killed you—haunt me, then! Be with me always—take any form—drive me mad! Only do not leave me in this abyss, where I cannot find you!

— **EMILY BRONTË,** *WUTHERING HEIGHTS*

20

Besides the owner of the laundromat, Mr. Paul, and a trio of gray-faced women watching their loads more than their children, Vivian was the only other customer in the laundry that evening. She came alone, armored in a gray, shapeless coat and wielding a wheeled plastic basket. Her hair she covered with a plain black scarf that she secured beneath her chin, and she wore nothing on her face save for a scowl.

"Evenin', Mrs. Rice!" Mr. Paul called to her with a wave.

Vivian nodded shortly in response. She didn't care for Mr. Paul; he was overfamiliar, the kind of person who thought his skin color and their close age united them. Where was all this camaraderie when she was showing up to church with black eyes, when her husband died and nobody came to look in on her, not even to see if there was something in the fridge? Wordlessly, Vivian approached the counter, dug into her pocketbook, and handed the man two singles.

"Nice night, ain't it?" He counted out eight quarters, held out his hand for Vivian to take them from him. She looked at the hand for several seconds before he flushed and placed them on the counter. As she picked up her quarters, he said, "*Say!* Where's that sister of yours? Seems like I haven't seen her out an' about in ages!"

"Phyllis ain't well" was all Vivian said. No need for Mr. Paul to know that Phyllis didn't leave the house nowadays, that even a walk to the end of the driveway was enough to cause fits. The last time Phyllis had left the house on Westmoor was the night they buried Ernestine. After that, she was content to sit in their shared bedroom and while away the hours with talk television, courtroom shows, and soap operas.

"Well, that's too bad. You know, if you have her put on the sick-and-shut-in list, I know folks down at the church would be more than happy to come by and pray for her."

Vivian pursed her lips, put her coins in the pocket of her coat. "Thank you, *sir*, but that's not necessary. Philly and I, we don't like nobody in our house."

She tracked down her usual set, an unbroken row of three washers and dryers near the back, and dumped the clothes out onto one of the plastic tables to sort the darks from the colors. She was silent as she worked, quick and efficient. Within ten minutes, Vivian had the whole of the basket sorted, her clothes and Phyllis's clothes arranged into neat piles.

This wasn't *real* laundry, not in Vivian's eyes. Laundry was what Ernestine used to do, massive loads of linen and uniforms, industrial-strength cleaners that turned her hands ugly. Laundry was vats of boiling water brought out to the yard, scrubbing clothes against a washboard with soap she'd made herself. They used to make games out of it, she and her sisters, singing as they worked, tossing the clothes between them until Momma told them off, lest they drop something. Vivian let one of Daddy's good shirts fall once, red Georgia clay staining the blue cotton. He wore her legs out, switched her until the backs of her thighs were all welts.

Still, even if it wasn't real, it was easier. These neat little bottles of softener and conditioner and detergent were better than lye burns, the stink of bleach. Vivian swung the door on the last set of underthings, caught a glimpse of something in the machine, and pulled it out before slamming the door shut. It was a headscarf, silken, chick yellow and patterned with yellow roses. She felt along its edge for the name she knew was embroidered there in blue thread—Ernestine Lily Rice.

She hadn't seen it in years, thought they'd burned it. Vivian brought the scarf to her nose and inhaled deeply. She thought she could smell her sister still, the tuberose and calamine lotion masked by the funk of age. Each sniff brought memories of Ernestine braiding hair, Ernestine at the stove, Ernestine patting her head soothingly after a particularly vicious beating. When she could take no more, Vivian gave the scarf a final squeeze and then tucked it into the pocket of her coat.

Vivian Rice was seven-one and tired. Her parents were dead, her husband was dead, her beloved sister was brutally murdered, and all that was left was her, Phyllis, and a house that hated them. Her beauty, what little of it she had, was long gone, drained away by grief and by malice. If anything remained of the young woman who wore flowers in her hair to wave her husband off to war, it was buried too deeply to exhume. She wouldn't want anything to do with that girl anyways. Too naive, too stupid, too bright-eyed and hopeful, and what was there to be hopeful for when only twenty years after she and her sister sat giggling over blue thread, that same sister would be cold meat in the kitchen?

Hope was a dangerous thing for a Black woman to hold, even more dangerous when she had a past like Vivian's. What little joy Vivian found in those days—hoeing hard ground, picking cotton bolls till her hands bled—she'd found with her sisters, digging it out the soil like earthworms. And, like earthworms, joy was easily killed, crushed, drowned out and flattened. A memory came to Vivian—the first time Ernestine had fallen pregnant, the dead look in her eyes as she regarded her bloodless underwear. She had asked Nessie if it was one of the boys from the neighboring farms or one of Mr. Humphrey's sons, even though she knew the answer.

"Is it his?" Vivian had whispered. The stifled, muffled weeping of her older sister was the only response she needed. Mercifully, it had died only a couple of weeks later, the splash of red on Ernestine's legs like a victory banner. *Not that it mattered*, thought Vivian. *Whenever he could, he did, and even when he couldn't, he did it still.*

There were four more after the first. Some were only blood in chamber pots and others had faces, little limbs. The one that was born mostly whole but with a twisted arm and cleft lip was what made Vivian think of nursing, less so for the baby itself and more for Ernestine after. Nessie was sixteen then, calcifying but not yet stone, and Vivian had sat between her legs, massaging her stomach until the afterbirth came away.

"Just a little longer now," she'd said. The thing—she hadn't wanted to call it a baby, didn't want it to settle in her brain as a brother or a nephew or whatever—was blue, hadn't even drawn a single breath. That was the one mercy. At least none of them lived, at least none of them lasted.

Well, Vivian supposed. All but one.

It all went to hell after Momma died. In 1916, Daddy bought land in Atlanta to build them a house, and three years later, Ruth Rice, thirty-six and worn thin after years of burying blood clots and nursing white babies, tried birthing a final child and died in the process. It was a boy, brown skin and a head of dark hair; Daddy named him Mason, after his own father and his brother, and buried him next to Momma, his parents.

Auntie Caroline lived with them for about two years before she and her husband migrated north, and then it was only the girls and their father. Two years after that, Daddy moved them into the house on Westmoor Drive, and somewhere between the shifting of furniture, painting walls, and planting gardenias, Daddy planted another seed in Ernestine.

Back on Humphrey's land, Vivian couldn't miss the sounds, the squeaking, the thump of the bed frame against the wall; she only wondered who it was beneath Daddy, dead-eyed Momma or dead-eyed Nessie. She didn't have to wonder on Westmoor Drive, and the knowledge that she was most likely sleeping peacefully in the room she shared with Phyllis while her father was smothering Nessie, forcing another damned baby on her, haunted Vivian through the years.

It wasn't as if she could've stopped it. There were things they didn't talk about, secrets they let hang over their necks like nooses. To say aloud, *Can't we run? Can't we kill 'im? Can't we do anything other than let it happen and happen and happen?* would be admitting that it was real, and if Momma didn't stop it, there wasn't much Vivian could do, was there?

(She would have though, if Ernestine had only asked. For all the times Ernestine took lashes meant for her and drew Daddy's attention so he wouldn't see how Vivian and Phyllis were filling out, she would've killed without question.)

When the baby was born, it was only Vivian and Ernestine in the room. Phyllis had wanted to help, but neither sister thought it wise for her to be there, though both suspected Phyllis already knew the truth. Alone, they handled things, Ernestine biting her tongue against screaming and Vivian once again between her sister's legs, muttering encouragements. *Hold tight to me, gal. Slow now, breathe* real *slow for me. There you go, Nessie! Now,* push, *gal,* push!

Out it came, dark and red and bawling. What an insult, what a sight! Of all their mother's children lost, buried, here was this ugly thing splashed out in a river of blood and amniotic fluid, staining Nessie's pretty yellow sheets. It wailed, balled fists striking the air. They hadn't expected it to live so there was no bassinet, nothing to swaddle it in; Vivian placed the baby in a dresser drawer, returned to her sister's side, and helped her pass the afterbirth.

With perfect clarity, Vivian recalled cleaning the baby and finding it well, uninjured. Ernestine wouldn't hold it, wouldn't so much as look at it until days after the birth, so it was up to her and Phyllis to keep it alive. She wouldn't name it either, so it was Daddy who took the baby, a girl, and named her Judith.

Vivian couldn't love her niece—her sister. How could she, knowing what she knew, seeing how Ernestine had labored to bring the cursed child into the world? Phyllis might have thought there was no such thing as bad seed, but Judith was conceived in evil, born in evil.

Vivian thought she'd feel a little differently after Daddy died, but her disdain for the little girl stayed the same. Even with their father six feet under, she couldn't shake the disgust, the hatred. She looked at Jude and saw Ernestine at sixteen, her thighs wet with blood. The girl cried and she heard Ernestine's pained groans, saw the angry band of black-and-blue around Nessie's wrist after she'd agreed to the stipulations in Daddy's will. Judith brought her rocks and stickers, any little thing to appeal to her coldest aunt, and despite the innocence in the girl's face, the open desperation, all Vivian saw was Daddy slipping his ring off Momma's cold hand and putting it onto Nessie's warm one.

It was a relief to leave the Westmoor house. Vivian didn't even particularly love Douglas, the man who courted and proposed to her, but she took his ring because it meant getting away from the memories, from the girl. That was back in '34, and a for a good, long while Vivian was happy. Nessie sewed her a wedding blanket and Phyllis wove flowers into her hair. They got married in a church, naturally, and Douglas's brother was kind enough to give her away. Even the addition of sullen Judith as a flower girl didn't dim the day's joy, and Vivian remembered feeling so happy, so hopeful of the future, that she pulled her little niece close and kissed her cheek.

"Might be you got another li'l cousin in a year," she said to Judith, winking. *Must've been the wink*, Vivian told herself, watching the laundry go around and around. *Too damn prideful, too damn happy.*

To hell with it. To hope was to die, and dying was the only reward after a life so mean.

Vivian took the bus home. The circuitous route brought her past her old house, the charming two-bedroom Douglas had bought her as a wedding present. The rosebushes she'd planted were dead, the lawn overgrown and wild with weeds. Vivian couldn't begin to imagine the state of the inside, but it must have been as she'd left it thirteen years ago, everything waiting for her as if she'd only stepped out for milk.

Looking at the house made Vivian feel silly. Who did she think she was, anyways, trying to live like she deserved lacy curtains in the windows? Every time Vivian reached above her station, tried to be more than dirt underneath her nails and blisters from farmwork, life knocked her flat on her back. Older, wiser, she could admit to herself that she was a fool back then for thinking that training as a nurse, having a husband and a house, would separate her. In the end, it was only a game of pretend, her uniform and wedding dress different costumes she put on.

The bus stopped a block from the Westmoor house, and Vivian got off grunting, laundry basket thumping behind her. When the bus pulled off, there was only Vivian on the street, dim streetlights, and the wall of trees her father had planted to separate his daughters from the world.

It was only because Ernest was so nasty himself that he could build such a nasty house. Its walls were either too tall or too short, the dimensions of each room somehow both cavernous and cramped. The stairs were too steep, the roof line irregular, and the slats of hardwood were off by mere and maddening centimeters. Ernest Rice didn't have to build his house far back from the road and at the farthest end of the street, but he did so regardless. His daughters were his treasures, and he hoarded them on his half acre of land surrounded by sweet gum trees that admitted no light. The Westmoor house stood alone, hateful as its maker, its foundations malicious and its furnace stoked by rage.

Undulating gray light covered Vivian like an infant's caul as she entered the house. She called out for her sister, heard no response, and called again.

"Philly?"

"In the bedroom!"

Vivian followed her sister's voice down the hall, up the stairs, and into the large room they used for everything from sleeping to cooking small meals. The rest of the house they left to its own devices, unwilling to contend with the horror of the kitchen or the bedrooms used by Ernestine and Judith. Though the room they once shared as young women was cluttered with furniture (a fridge, a hot plate, two twin-size beds, a nightstand for each sister, a chest of drawers, a wardrobe, two plastic chairs, and a small collapsible dining table they kept folded under the window when it wasn't in use), it remained neat, spotless. Even the flotsam from the sisters' respective homes sat tidily on their nightstands, the glass angels and combs and framed photographs dust-free and arranged thoughtfully.

Phyllis stood over the television, rocking and mumbling prayers under her breath. Vivian saw that the TV was on the fritz again, the signal roaming from Phyllis's preferred wholesome programming to scenes out of horror movies, near-naked women splashed with blood scrambling from chain saws, a little girl rotating her head like an owl, spewing pea soup. Vivian dragged the laundry basket into the corner, checked that the TV was unplugged (it was), and then helped Phyllis throw a tarp over the screen. Much like a caged bird tricked into sleep, the television settled, the red glare softening into fuzz, then into blackness.

"Has it been acting up long?" asked Vivian.

"Only for the last twenty minutes. It was the bathroom in Nessie's room before—I already put the towels down." Phyllis took in deep breaths and put a hand to her heart as she sat on the edge of her bed. "I don't think I did anything to kick it off."

"It wasn't you," Vivian said flatly. "Found one of Nessie's scarves in the laundry. The yellow one, with the yellow roses? Got me thinking about her and about Daddy." She took off her shoes, rolled down her stockings, and draped them over her headboard. "About the girl."

Phyllis's flinch was so minute a stranger would've missed it, but Vivian knew her sister well. Talking about Ernestine was hard on a good day; bringing up Judith, talking about what their father had done to them all, was almost always impossible.

She put a hand on Phyllis's head and said, "No need to dwell on it. Come help me with this laundry."

They worked together in silence, folding linens and hanging up shirts, dresses. Once the basket was empty, Vivian made them a simple dinner of canned soup and crackers. She wished the kitchen was friendlier, but as it stood, just thinking about the room made her woozy. It was a vile place, prone to throwing glasses and gas leaks, and between the blood caught in the grout and the corpse-shaped stain in the tile, neither Vivian nor her sister could handle the kitchen's ire.

After rinsing their dishes in the bathroom sink and leaving them to dry in the bathtub, Vivian crawled into bed.

"No music tonight?" asked Phyllis softly. When the television rebelled, she liked to listen to the gospel station or to chorales, but Vivian couldn't take the noise.

"Maybe in the morning," Vivian responded. She clicked off her light and Phyllis clicked off hers. Vivian reached her hand out in the dark, feeling around for Phyllis, and when Phyllis grabbed hold, she squeezed tightly. "In the morning, I promise."

Sleep didn't come easy for either sister. The house was restless that night, roiling with anxious energy. The television flicked on and off at its leisure, stretches of silence and near sleep broken by earsplitting screams and lascivious moans. Their father's voice boomed from other rooms, and Vivian cowered like a child under her blanket, listening to the stomp of his heavy work boots against the hardwood.

As always, just when Vivian was sure her head would burst from the noise, the wailing and bellowing too much for her weakening senses, Ernestine's clothes began their march. She heard them leaving their wardrobe, the click-clack of sensible heels down the hall. With wide eyes and clenched teeth, Vivian watched the parade of empty church dresses, footless shoes, gloves without hands to flesh them. Ernestine's crisp white usher's uniform sidled past the open bedroom door, and in the bleak light of the hall appeared as if it were looking directly at Vivian.

All throughout the parade, the television roared, its static merging into one sound, a single name repeated—*Judith, Judith, Judith.*

21

Nessie's girl stood on the porch, tall and dark and wearing her sister's face. Everything was the same, the differences too minute. Same chin, same cheeks, same eyes and mouth always so serious, so disdainful—she even held herself like Ernestine, shoulders back, assured of her own strength. When she faced Phyllis, she was struck with a sense of déjà vu; the gashed face, the obscured eye.

"Lord, my God," whispered Phyllis. She held on to the doorknob for strength and put the other hand to her pounding heart.

"Evenin', Auntie Phyllis. Mind if I come in and sit a spell?" asked Judith.

Dumbstruck, Phyllis could only stare at the girl. She tried blinking her out, like an eyelash or a speck of dust, but Judith remained. Phyllis swayed, felt the world tilt beneath her feet. Judith was at her side in a flash, quilted bag abandoned as she took Phyllis by the arm and steered her into the house. She was placed in the front room, the couch's plastic covering sticking to the sweaty backs of her legs, and when Judith came to her with a glass of ice water, she downed it all.

"Slow now," Judith said. She laid a hand on Phyllis's shoulder and Phyllis flinched away.

Judith hummed and took a seat in the armchair beside the couch. She stretched out her legs, stretched her neck from side to side. Her clothes—blue jeans and a shirt that bared her thick, scarred arms—were incongruous to the tidiness of the room, the rose-patterned upholstery and scrolled rug.

Questions gripped Phyllis's stomach like constipation pains. Why, *why*? Why kill Ernestine, why run, why not *tell* somebody? Why'd you slit her throat, why'd you halve her face? What happened in this house that warranted so much ugliness? Words crowded her mouth, crowded on her tongue, and Phyllis had to force herself to breathe slow, to let things come to her one at a time.

"I . . . You . . ." Her hand trembled as she set the empty glass down. "My *God*."

"I called your place. It was the only number I remembered," said Judith. Her voice was a hoarse whisper, not much louder than it was when she was young.

"Not your mother's?" whispered Phyllis.

Judith shook her head and said, "Forgot it years ago. 'Sides, I didn't think anyone would be here. Thought I'd be able to see it alone."

"Your auntie Vivian and I been living here since . . ." She swallowed, tried to look Judith in the face, and found she couldn't. She focused on the empty stretch of wall above her head instead. "Since you left."

"It's, um . . ." Judith glanced around the room, taking it all in, and Phyllis saw through her eyes the decay, the ruins of a house that for five decades was as proud and imposing as its builder. Cracks in the ceiling, cracks in the plaster; the windows greasy with fingerprints, some splintered from frosts. The framed photograph of Daddy, the furniture, the woodwork—all of it was covered with a thin layer of dust, age keeping Phyllis and Vivian from wiping the house down daily.

Embarrassed, Phyllis cleared her throat and said, "It ain't as neat as your mother used to keep it, I know, but—"

"I kept it clean," interrupted Judith. Phyllis looked at her head-on now, taken aback by the bluntness. "*I* kept it clean, Auntie. Scrubbed the floors, stood up on that high ladder to get the grime from the crown molding. Smell of lemon Pine-Sol used to make me gag how much I used it, shining the wood railing and the brass and . . ." She puffed through her nose. "It don't matter. It's just a house."

It stung to have her sister's home—her home, for many years—flattened so, but it was true. Her father had built an ugly house, and no amount of painting, decorating, or furnishing could make it lovely. Phyllis had tried her hand at beautifying the awkward rooms, propping open windows to permit what little light broke through the tree line, and soon learned the uselessness of trying to turn pig shit into pearls.

Phyllis studied her niece. She was different, *much* different, more haunted in the eyes and far more solemn than she used to be, but there was a resilience in her too, the sort of fortitude a person exudes when they've clawed up nine circles of hell. Knowing that her own sister was one of the hells Judith crawled through rattled Phyllis, made her twitch in her seat.

"That night," Phyllis began. She palmed her sweat off onto the plastic, onto her robe. "That night, when you called me, you said you had to do it. Said you weren't sorry. Why me? Why call me?"

Judith regarded her plainly. Phyllis, unaccustomed to being observed baldly by folks younger than her, adjusted herself. How did she look to her niece, a woman so distanced from her she was nearly a stranger? Was she old and stooped? Was she a cruel judge, like Vivian, or was she kinder, more forgiving? Her niece's eye upon her left Phyllis flayed, and her stomach twisted as she considered myriad reasons why Judith might hate her.

"I don't know," Judith admitted. "I think I needed somebody to hear me, to know what I'd done, to tell me what to do or that it was gonna be alright, but—"

"But I didn't. I told you to stop coming to me with stories, to stop spreading rumors." Uncut, unadulterated shame gripped Phyllis, made her sweat and squirm. Many things had slipped her mind over the years—the names of old friends, her grandmother's eyes, the sound of her mother's voice—but she never forgot the ease with which she'd dismissed Judith's tears, her bruises, how even on that fateful night she waved off the panic in the woman's voice. So many times, Judith had come to her house as a child, as a teenager, eyes wild as she showed Phyllis the lashes on her legs, described to her the thrashings and whippings just as, if not more, brutal than the whippings Phyllis and her sisters had gotten from their father. Tears welled in Phyllis's eyes and she let them roll. "I left you to it."

Judith barked out a sharp, mirthless laugh, revealing a mouthful of irregular but strong teeth. "You left me to it. Probably for the best. If I'd let myself be talked down, I would still be here dying instead of out there living."

Softly, Phyllis said, "Was it really so bad?"

Her niece's sardonic smile softened and turned sad. "Hell would've been sweeter."

Whatever more there was to say was cut off by the crunch of gravel. Phyllis jerked to attention, hopped to her feet, and rushed to the front door just as Vivian opened it. There was no separation between the entrance and the rest of the house, the front door leading directly into the front room that served as a living area. Phyllis stood in Vivian's path, blocking her view to Judith.

"Philly, what is this?" asked Vivian. She had her little shopping cart beside her, plastic grocery bags laid over brown packages from the liquor store. "What's that car out in the driveway?"

"Now, Vivian," said Phyllis. She held her hands out in front of her as if she were subduing a wild animal. *Not too far off*, she thought to herself. Vivian's temper was almost as fiery as Ernestine's, as Momma's, red-hot and blasting in all directions, liable to burn up anything that got in its way. "Now, Vivian, I need you to comport yourself."

"*Comport myself?* Girl, if you don't get out my way!"

Vivian nudged Phyllis aside and the room stilled as she laid eyes on Judith. The woman was standing with her chin raised, almost daring for harm to come to her. Vivian, never one to be tested, puffed air from her nose and barreled toward Judith, Phyllis hurrying after her, pulling on her sister's arm.

"*Devil.* A damn devil, to come to *this* house, you must be out of your damned mind, you low-down, trifling, evil *bitch*!" screamed Vivian. Her hand was raised to strike, and Phyllis knew despite Vivian's age she was still strong enough to knock a grown person to the ground. There had been incidents: folks cutting her off at the grocery store, folks aggravating her on the bus. When Vivian got angry, she swung.

Just as the powerful hand came swinging down, Judith blocked it with her own, gripping Vivian's wrist and holding it aloft. Her eyes were tar black, her mouth pulled into a snarl, and when she shoved Vivian off her, she did it with enough force that the old woman landed on the couch with a grunt.

Stillness again, and silence, Phyllis holding on to her chest and muttering prayers, Vivian glaring up at Judith from the sofa, and Judith glaring down at Vivian. Panting heavily, Judith took a step back, eyes never leaving Vivian's.

In a low, stony voice, Judith said, "*Now*, now look here. Cuss me, damn me, yell and scream at me all you like, it don't matter to me none, but I'll tell you now." She nodded, chuckled without meaning it. "You ain't gon' raise your hand against me, you just ain't. I'd take it all but not that. Not from your sister and not from you."

She's the spitting image, thought Phyllis. There was Ernestine's rage, the hard set to her jaw, the unflinching fierceness that suffered no fools and fought life like a bear. Phyllis stood with her back against the wall, tried to steady her breath.

"I knew you weren't no good. I knew it, I *knew it*!" said Vivian. "Why are you here?" Sharply turning to Phyllis, she asked, "*Why* is she here? Why'd you let that thing in?"

"It's my house by rights," replied Judith. "I got the right to come back to my mother's house."

"Your mother! *Your* house!" Vivian laughed. "You gave that up the *minute* you ripped *my* sister's face apart." She smacked her chest with her uninjured hand, bared her rotted teeth. "Should've gutted you when we had the chance."

"Vivian!" Phyllis moved to stand in between her sister and her niece. "Enough. Both of you, please, enough. We'll figure this out, but not with . . . not with all of this." To her niece, she said, "Judith. How 'bout you set here, let me and your auntie work something out, hear?"

Judith nodded once and returned to her armchair. Turning to her sister, Phyllis lowered her voice and said, "Vivian, a word?"

Upstairs in their room, Vivian paced, and Phyllis sat on her bed with arms folded. She was tired of watching Vivian go from the door to the window, from the window to the door, but she was tired of arguing as well. It was too much excitement for her heart, too much pressure on her head.

"I won't have her stay here," said Vivian for the tenth time. "I *won't*, Philly, I just won't. I rather walk on down to that kitchen and plant my face on the floor fore I let it happen."

"It is her mother's house, Vivian. No matter what she did, this is her mother's house."

"God, you actin' like she told a lie or skipped town. She killed our sister, Phyllis! Don't you remember that? Don't you remember the mess she made of her face?" Vivian's voice rose and cracked with tears. "Her *eye*, Phyllis! We buried her without her eye!"

"Maybe she . . ." And the words froze in Phyllis's throat, choked her. She felt Vivian's eyes narrowing in on her, felt Vivian stalking closer to where she sat.

"Maybe she *what*, Phyllis?"

Phyllis raised her head, met her sister's gaze. She was trembling, inside and out, and behind her eyes, she felt the familiar needlelike migraine growing, growing. In as calm and even of a voice as she could manage, Phyllis steeled herself, saying, "Maybe she deserved it."

Vivian threw up her hands, aghast, shaking her head, shaking away even the idea of it, but Phyllis pressed on. Too long they'd deified their sister's ghost, called her holy and pure when so many times, countless times, she was anything but. There was a coldness in them, a violence sewn into them by their father and their mother, their father's father and mother's mother, and on and on, back and back, until the first Rice, not even a Rice then, had the misfortune of being snatched from the motherland. Even there too, Phyllis supposed, there were ancestors and many-times-distanced relatives stitched with the same bloody patches. Dyed in the flesh, dyed in the wool—the ugliness was native to them, as hereditary as eye color and set of mouth.

"Take her off the pedestal, Vivian. Just this once, just now with only you and me here, and think about it. Really, think about *her* and how she was. Think of how she beat that girl for anything from speaking too slow or smiling or dancing. Things in her *nature*, Vivian, she would punish her for. The girl can't help whose face she has, who she resembles, the pitch of her voice, and still she beat her. Whupped her, tore her up—you can't tell me that's right."

Vivian wouldn't meet Phyllis's eyes. She stared down at the floor, shoulders shaking and jaw working. Arms folded over her chest, she said, "We had it worse. That girl, she don't know nothing about it, not even the first clue—*we* had it worse and we didn't—we *wouldn't* think to do something like that to Momma. Not even to Daddy."

"Maybe that's on us then," said Phyllis. "But it wasn't on Judith to take it just because we did."

"You are defending the animal that killed your sister."

"No, Vivian, I'm defending my niece, that little girl we shoulda protected. If we had stepped in, if we stood between her and her mother, Ernestine would be alive."

Vivian kissed her teeth, turned so that she was facing Phyllis as she leaned against the dresser, body blocking the television entirely. "You think Ernestine made her the way she is?" She let out a puff of laughter and shook her head. "Girl, there weren't nothing Nessie could do to that child to make her anything other than what she is."

"You blaming the child for something she ain't have no part in, Vivian!" cried Phyllis. She knew they were being too loud, knew Judith could probably hear them from downstairs, but she didn't care. "For something done *to* her, not *by* her."

"What's the difference?" asked Vivian. The wind left her, shoulders dropping, and she crossed the room again to fall onto her bed. Phyllis saw clearly the bracelet of bruises Judith had left her with, but found she could not feel any pity for her sister. "She killed Nessie, over and over and over. Since birth, since conception—I *hate* her, Philly. It's wrong, I know it's wrong, and I know she ain't the one who deserves my hatred, but I can't..." Her voice cracked; she sobbed. "Where am I supposed to put it, Philly? The anger? The love? Where's it s'posed to go?"

Speechlessly, Phyllis watched her impervious sister break into tears. She had seen Vivian cry before, had seen the stoic mien collapse, but always she pulled it together, snot and tears cleared away before Phyllis could think to comfort her. Now, Vivian was inconsolable, keening, wailing into her mattress like she hadn't since she was a little girl.

Phyllis went to her sister and held Vivian, hands clasped around her waist and head resting on her back.

22

While her aunts argued over her coming and staying, Jude reacquainted herself with her mother's house. Like a cat upon meeting a stranger, the mood in each of the rooms downstairs was cautiously hostile, all arched back and hisses. In the front room, the plastic peeled itself off the sofas and the coffee table trembled ever so slightly. Jude ignored it—she didn't feel comfortable yet, chastising furniture she didn't know—and took in the dust, the grime. Her grandfather regarded her coolly from his place on the wall, his eyes flat and joyless. She shrank from him; even in death and years older, he unnerved her, this tyrant who frightened even Ma'am.

Unable to sit another minute under Pappy's glare, Jude peeked into the other rooms, the dining room and half bath, the kitchen. She stood at the room's threshold, stomach knotting, unable to place even a single foot inside. It smelled of blood and of dry rot, the cabinetry warped and every surface covered in powdery gray. At the room's center, a perfect outline of her mother's corpse was set, intaglio, into the green-and-brown wicker-weave tile.

Jude stepped into the kitchen. She burped, felt the vomit rising in her throat, and got to the sink in time to spit it there. On her tongue was the taste of bile and of jasmine perfume. Jude turned on the tap and rinsed her mouth, glanced out of the greasy, fingerprinted window. In her mind, it was '65 again, the opening chords of "Don't Let Me Be Misunderstood" tinkling in her ears. She heard Ma'am calling for her, heard Billy Graham, but she heard birdsong too, her aunts upstairs arguing and someone weeping. Tentatively, Jude put a hand to her own face, just to be sure it wasn't her carrying on, but her eyes were decidedly dry.

Out of body, Jude watched herself touch dishes, plates, and cups. She was in Candle; she was on Westmoor Drive. She was in her own kitchen grinding herbs, she was in Ma'am's house cooking beef stew. She needed to feel things, to anchor herself. Jude grabbed a glass angel and held it tightly in her hand, the brown cherub's pointed wings cutting into the scarred palm. Blood would be better, a little trickle of red to release the steam building behind her eyes. She imagined cutting open her palm, red coming out and Ma'am's spirit slipping in, poisoning her bloodstream, the thought so powerful and big, it almost seemed true.

"We don't usually come in here."

Jude yelped and dropped the angel. Its face cracked down the center, the wings skittering across the tile. Heart pounding painfully in her chest, she bent down to retrieve the pieces, the angel's shattered body. Aunt Phyllis stood watching as Jude settled the pieces on a countertop, and then said, "Didn't mean to startle you."

"Jumpy as a rabbit, me. Always have been." Jude turned to her aunt, put her hands into her pockets, and said, "I don't mean to stay long."

"I don't think Vivian wants you to stay at all."

"I get that, Auntie. I really do, but . . ." She gave Aunt Phyllis the whole of her gaze. How to explain to the woman her need for resolution, completion? How to make her see that the Westmoor house was like a bruise to her, tender and sore, pained pleasure to touch? Jude wouldn't leave until she had a better sense of herself, of Ma'am, the miseries and misfortunes that made the Rice blood run hot. At last, Jude repeated, "I won't stay long."

"Couple'a weeks?" tried Phyllis.

Jude granted her a small smile. "Try a month."

If her shouldering her way into the house discomfited Aunt Phyllis, she was good at hiding it. She led Jude upstairs and to her old bedroom, said they'd try to find something for her to eat in an hour or so.

"You don't cook?" asked Jude.

Phyllis shook her head, hand hovering over the knob to Jude's room as if she were afraid that it'd burn her. She put her hand behind her back and said to Jude, "Like I said, we don't like to go into the kitchen. We have a little hot plate in the bedroom or we'll order out. You like Chinese?"

"Haven't had it in years," admitted Jude. She listened as Phyllis recommended combination plates and house specials, what she liked and what Vivian liked, what place they preferred to order from since the other Chinese-takeout place was too far, and anyways, the employees weren't kind to Vivian when she picked their food up. She let Phyllis ramble, seeing within the old woman a desperate need to be heard, to have some ear other than Vivian's to receive her stories. When the woman was through, Jude closed and locked the door behind her before turning and facing, at last, her old bedroom.

It hadn't changed. Dreams distorted it, made everything red and too small, but it was as she'd left it—a decent-sized bedroom, closet on that wall and her four-poster bed on the other, lace curtains, pink rug, staid painting of flowers over her dresser. On top of the dresser were the porcelain dolls she remembered and the jewelry box. Bracing herself, Jude opened the box, but there was no rolling eye in there, only earrings and a little ring, a brooch she didn't recall having before. It was childish, even for a child, and insultingly juvenile for a woman of forty-one, now fifty-four. She took everything she didn't like—the lace curtains, the dolls, the painting, the pink rug, the fluffy and frilly pillows—and threw it into the closet. Everything else could wait until morning.

Jude unpacked her bag, the handmade articles of clothing and carved pieces of jewelry charming and colorful against the plain pink-and-white color scheme of her childhood bedroom. She dumped a bundle of clothing on the bed, loose dresses and overalls and beaded blouses, and as she worked through it, she found a bangle. Jude knew immediately it was one of Nemoira's, thin and silver, the type she liked to stack five, six bangles high and accentuate with ceramic and clay bracelets. So numb had she been in Candle, she didn't think herself capable of tears on Westmoor Drive, but Jude cried anyway, sniffling and suppressing her bigger sobs, burying her face in her hands to dampen the noise.

Dinner was a stilted affair, real forks and a table runner paired with Styrofoam containers and take-out boxes. Phyllis and Vivian sat across from her and ate like birds, pecking at rice and broccoli, saucy pieces of chicken. There was only water to drink, but every so often, Vivian rose, disappeared into the bathroom, and returned wobbling, eyes blearier each time she left. Jude was less reserved in her eating; she knew this meat to be what it promised to be—beef and chicken—and knowing that the food came from somewhere far from her own tainted kitchen heightened the taste.

They didn't talk over dinner, and Jude was grateful for it. Whatever questions were pinging in her aunts' brains could wait until she was settled in. Afterward, Jude cleared the table, the paper bags and Styrofoam, as Phyllis gathered up the cutlery, putting it into her pockets. It was only later, as she was walking upstairs to prepare for bed, that Jude saw Vivian up to her wrists in dish soap in the bathroom, the unsteady pile of plates and bowls and cups in the tub.

The house fell silent. Jude sat in the dark of her room, cross-legged on top of her duvet. The window was open, spring air pouring in with the sounds of crickets, cicadas. She heard few frogs, and the absence of loons' calling left her feeling lonesome.

She missed Candle. Thirteen, almost fourteen, years she'd lived in that farmhouse, loving its dereliction, adoring the noise and restlessness of its ghosts. The haints were harmless once they were used to her, and Candle, once tamed, was as doting to her as a dog. How would it treat her now, Jude worried, now that she had abused and abandoned it, left it to fester as she grieved? Could a house forgive?

Sleepless, Jude read. She allowed herself to be swept along James Baldwin's winding river of words, the story of the gospel singer and his lover so touching, so tender that it almost made her weep. Escape, reflection; those were the joys of reading. No matter how desolate she'd felt under Ma'am's rule, she knew there was a cache of hidden worlds in her closet, novels and dramas, slim books of poetry she marked with pen.

Around nine, the house came alive with noise. From down the hall, she heard a television screeching, squealing, news channels and squeaking cartoons blaring over the national anthem. One of her aunts—Jude couldn't tell which one—moaned long and pained, and yelled, "Turn it off! Turn it *off*!" There was silence for a moment and then the noise began again, ratcheting louder and louder. A man's voice cracked like thunder in a room on the other side of the house; Jude flinched, inched back against her headboard. One of the aunts shrieked, the piercing note vanishing beneath the man's angry voice.

The man said, "Ernestine! *Ernie!* Girl, I won't call for you again!"

Was that Pappy talking to Ma'am so meanly? And who was that blubbering, voice wavering and thin, begging, "No, no, no, you can't, you *can't*"? Jude put her hands to her ears and tried to will the overwhelming noise away, but on it went, through the night and into the morning—shouting, sobbing, begging.

Like nuns they were, Phyllis and Vivian, stooped and ascetic, their entire lives confined to their shared bedroom, the bathroom, the dining room. Alone in their room, they ate canned meat and watched Christian television, listened to sermons on the radio. There was no church, no quilting circle; Vivian left the house very rarely, and Phyllis not at all. When Vivian did go out, she returned with clean laundry and with groceries, her metal cart tinkling with poorly hidden bottles of liquor. Her aunts were about their money, cheap with clothes and food but cavalier when it came to their interests. Phyllis, for example, spent hundreds on televangelists' schemes, miracle cures, end-of-days paraphernalia, vials of holy oil (olive oil, Jude learned) and holy water, made-to-order illuminated Bibles. Vivian was more prosaic, practical; she spent her late husband's military pension on rum and wine and gin, on glass angels to replace the ones always breaking.

Theirs was a unique sort of misery. Joy did not penetrate these walls, nor did light, color. Losing their sister devastated them, their past tribulations paling in comparison to the havoc Jude had wreaked in her desperation to free herself. Small parts of Jude were pleased to see them brought so low—revenge for never having protected her from their dear Nessie. Still, she pitied their self-afflicted isolation, the desolation of the house they'd once called home. The rooms echoed with their sister's voice, her smell, and many times Jude came across one of the aunts in a fit of tears, tearing at her limp hair, beating her chest as if the sister-wound were new. It pained Jude, and though she did not regret saving her life, she wished there had been a way to free herself without having to kill Ma'am and, by extension, her sisters.

There was no use in trying to talk with Aunt Vivian, the woman having made her hatred of Jude no secret. Vivian was openly hostile, every invitation to conversation ending abruptly with a hard look and a door slammed in her face. Of the two aunts, Vivian reminded Jude the most of her mother, the uncontrolled temper, the way she seemed always moments away from committing some gross act of violence. She kept herself in check though; Jude's threat must've rattled her.

Phyllis, for her part, seemed eager to know her niece. Over a series of dinners (Chinese takeout, as usual, the women eating directly from the Styrofoam), Jude fielded questions about her past thirteen years, where she'd lived and who with, if anybody, and did she like living so far south, and what had she been doing with herself all these years. She liked talking about the Okefenokee, and she painted pictures for her aunts of the cypress dome, the Spanish moss, the marshes and fields of wildflower, the constant whoops and chirrs and croaks. She told them a little about Whitnee, and nothing about Nemoira, the woman a wound too raw to disturb. When Phyllis asked for a second time what she did out there in the woods, Jude said that she minded her house, her land, and did herbalist work.

"Like Ma'Dear!" exclaimed Phyllis. She clapped her hands together, turned to Vivian. "You remember them nasty potions Ma'ammy used to force on us? Castor oil and cohosh, weren't nothing like it."

"Nothing else for it on Humphrey's," said Vivian flatly. She closed her box of food and pushed it to the side, all her words pointed directly at the wall. "White doctor wouldn't come even if you lost a hand, a leg…"

"My Lord, if Ma'ammy didn't treat that garden like it was her own personal pharmacy." To Jude, Phyllis said, "Whatever ailed you, she'd reach down into that there grass and pull up something to set you right. Pennyroyal, licorice, anything she put her hands to, she mended."

"I never met Ma'Dear," Jude confessed. Ma'am didn't talk about her mother, not to Jude at least. She had asked after her grandmother and the rest of her people, had begged, even, to be let in on the great secret of her lineage, but to no avail. It was as if Jude and Ma'am, her aunties, all came from nowhere and no one, empty spaces suddenly occupied. "What was she like?"

Phyllis opened her mouth to speak but closed it directly after. Jude looked to her, then to Vivian. The woman's face was stormy, eyes narrowed in contempt. She thought there'd be more; the women often bickered in front of Jude—about when she should leave, about what she was allowed to do in the house, what things should and shouldn't be said in her presence. It was a surprise, then, that Vivian threw back her chair and stomped from the room.

That night Jude was too tired to resist the sleep that came to her. Her dreams were green and full of brown women, her mother and her aunts skipping in circles, jumping rope. When Jude rose in the night, her feet were confused by the layout of the house. Reoriented and remembering, they took her past the open door of her aunts' bedroom, down the precariously steep stairs, and into the kitchen where, she crawled onto the counter and out the window. In the yard overgrown with grass, weeds, Jude stood staring blankly out to the wall of green that kept the world out and the Rices in.

23

There were no woods to wander in the city, so Jude contented herself with walking the span of the yard, picking wildflowers. Color for the sake of color, beauty without purpose—she held a bouquet of lobelia and violet, delicate pink milkweeds, and drooping Solomon's seal. The vases in Ma'am's house were full of false plants; Jude emptied a few to refill them with freshly cut blooms.

Standing in the kitchen carefully clipping the stems of her haul, she considered how to go about constructing an altar. There were plenty of consoles and sideboards scattered around the house, pieces carved by her grandfather, but Jude was reluctant to use any of them. If she took the car into the city, she could find something more to her taste, with enough room to display the china bowls, cups, plates, candles, flowers, offerings of food and libations, coins and trinkets needed to appease the sticky, staticky energy in the house. Decision made, Jude took a vase, filled it with water, dropped in half an aspirin, and then arranged in it a hectic spray of purple, yellow, and bright red.

It'd be one of the first things on the altar when she was finished.

Jude washed her face, chose an outfit of overalls and her heavy boots, and then tracked down her aunts to let them know she was going. She waved off their questions, uninterested in either aunt's opinion about her clothes or her wild plume of coiled hair.

"You at least want to tell us when you *might* be back?" asked Vivian testily.

"No more than an hour or so, I reckon," Jude replied. "Should I bring in something for dinner?"

"We don't use the kitchen," said Vivian. Her gaze hadn't thawed from the night before, and she held her wrist very carefully, minute shifts raising her shirtsleeve so Jude could see her brand.

"I'll cook. Neck bones tonight?"

She left before she got an answer, tired of talking and ready to be out in the city she hadn't seen for over a decade. As she backed the car out from where she'd parked it, Jude saw the house's gray, trembling membrane and wondered if either of her aunts ever did anything to remove it or make it easier to pass through. *Not likely*, thought Jude. Either they didn't know what to do, knew what to do and were afraid to do it, or else they were like Ma'am, stubbornly sitting in their own filth to spite whomever.

The city of Atlanta as Jude knew it no longer existed. Old buildings she visited in her youth were boarded up or gone entirely, replaced by sleek modern office buildings, apartments. Gone were the "No Coloreds" signs, the "Whites Only" signs; everything was for everyone, and Jude needn't cross the street when a white person passed, nor did she have to walk around the back of a business to receive service. She got no odd looks for her big afro, her dark skin; in fact, there were more folks like her, women with coils and curls, beaded braids, women in jeans and men in dashikis, men with locked hair, bangles, wooden earrings, picks in their hair. In this new Atlanta, Black was king, and Jude blended into the crowd, her appearance that won her disdain in Whitnee par for the course in the city.

From a brightly lit grocery store, Jude purchased pinto beans, collards, neck bones, flour, sugar, a few shakers of seasoning, baking powder, baking soda, a cache of cleaning supplies, and a carton of strawberries to serve as dessert. A trip to a botanica provided her with a little glass bottle of Florida water and tall, thin candles to use on the altar. Her final stop of the day was to an antique store, where she purchased a long, narrow console stained a deep mahogany. On her way home, she drove past a woman selling wooden beads and other carved curios from a plastic table plastered with images of missing Black children and purchased a package of brown-and-tan beads, a balsa-wood bear with yellow stone eyes.

Jude returned to Ma'am's house and set the console in front of the framed photograph of Pappy. She covered it with candles, china from her mother's cabinets, dainty teacups, glass angels, and the bouquet she'd made. In the dishes and cups, Jude placed coins and dried petals, a dram of Florida water, some beads, a few strawberries.

Footsteps approached her from behind. Jude held her shoulders still, continued with her task.

"What's this?" asked Aunt Vivian tersely.

"An altar," replied Jude. She lit a candle and used it to light the others, the console washed in yellow flame. "You got any liquor?"

"Nobody *here* drinks." Vivian stood over her shoulder, sneering. "An *altar*? What is all this stuff?"

Jude considered the empty bottles of gin she'd seen in the outside garbage can, the reek of alcohol she often caught on Vivian's breath. Smoothly, she replied, "Little things to honor the house. I do it at my own place—helps it settle some, knowing someone respects it."

"*I* don't know what sort of mess you get into in whatever hell you crawled out of, but in *my* sister's house, we don't hold with none of this satanic nonsense."

Vivian wanted a response, but Jude didn't give it to her. Instead, she asked if there were any photographs of her mother she could have, or something with the family all together, her late grandmother and grandfather included.

The puff of breath from her aunt's nose was almost bovine. Arms crossed, Vivian snapped, "Like I'd let you put any picture of Ernestine up on this devil's altar!"

There was something on Jude's tongue about venerations, about honoring the dead, but it was promptly swallowed when Vivian took hold of the console and threw it onto its side. The china, the glasses, and the angels broke, their shards traveling the length of the front room, under the chairs and sofa. The candles extinguished themselves as they fell, hot wax pooling on the hardwood. Beads and coins, the two or so dollars Jude had put on the altar, swam in a small puddle of Florida water.

Jude steadied herself. *Snap*, her mind said. *Snap! Take that old bitch by her throat and show her what kind of thing you* really *are. She think you a devil? Show her!* Show her!

Unable to speak lest she say something unforgivable, Jude squatted down and picked up pieces of glass, beads, petals. She kept her eyes down; if she looked at Vivian, she'd kill her. Take any old sharp off the floor and jam it into her neck, let her wet her sister's floor with her blood, to hell what scary ol' Phyllis thought about it.

Towering over her, Vivian said, "I know what kind of person my sister was, gal. Don't you ever think I didn't know who she was."

Coin, petal, bead, coinpetalbead, shard of glass, angel wing, porcelain harp. *If I look at her, if I even so much as look at her.*

"Thing is: I know what kind of person you are too. You think

I don't, but I see right into the pit of you, can see your soul as clear as I see your face. *Yes, I* know *you*."

"Vivian, that's enough." Phyllis stood in the arch between the front room and the hall, hands flexing at her sides. "Please."

"Spoiled, ruined—"

"Vivian!" shouted Phyllis. She tried again to come between her sister and Jude, but to no avail. Vivian nudged her aside, and Jude rose, finally meeting Vivian's gaze. The jagged piece of china she held cut deep into her palm, red flowing down her wrist and over her fingers, dripping onto the hardwood.

Vivian flicked her eyes down to the glass and smiled. "You your daddy's child all right. First thought, hit 'em; second thought, kill 'em. You think you got it from your ma'am?" Vivian laughed. "No, child, *no*. You got it from *him*."

Vivian pointed to the photograph on the wall—the framed picture of her grandfather standing in front of his shotgun shack on Humphrey's land. Same eyes, same nose, same mouth; what Jude thought was Ma'am's, what she thought was her own. The glass piece fell from her hand, and Jude staggered backward, away from her aunts and the photograph, shaking her head.

"You just saying this to be cruel," Jude whispered. "You just like her—you'd say anything to hurt somebody. To hurt *me*."

Vivian retorted, "Why would I waste my breath on a lie? You is your granddaddy's daughter—bad seed. You was born ruined and you gon' die ruined."

Jude's eyes jumped from Vivian, satisfied and smug; to Phyllis, grimacing, cringing with horror; to her grandfather, her father, stoic and dead eyed in his bronze frame.

"*Oh!*" Jude gasped. Her mind was empty, shining, flashing red and green and blinding white, and she pushed past Vivian, past Phyllis, to rush out the front door. The cool spring air offered no relief to the heat in her face, in her chest, the roiling in her stomach. Staggering, limited vision limited further with shock, she crossed the yard, blinking. When her legs could take her no farther, Jude collapsed onto the grass, hunched over, and vomited.

How clearly she saw it all now! Of course Ma'am never loved her—how could you love something that poisoned you? Of course there were no stories or pictures! Blood bonded Ma'am and Jude, but too much of it, mother-blood and father-blood and grandfather-blood and sister-blood all mingled together, making something... *Something like* me, Jude thought.

She put her face into the earth and moaned, wept. Tears and dirt blended with the snot on her cheeks, and she let the mess remain there, the foulness on the inside matching the foulness she felt inside. Jude wanted, she wanted—she wanted to be home but she was already home; she wanted to die, but nothing inside of her was alive; she wanted Nemoira, but she'd killed her; wanted to cut her father out of her, but he was too deeply embedded; wanted Ma'am to come from the house and set beside her, touch her face with a tenderness the woman had never shown in life.

When Jude rose to her feet again, the sun had disappeared behind the fence of trees. She made her way back to the house with its grim and unlit windows, softly closing the front door behind her. The front room was empty, cleared of the glass and spilled water, the console returned to an upright position. Jude's bouquet sat in a new vase, the petals and stems crushed but still pretty; there were different dishes on the altar as well, coins on a plate and a little brown liquor in a teacup.

Jude locked eyes with her father-grandfather. There was no mirth in his face. She never remembered his smiling, but she recalled how her mother deferred to him, how Aunt Vivian and Aunt Phyllis turned into girls when confronted by his booming voice, his penetrating stare. How unflappable, impregnable Ma'am would cower, go white with fear when Jude so much as crossed Granddaddy in the hall without her escorting.

"Don't let nobody look at your legs," she would say. Jude thought it was because Ma'am was ashamed of what she'd done to her; sick rose in her stomach as she realized two things could be true at once.

Bilious spit on her tongue, belly fiery with wrath and with disgust, Jude tore the framed photograph off the wall, threw it to the ground, and ripped the picture from its framing. She shredded it, ripped the face in two and then four, until there was nothing recognizable about her father-grandfather, and threw the scraps into the fireplace.

interlude: sister-auntie

Sister-Auntie knows she shouldn't have said it the minute the words leave her mouth, but the words did leave her mouth, and now there's nothing for it 'cept feel sorry. Feel sorry for her poor, dead sister, feel sorry for her sister-niece, feel sorry for herself for getting so worked up, now why did she get so worked up?

It's the cooling off that's embarrassing. After the rage is gone, once she clears all the red from her eyes, Sister-Auntie sees plainly what she's done and it shames her. Nobody raised her to be like that, to say those sorts of things to anybody, not even anybodies she can't love. Once she said her uglybuttrue things, Sister-Niece ran out the door, went into the yard to throw up and throw a fit. She hears her screaming and carrying on from the house, hears it over the angry stare Alive-Sister gives her.

"Now what did you gain from that?" she asks Sister-Auntie, and Sister-Auntie can't say because whatever satisfaction it brought her to see her sister's killer go white is dulled by the knowledge that she broke her promise to Dead-Sister.

Lying on her bed like a scolded child, Sister-Auntie considers what's to be done. Talking to the girl is out of the question. Some broken things you repair—the witchy altar thing she'd been putting together, for one—nice dishes and plates, a little of her good liquor in a cup—and others you burn. She wants to say something to Alive-Sister, but Alive-Sister is mad at her, has gone into the spare room and slammed the door shut behind her.

Never, ever has Sister-Auntie felt so lonely. There has always been somebody beside her, somebody to cheer and console her. Only empty space now, no sisters, no nothing, so she digs under the bed, pulls out a bottle of rum, and pours herself a glass.

The Bible says everything in moderation. If Sister-Auntie's concept of moderation is glass after cup after mug of white liquor, dark liquor, wine, gin, beer, rum, whiskey, enough to blot out everything uglybuttrue, enough to knock her into blackness, it's nobody's business but Jesus. Didn't he turn water into wine? Sister-Auntie thinks he might've turned it into something stronger if he knew what was coming for him, something with a bite to take away the sting of mean ol' Golgotha hill.

Sister-Auntie finishes a bottle, two bottles. At three and a half, the room is dancing, a little one-two-three waltz like what she used to dance with her husband. Foxtrot, Lindy Hop, whirling whirling, husband throwing her in the air, tossing her, sliding her across the floor, felt like flying, felt like being on a whole new planet. Sister-Auntie can forget, dancing, that her ma'ammy was barely cold when her daddy put her wedding band on Dead-Sister's finger. Can forget what she heard in the night, pain-pleasure, Dead-Sister dead silent and the hoglike grunting. Swing, girl, swing! Push, gal, push!

Sister-Auntie reaches for another bottle and grabs air instead. Her eyes are waltzing one-two-three onetwothree as she looks out the window and sees, standing in the yard, a pillar of jade light. There are no other words to describe it; it stands like a person, glowing, shimmering, its green halo throbbing, and though it is all the way out there, Sister-Auntie knows if she reaches out, she can touch it, feel it warm and sticky like sap on her hand.

When's the last time she glowed anyway? When's the last time light pierced her center, left her feeling clean inside? Maybe tangling blue thread with Dead-Sister? Thinking about time makes Sister-Auntie's head fizzy like television static. She presses her fingers into her eyes, and when she opens them again, she sees the green glowing figure beckoning to her, one arm extended as if to say, Come on, come on.

Walking is hard, but she tells herself she's dancing instead, and then it's easy to make her way down the too-long hall and the too-steep stairs, another hall, and through the front room, and out into the cold night. Now she's alive, now she feels long-forgotten parts of herself, her eyelashes and nipples, her knees and thighs come to life. She goes to the glow and it steps away from her. Goes to the glow and it walks back and back, and Sister-Auntie chases it, stumbling over herself, righting herself, never letting the light leave her sight.

It brings her to the wall of trees and of kudzu. The princess trees look like people with their heads down, people dancing. She wants to dance again, to feel herself swingswingswing and fly, her husband's hands strong on her hips, lifting her into the air, making her feel so small, and so when the green glow beckons her deeper, she follows it. Goes with it into the kudzu, and when the green enters her, absorbs her, fills her with light and leaf, she feels so! Feels so—

Well, at least Nessie is there. She would've been lonely otherwise, green and leafy and glowing alone.

24

Come Monday morning, there was no sign of Vivian. Phyllis, still seething, pointedly ignored her absence until afternoon, her irritated sighs and muttering morphing into fidgeting, pacing. Jude kept a cooler head. She slept little and woke exhausted. Last night's wounds oozed resentment, and she listened distracted as Phyllis rattled off her concerns.

"She's never been gone for so long," she said. The weak mug of tea Jude poured her was cooling at her elbow, and she worried the neckline of her robe. "An hour or so, here and there, but never this long."

"Might've been held up at the store," suggested Jude. Her own cup was drained and she considered getting up for more. "Can't she have seen a friend?"

"What *friend*? She don't like nobody. Only *friend* she got beside me is them bottles she 'sneaks' in the house."

Jude made no attempt to fill the silence that followed. She had a picture of Vivian in her mind, an unflattering and pathetic portrait of a woman too proud to admit to loneliness comforting herself with booze and distorted memory. Jude sat with the discomforting similarities between her and her aunt, let the knowledge that only years and a willingness to drink separated them.

Neither woman wasted her breath suggesting involving the law. There were certain things one did not share, certain things handled in-house. Dirty laundry, recalcitrant children slaughtering their mother, fathers who were grandfathers and sisters who were mothers, busted lips, broken bones, backs patterned with bullwhip lashes—these were their burdens, and no one but niece and aunt would lose sleep over them.

"We should search for her, then," said Jude. "Just you and me."

Phyllis's lips quirked into a half smile and she shook her head, pulled her cold mug close to her. "I haven't so much as crossed the tree line in thirteen years. I can't go out there."

"You fraid of folks seeing you? Of knowing what happened, with Ma'am?"

"*Ye-ess*, but it's . . . it's more too, it's . . ." She licked her lips. In her quest to look anywhere but Jude's face, her gaze landed on the arch leading into the kitchen. "I'm scared of going outside and the world having gone on. Scared of it being different. Only thing worse than people looking me in my face and knowing what happened in this house is people looking me in my face and not knowing at all. Folks I went to church with, prayed with, smiling and carrying on, not even guessing what kept me indoors for so long."

Softly, Phyllis said, "I wish we had done what you did. Feels evil saying it, even now, but I do. I wish we had . . ." The word *kill* floated in the air above them, Phyllis unable to speak it aloud and Jude determined not to say it for her. She scraped her chair away from the table and unsteadily got to her feet. Suddenly she seemed very frail to Jude, her wrinkled hand on Jude's shoulder as she made to leave the room bony and cold.

Once Phyllis was gone, Jude took their cups into the kitchen and washed them. From her position at the sink, she could see the kudzu-eaten tree line, the winding path that led to the outside world. She tried to imagine Phyllis walking the path now and found she couldn't. There was no place for her aunt out there, nowhere a woman so frail and with eyes so sad could be at peace. There was only the Westmoor house, Jude realized, and Phyllis would be there for as long as the miserable place stood.

Unafraid of the world or, at least, less afraid than Phyllis, Jude went out into the city again. She went to the places Phyllis said Vivian frequented—the package store, the underwhelming local food mart, the laundromat, the church—and asked about her aunt. The man at the package store didn't know her name, but he knew she came in every Sunday and always bought a box worth of liquor to hide under her groceries. Some folks at the food mart (Rich's, Jude remembered) said they hadn't seen her since her last visit, three days ago. The laundromat was the same, a man called Paul relating a story of a terse Vivian coming in that past Friday, and the church offered no answers, the secretary there having not seen Vivian in over a month.

"She don't come to church no more?" asked Jude. Laxity in faith didn't match the image she kept of her Holy Roller aunt, Vivian's religious devotion bested only by Ma'am's. "You sure? Vivian Rice?"

"I'm sure," said the secretary. She was younger than Jude, pressed hair and nails painted a neutral, unoffensive pink. It was hard to imagine the woman remembering her mother. "It happens sometimes. Some old folks, they stay with a church they whole life. Others, they just stop coming." She shrugged, gave Jude a once-over, and then asked, "Would *you* like to join us this Sunday?"

It was still early in the day after Jude visited Vivian's haunts. Lacking leads and with waning interest, Jude boarded the nearest public bus and let it take her on a slow tour through Atlanta as she made her way home. She let herself miss Candle, the constant natural noise of the woods. Her time in the city was wearing on her, and the exhaust fumes and cigarette smoke, the funk of marijuana, of body odor, was beginning to fray her nerves. It didn't help that everywhere she looked she saw women wearing Nemoira's face, heard her voice coming from the mouths of strangers. Nemoira stood on the sidewalk holding a child's hand, laughed with a group of friends, smoked a cigarette, leaned against a telephone pole. At the stop three blocks from Ma'am's house, Jude saw her bend to pick a penny off the ground; she lifted her head, braids falling back to reveal her face, and with no small amount of disappointment, Jude realized the woman was too young and too light to ever be her Nemoira.

Phyllis was in the front room when Jude returned. She was seated on the sofa, a large photo album on her lap and a mess of unsorted photographs fanned out around her.

"What are these?" Jude asked. She removed her shoes, tentatively took a seat beside Phyllis.

"I found 'em under Vivian's bed. Always wondered where these were hiding—think she must've had 'em at her house before and brought them over when we moved in." She passed Jude a black-and-white photograph of three smiling dark-skinned girls with their arms around one another, and then another of a woman staring annoyed into the camera.

"I never seen any of these," said Jude. She pointed to the girl at the center of the trio and then to the annoyed woman, and asked, "Is that Ma'am?"

"The first one, yeah. I think Nessie was fifteen or so here, so Viv was twelve, and I was six. That's the house in the back, that's where we grew up the three of us. We shared a bed." Of the other photograph, Phyllis said, "This here is Ma'Dear, Ruth. I was about the same age I was in that picture when she passed. We never knew much 'bout her side of the family, 'cept for all of 'em was dead or out west."

Slowly, Phyllis flipped through the photo album and through the stacks of loose pictures, pausing every so often to show Jude a relative or to relate a story about the photo's subject. Here was one of her grandfather with his brother, Mason, and his sister, Caroline, who Jude's middle name came from; the sister, said Phyllis, was heavy-handed, and the brother had been lynched. Vivian's wedding pictures were some of the first in color, Jude herself outfitted in a puffy yellow dress and a solemn expression. Afterward, the world was a kaleidoscope of pinks, blues, purples, reds: Vivian in her nurse's uniform, grinning into the camera; Pappy's wake, the dining table overburdened with food; Phyllis's wedding to her husband, the Uncle Cephus she remembered liking for his pockets full of candy; a photo of her cousin Monrose as a newborn, and then one of his funeral, his tiny little coffin overlaid with purple cloth.

More pictures were passed, among them daguerreotypes of her grandparents' wedding and monochrome photographs of her aunts and mother as children. Chuckling, Phyllis showed her Ma'am as a young woman working in the laundry, Ma'am beaming, holding up a first-place ribbon in front of a quilt she'd sewn, Ma'am not as her mother but as Ernestine the girl, Ernestine the teenager, Ernestine who liked sweets and playing hand games with her sisters.

Save for the photograph of Jude at her Aunt Vivian's wedding, there were only three pictures of Jude—one of her at a couple of months old in a christening dress, *Judith in her little gown* written out in her mother's neat script; another, Jude at age seven at her baptism, hair plaited, serious and unsmiling with the Chattahoochee River behind her; and the last, the only picture with Jude and Ma'am together, the only one with anything resembling joy on either person's face—Jude and Ma'am holding ribbons from another quilting competition, a blue-and-green brick variation dotted with embroidered daisies stretched between them. She didn't even know she was working toward tears until the first drop fell onto Ma'am's face.

Phyllis made no attempt to soothe her or stop her tears, and Jude was grateful for it. Crying silently, Jude smoothed her hand over the photograph, over Ma'am's smile.

"Is this why she hated me?" she asked Phyllis. "Because of him?"

"She didn't hate you. She didn't love you, yes, but she didn't hate you either. Nessie, she just couldn't—" Something flickered in Phyllis's eye, a passing thought, and she turned her face away from Jude's. "Some women ain't meant to be mothers. Your ma'am, she was one of them."

"She didn't have to take it out on me. I was just a girl," said Jude. Tears rolled down her cheeks and onto her hands, pooled on Ma'am's face. "I was her girl."

Aunt Phyllis tidied her stack of pictures. She whispered, "She was ours too. Our protector and our friend, our world, and you took her from us."

"I'm sorry," said Jude, and it surprised her to find that she meant it. Her aunt met her eye, and it pained Jude to see her so gray and drawn, the grief in her eyes palpable. "I'm not sorry for killing her—she put a hand around my throat to stop me from leaving, would've killed me just to keep me in this house with her—but I am sorry you lost your sister. I wish I knew her like you knew her. She seemed . . ." Jude dragged a tear over her mother's face, obscuring it. "She seemed sweet, before me."

"I think . . . I think if you were only her sister, if you were only *our* sister, she would've loved you with her whole self. It wouldn't have been a question."

There was nothing else to say. Jude held in her hands and her mind Ernestine and Ma'am, both sides to a woman she in turn despised and adored. Her mother whipped her, ruined her; her sister had once held her in her arms, looked down at her with warring emotions, unable to decide whether to love or loathe the baby she held. Jude handed the photo of her mother back to Phyllis and wiped her face.

She sniffled and cleared her throat, and said, "You never did say where you buried her."

Phyllis took the picture and slipped it back into the album, used a rubber band to secure the loose stack. She let out a long, breathy sigh, regarded Jude with misty eyes of her own. "We buried her on Humphrey's plantation. It was in your... *his* will, and it was the only way he'd let her have the house and the money."

Anger surged through Jude, and it took all her willpower to stay seated, to not jump to her feet and scream. As calmly as she could manage, she said, "No churchyard, no quiet field? *Nowhere* else? Phyllis, how could you?"

"We didn't know what else to do. I didn't want it, wanted to put her somewhere else, but... Where else could we put her that wouldn't ask questions?"

Jude squeezed her eyes tight against the fresh wave of tears threatening to fall. If she had a blade or a flame, she'd tear her hand to shreds, draw ugly patterns on her legs and stomach, ruin her forearms with head-splitting wrath. "I would've taken her." She shook her head, sniffed hard against the snot wetting her upper lip. "I should've taken her."

"We can't change the past," said Phyllis. "'Sides, if you had taken her, we wouldn't have been able to say goodbye."

Phyllis held out her hand and Jude placed her own in it, and for a good while, Jude let herself be held by her sister.

Later, Phyllis sat on the sofa with Jude on the floor positioned between her knees and dragged a brush through her hair.

"Don't you do anything with this mane of yours?"

"I comb it," answered Jude. Phyllis wasn't heavy-handed like Ma'am was, her touch surprisingly light as she worked through tangles and knots. When she washed Jude's hair earlier, the feel of her bony fingers working shampoo, conditioner, and coconut oil through her coils was the kindest touch Jude had felt in the month and a half since Nemoira's death.

"Like hacking through a jungle," muttered Phyllis. She made Jude hold on to the pot of hair grease that she took dabs from every so often. For all her complaining, she was a deft hand, patiently separating and weaving Jude's thick hair into thirty or so braids. Jude brought her the remainder of the bag of wooden beads, a handful of cowrie shells, and Phyllis decorated the ends with them, sewed the cowries in at the roots.

It'd been years since Jude had seen herself in a mirror, her sole reflective surfaces for the past decade being ponds, swamps, and, for the briefest time, Nemoira's eyes. Faced with her reflection, Jude was surprised to find not a copy of her mother or even of her aunts but herself as she remembered, more lined and wiser in the eye, but undeniably Jude.

Phyllis smoothed her hands over Jude's braided head, the pressure of her touch a relief from the new-braid tension. Jude relaxed into the sensation and had just closed her eyes when Phyllis said, "I think you should go home."

Jude straightened, turned to face Phyllis. "You don't want me here?"

"It don't matter what I want. It matters that you left here, and you don't belong no more. It don't suit you."

"Nowhere suits me," said Jude flatly.

"But that place, wherever you come from, it suits you more than this, don't it?"

Jude considered Phyllis's words. In her mind, she saw the woods, bright and loud and verdant, heard the melodic call of waterfowl and wading birds accompanied by frogs' ribbits and insect songs. She saw Candle alight on a Sunday evening, saw herself walking through the house and soothing the restless furniture to sleep, her hymns a lullaby to the haints. And though Jude knew Nemoira wouldn't be there, would maybe never be there again, she saw her sitting in front of the fireplace, digging in the garden, smiling or singing, trailing Jude like Mary's lamb.

"What about you?" Jude asked. "You really want to stay in this ugly house forever?"

Phyllis shrugged, smiled sadly. "I don't, but what can I do? My mama, she gone, and my father, and two of my sisters." Jude started to speak, to say that Vivian very well could come back, but Phyllis dismissed her with a wave of the hand. "I got no kin now, 'cept the one sister-niece sitting in front of me." She tilted Jude's face to her, cupped her cheek. "Where else do I belong in this world save for my sister's house?"

25

Though Jude doubted there'd be anyone left alive to stop her from going onto Humphrey's land and digging up her mother's bones, she went to Sparta at night. All that she needed—a shovel, a flashlight, a craftily drawn map showing where Ma'am was buried—was packed into the Studebaker along with Jude's bag and another suitcase bulging with supplies to take south with her. Phyllis, though impressed with Jude's self-sustaining nature, loaded her with old clothes of Vivian's, two pairs of flat shoes ("You can't wear them boots *all* the time!"), some of Ma'am's china wrapped in newspaper, the pink-and-purple quilt from Ma'am's bed, as well as a slim stack of photographs, including the one of her and Ma'am smiling.

She found a station playing soul music, and for two hours, Jude listened to Stevie Wonder and Donna Summer, Aretha Franklin as she rode highways into narrow streets, narrow streets into even narrower dirt paths. When she came upon Humphrey's land, it was a little past eight in the evening, the sky dark and the moon's light blocked by clouds. She drove the Studebaker past a manor blackened with soot, its roof all but gone, and row after row of slave cabins. Some of the land was long dead, useless, and on some of it cotton and sugarcane grew tall enough to hide grown adults.

Jude followed the map's instructions to the southwest corner of the plantation to the Rice plot. It was ten acres, massively larger than the land she managed out in the Okefenokee. No sugar grew on the land but the cotton was waist-high, and an overgrown vegetable garden hosted snap peas, string beans, a few struggling strawberry plants. Little remained of the shotgun shack her mother grew up in, time having turned the sturdy structure into so much firewood. Jude walked through the rotten arch that must've been the front door and stood in the house's corpse, hands in her pockets, heart in her throat.

So this was it, she thought to herself. This was the land that raised and broke her grandfather, that raised and broke Ernestine, scarred her back and made her cold. Here was their nursery, their roots nursed with blood, strengthened by the bones of slaves killed before them.

There was a little graveyard on the plot, two rows of Rices marked by bushes. The map told her who was buried where—Ma'Dear and Pawpaw, her aunts' grandparents, nearer to the left, and the unfortunate eleven Rice miscarriages, stillborns, all crowded into two graves to the right. Ma'am rested between her father and the children's graves, her own mother on the other side of her father.

It'd taken Jude's aunts five hours to dig their sister's grave. Tired but stronger, fortified with a determined rage, Jude dug her mother up in a little under four. She was soaked through with sweat by the time she got to the discolored linen that held her mother's bones. The smell of the grave, untouched earth and a body rotted down to nothing, didn't sicken her like she thought it would. Fortification, Vivian would call it. Past troubles coming to strengthen you in the present.

By flashlight, Jude brought the shroud and shovel to the Studebaker and gingerly placed Ma'am in the back seat. She buckled her in, and as she laid a hand on what felt like her skull, Jude saw the golden band on her finger. She recalled the pictures Phyllis had shown her, the wedding photograph with her grandmother Ruth wearing the ring, and then the ring on Ma'am's hand. Feeling it heavy on her hand, Jude yanked the ring off her finger and threw it away from her, far into the night. Where it landed, she did not care.

All that mattered lay still in the back seat, waiting to be brought home.

Jude returned to Candle early in the morning, exhausted beyond all measure and relieved to be back. Candle howled when she entered it and Jude put her hands up in apology, saying, "I know, I know. Let me sleep awhile and I'll put things to right, hear me?"

Candle rumbled, seethed. After a couple of hours of sleep, Jude started clearing the rooms, one by one. In Nemoira's room, she scrubbed her blood from the hearth and considered the damage to the floors, the furniture. It'd take time to repair the dining room's floor, to make sense of the destruction, but in the meantime, Jude would do what she could, salvaging and restoring some pieces and burning the rest.

She took her time, taking breaks to sleep and to eat, to lazily walk the yard in search of a good spot to bury her mother. All throughout the cleaning, Candle stormed, indignant at being abandoned for nearly a week. Jude apologized, not with words but with action, mending what she and Nemoira had broken, tenderly nursing what she had neglected.

Jude found the chaos in the cellar. The shelves were knocked over, a good deal of the preserves and jams dashed across the floor. The hole in the cellar's ceiling was like a skylight, sunshine from the dining room coating the stained concrete, the broken wood with cool, clean light. In the prayer closet, the altar was thrown on its side, its offerings and dishes strewn about. Clicking her tongue, Jude righted the table. The china she replaced with the dishes pressed upon her by Phyllis, and she filled the bowls with new liquor, a handful of coins.

"I'll bring dinner down after I bury the bones," Jude told the altar as she set in place the candles, the photograph of Ma'am and her with their quilt.

By the time Jude was finished with her cleaning, Candle was tidy if barren, the rooms stripped of their furniture. Only the bathroom and Nemoira's room remained the same, the latter's only change being the removal of its gory decor. It was if the house was new, emptied, with few traces of its former life—Jude could, if she liked, begin again.

After a fast dinner of roasted bear meat (little plate for the altar, little plate on the porch), Jude went out to the garden and dug a grave. She went slowly, stopping whenever exhaustion or sorrow sapped her, and returning to the task when she felt strong again. The hole she dug was just under four feet, deep enough to prevent rabbits and raccoons from disturbing Ma'am's bones, and when she was through, she laid the linen shroud in the grave as gingerly as she would a newborn. Singing softly, Jude filled in the hole, hand after hand of soil spilling through cold fingers.

> There's a leak in this old building
> And my soul has got to move
> I've got another building
> A building not made by man's hands

No man's hands built Candle, raised its walls nor its roof. Its garden and its field, its insides and its haints—these were women's work made holy with intention, made sacred by year upon year of practice, of dedication. The peace her mother (*my sister*, Jude reminded herself) was denied in life and temporarily in death could be found here. If heaven did not have her, Jude would keep her, plant hydrangea and gloxinia upon her, and make the earth that held her grander than any gold-paved street.

Seated on her knees, Jude folded her hands in her lap and said to the bones, "I didn't have anything to say after I killed you. Figured I got it all off my chest when I opened your throat, but there's other things, things I didn't know how to say until now." She thought of her mother as a young woman smiling, thought of her in a cluster with her sisters. "I loved you, Ma'am. I don't know why—same reason you loved your own mother and father, I guess, 'cause you don't think there's anything else out there. I know that's why you stayed; that's why *I* stayed, at least. I couldn't imagine a world where anyone could love me if my own mother didn't. And I guess you thought so too; who could love you, who could want you, if your own father would treat you so nastily?"

Jude looked around herself. The noise of the forest engulfed her, its smell rushing down her throat, filling her, swallowing her. Jude exhaled. Within the Okefenokee, within the stink of swamp water and peat, the comforting trill of thrushes and mockingbirds, her shoulders dropped and her soul settled comfortably in her body.

"I wish someone had told you the truth, that there's more to life than what's done to you. I wish you were here, *really* here, so you could see what I see, the flowers and the frogs, the trees that come up over you like the roof of heaven. I think you would've loved the world if you knew there was more to it than your father's houses. Think you would've loved me too."

Jude's voice cracked upon finishing and sorrow echoed through her like a pressed bruise. No tears came, and there was only the wind whistling, the feel of grass against her ankles. Joints popping, groaning, Jude rose and dusted dirt from her jeans. She let her mother rest.

PART 4

And she was loved!
— **TONI MORRISON,**
SONG OF SOLOMON

26

Spring
1990

Sundays were still for picking flowers. Jude, aged and changed, liked her routines and her rituals, liked the traditions that put shape to the shapeless days out in nature. After twenty-five years in the Okefenokee, she never tired of returning again and again, Sunday after Sunday, to the cypress dome, the bowed tree that cradled her like a child.

Slower and with steps more cautious, Jude entered the woods. It was springtime in Georgia, the weather just on this side of chilly, and Jude wore her coat of many colors and carried a basket laden with her sewing materials and lunch. She trod the familiar dirt path, the road so common she'd know it blind, her feet instinctively taking her past the pitcher plants and over the fallen sweet gum tree.

Waterfowl calls brought her to the cypress dome, the water high with rainfall. Jude removed her shoes and waded into the brown water. She sighed at the coolness, the feel of water snakes and tadpoles swishing around her ankles. Birdsong and the lap of water were the only sounds as Jude picked bushels of iris and lily, dittany and goldenrod and violet. She imagined bouquets, sprays of orange and pink and purple and yellow sat in the dining room, butter-yellow sunlight refracting off a cut-glass vase.

Spry at her sixty-six years, Jude hefted herself onto the bowed cypress with a grunt. The combined perfume of cut flowers, fresh dew, and green water was heady as summer wine. She slept, she wandered, she sat down to eat her lunch of rice and broth; Jude dug through bushes until she found muscadine grapes, and treated herself to a bunch of them, joyfully crushing them with her teeth, staining her fingers with their juice.

Once she swallowed the last mouthful, Jude removed from her basket the makings of her newest quilt. She had been sick for most of the previous year, a flu and back-to-back colds confining her to bed, and so her yearly quilt was a simple square-and-circle pattern she made using old bedding and clothes. This year, however, she planned to pull out all the stops with a gigantic story quilt, the tapestry representing each of her twenty-five years in the forest. Already, she'd cut and stitched together countless fabric trees, shrubs, flowers, not to mention the wildlife; the gators and ibises, boars and mountain lions. Jude fingered the largest of the animals, a five-inch grizzly bear she'd cut from Nemoira's black-brown pelt.

In the eleven years since she killed Nemoira, Jude had not numbed to the grief of losing her. Time only heightened the pain, the love unexpressed flattening her, smothering her. Innocuous things made Jude weep—a rabbit crossing the field, a flash of fuchsia in her fabric drawer. She once fell to tears and to her knees upon hearing the opening chords of Nina Simone's "Wild Is the Wind." Something about the piano, the nauseating and head-splitting neediness of Nina's crooning pierced directly at the center of her, left Jude gasping for breath on the kitchen floor, hand clenched at her heart.

There was no fighting it, the loneliness and the longing, and Jude didn't want to fight it. She missed her beast, she missed her woman, and she would, she thought, until the day she died.

In the meantime, Jude carried on. She kept Nemoira's promise and used all of her: the pelt she used to line her winter clothes, gloves, and coats, or else she used it as backing for blankets. For almost two years, Jude ate Nemoira, working her way slowly through the massive bear's meats and organs, making stock and stews from her bones, roasting the marrow as a treat. Whatever she couldn't wear or eat, Jude ground up and used in the garden, the visceral remains of her lover fertilizing the land.

Occasionally, Jude found herself craving a flavor taboo. Nothing else satisfied, nothing touched the taste of that particular pig, gamy and fatty and tender. When pickings in the woods were slim and Jude was forced to rely on the butcher, disinterestedly looking over the man's paltry selection, she'd catch sight of a passerby, a customer, and for longer than she liked, Jude would consider the fat of their thighs, the health of their heart and lungs and liver. She wondered what Nemoira would bring to her first.

Jude blinked, distracted herself from her watering mouth by swigging some tea and throwing herself into her sewing. She stitched together a few more trees and foxes, working until her mind was clear, until it was sunset.

Even now, the woods did not baby her as she walked home at night. Age mattered not to a place inhabited by waters and trees older than bone, so Jude watched her step when traversing the treacherous undergrowth, the roots jutting up through mulch.

As she crossed the field and neared Candle, she saw a figure waiting for her on the porch. They were sat on the steps with a bundle on their lap, legs spread indecorously, dressed in a heavy brown leather coat. Jude approached the figure, and they lifted their dark head, revealing glossy, black stone eyes and a slight smile.

"Hello, Judy," said Nemoira.

If she weren't so tired, if her hands weren't full with the flowers and her basket, Jude would smack the woman. It would be the least she deserved—the nerve of her to submit to the blade, to take so long to return to her, and only say hello now that she was back. Jude huffed through her nose, set the basket down on the porch, and gestured to the bundle in Nemoira's lap with her chin.

"What's this?"

"Dinner," replied Nemoira cheerily. She let the wax paper bundle fall open and showed Jude the marbled cut of meat still weeping blood. "Nothing funny, I swear. It's deer." Her smile broadened ever so slightly, eyes sparkling with mischief. "You always did like deer."

Jude made a little nothing noise and looked Nemoira over. Standing so near to her, seeing her dark and lovely face dizzied Jude, made her hot with anger and confusion and lust. Memories of the sweet times stood alongside memories of the sour. She wanted to take the woman's face in her hands and kiss her; she wanted to take the woman's face in her hands and smash her smile into pieces.

"You been sitting here long?" asked Jude.

"Only an hour."

Jude looked over Nemoira's shoulder to the sunken red spot on the porch where she'd laid her kills for thirteen years. An empty bowl sat there now, the dregs of last night's dinner coating the sides. Nemoira followed her gaze, and almost bashfully, she confessed, "I mighta been coming for the past couple of weeks just to eat."

"What? Big ol' bear too scared to say hello?"

"I wasn't ready. Every time I thought I was, I saw your face and I . . ." Nemoira held her mouth open but no words left it. "I couldn't do it."

"Imagine that," said Jude dryly. She came onto the porch, picked up the basket and the bowl, and stood by the front door. "An animal with a guilty conscience!"

"Me guilty?" Nemoira turned to Jude sharply. "*You* was the one that killed me!"

"You lied to me, fed me human meat, filled my house with corpses and bones, and told me to my *face* you meant to eat me next. What was I supposed to do? Let you?"

Jude and Nemoira stared at each other, Jude with a brow raised and Nemoira with an annoyed, frustrated expression. Finally, Nemoira broke the contact, and Jude pushed open the front door. Over her shoulder, she said, "Come in if you want. I'll have dinner done in an hour."

A minute passed before Jude heard Nemoira enter and the sound of the door closing behind her. Nemoira removed her shoes and followed Jude into the kitchen, put the package of meat down on the counter before finding a chair to sit in. The woman's eyes were a brand on her back, tracking Jude as she went from counter to icebox to shelves of seasoning. She cleared her throat as she chopped celery and carrot, meaty chunks of potato.

"Took you a while to come back."

"I warned you it was harder coming back from bigger deaths. You used all of me; I had to grow from nothing." Nemoira came to Jude's side, brushed a knotted loc back from her face, and said, "You look good. Different, but good."

"I look old," she responded. Flames jumped beneath the stewpot, the smell of cooking venison and thyme and bay leaf filling the kitchen. Jude scraped the vegetables off the cutting board and into the pot with her knife. "Old and tired and beat up."

She gave Nemoira her face, showed her the deep brown scars that marked the right side of her face, that stiffened her speech. Where there was once an eye was now only wrinkled, knotted skin. Nemoira put a hand to Jude's scarred cheek and rubbed it with her thumb.

"I can make us match, if you like. You left me with plenty," said Nemoira. As she held Jude, her face changed, the smooth, unlined skin falling away to reveal the burns left by the buckshot, the myriad scratches and slashes from where Jude had dug in her nails. Across her throat, dainty and fine as a thin silver chain, was the line Jude had drawn across her throat with the cleaver.

Jude turned her head away, returned to cooking. When arms came to circle her waist, she resisted the urge to lean back into the touch, to sink without thought into Nemoira. Tears fell into the pot, oversalting the venison.

Dinner was strange, all furtive glances and stilted conversation. Every time Jude thought to say something to Nemoira, she was struck with a memory of Nemoira as the bear, the total terror she'd felt when confronted with those claws, those teeth. She listened with half an ear to Nemoira's compliments on her cooking, to tedious small talk about the changing weather and the look of the garden.

Finally, Jude pushed away her bowl and said, "I still don't understand why you did all you did. Why lie to me?"

Nemoira swallowed, wiped her mouth. "I thought it was the only way to keep you. I thought if it went on long enough, you'd come to like it, that I could change you even more than you already had. You were already so *unhuman* I thought, if I couldn't eat you, I could get you to eat the world."

Jude considered Nemoira's words, the truth of them. She knew she wasn't the same woman she was twenty-five years ago, that something within her had transformed and that she was now something entirely new. Memory alone bonded Jude to that old version of herself, to the woman who cowered and flinched and feared. Still, the violence inflicted on her, the violence she inflicted on others, the blood she spilled and the blood that ran through her veins, none of it defined or unhumaned. She was still Jude, human even in her peculiarities, worthy of the title of person despite what she'd done and what had been done to her.

"I guess I was more human than you thought," said Jude.

Nemoira's eyes lit up, her smile grew, and Jude couldn't resist smiling along with her.

"I guess so."

While Nemoira did the dishes ("It's the *least* I can do!"), Jude carried two bowls of stew, a bottle of gin, and a pocketful of treasures down into the cellar. She lit the candles framing Ernestine's photo, and then filled the dishes with pennies, quarters, beads and cowrie shells, stones she found in the woods, a gray loc twisted too thin.

Honoring Ernestine, her sister, took nothing from Jude but time and sometimes tears. Jude couldn't love her mother: There was too much bad blood between them, too much anger and spite and bile, but she could try to love her sister. Nessie was long-lost, buried on evil land but now exhumed. Jude let herself feel for Nessie what she could not feel for Ma'am—tenderness, patience, forgiveness.

"Evening, Nessie," started Jude. She set down the bowls of food, one for her mother and one for the nameless haints. "Here's dinner. Looks like the plums will be ready to pick tomorrow, so we can have them then. Phyllis, she said you liked your plums stewed." Jude grimaced. "Not *my* taste, but I'll bring them like that, if you want."

She told her sister other things, anything that came to her mind about her walk and about the quilt. She told her about Nemoira coming back, about falling in love with a monster and fighting it, killing it with the same cold determination that she'd killed Ernestine with. If the woman did not like to hear about her sister-daughter's taste in bedmate, she was respectful enough a ghost to keep her reactions tapered to petering candlelight.

"What you think, Nessie? Think I'm being a fool 'bout this woman?"

The candle flames flared, then settled. Jude laughed, blew out the candles.

Nemoira was waiting for her in the living room, feet tucked beneath her as she stared into the lit hearth. Jude sat on the couch beside her, and when she patted Nemoira's knee to draw her attention, the woman took her hand in her own.

"Look here. I want you, Nemoira. There's no reason to it, I just do, and because I want what I want, this is how it's going to be." As always, Jude's voice was gentle, soft as leather, but there was no give in her expression, no room for misunderstanding in her tone. "One, you not gonna lie to me. Whatever the truth is, you give it to me straight, let me decide whether I want to accept it or not. Understood?"

Nemoira nodded and Jude continued: "Two, you keep your claws to yourself. Next time you so much as scratch me without permission, I'll put a bullet right between your eyes. I did it before, Nemoira, and I don't wanna do it again. Don't hurt me and don't make me hurt you."

Nemoira canted her head and narrowed her eyes. "Who defines what hurt is?"

"We do, together, but in broad strokes—smashing my head into a hearth and clawing out my eye are noes. You stay in my house, you stay sweet to me. I only wanna see your teeth in *very* specific circumstances."

For a moment it seemed like Nemoira had more to argue,

but she only nodded, gestured for Jude to continue. "What else? What other house rules?"

"Only one more," said Jude. "Under no circumstances will you eat human flesh, and under no circumstances will you feed me human flesh."

Jude watched Nemoira still, watched her eyes shift and flash with warring emotion. "You denying me my nature," replied Nemoira at length. "You want to make me something I'm not."

"I am," Jude admitted with a nod. "And if you don't wanna do it, if you can't give up the meat, you can leave. I won't hold you, woman, and I won't beg. I'm over it, begging love and decency from people who won't give it freely." She was taking food from Nemoira's mouth and she knew it, but she also knew there were other meats, other tastes, flavors Nemoira liked better than blood. Jude looked at Nemoira head-on, unflinching, and tried with her eyes to convey her seriousness, her resolve. "But I tell you this—you stay here, you stay with me in my bed under my roof, and you won't go hungry. If it's flesh you want, skin and bone and blood, have me. Keep me."

The silence that followed was broken only by the women's labored breathing, the crackle of firewood. Long gone were the days that Jude could look at Nemoira and know immediately what she was thinking, what she wanted and needed. If only she could read the woman like pages of a book, or like tea leaves, swirling and sifting the minute changes in her brows, her posture.

Finally, Nemoira rose and stepped out of her clothes. She stood in front of Jude, backlit by firelight, and slowly, smoothly, she transformed. Her mouth and nose softened into a muzzle, hands and feet melding together to form paws. Jude watched Nemoira's bones change shape, the woman lowering herself onto the ground as she sprouted black fur, a tail. An off-white patch of fur traveled from her throat down to her belly, and when she was through, she rested her chin on Jude's knee, ears relaxed and tail swinging slowly. A herding dog Nemoira was, a mighty Great Pyrenees, enemy to wolves and cougars and grizzly bears.

Jude eased to her knees so she and Nemoira were at eye level, and ran her hands over the dog's furry flank, her ears, her wet nose. She pulled back the black lips to see the teeth glistening with spit, the lolling pink tongue. She looked into the dog's black eyes and saw her woman in them, the tenderness and patience, a fire Nemoira's own.

"Good girl," Jude murmured. "Good, beautiful girl."

Nemoira rumbled, flopped down with her chin on Jude's lap. Laughing softly, Jude petted Nemoira. Illuminated by lamplight, by firelight, the bear-fur rug warm beneath them, Jude dug her hand into Nemoira's fur and did not let go.

ACKNOWLEDGEMENTS

From the bottom of my heart, I'd like to thank my agent, Valentina Sainato—who gave *On Sundays* a chance, and started me on this adventure—as well as the entire editorial, publishing, and marketing teams at Saga, who have made this debut such a beautiful, surreal experience for me. Very special thanks to Nivia Evans and Jéla Lewter, my editors, for seeing the vision and tolerating my backtalk in the revisions.

Thank you to Sandra T., who first pushed and inspired me to write this story. To B. Umaia Perlin, who has been, essentially, Jude's doula into this world; Baya, girl, I am not joking when I say Jude would not be who Jude is without you.

Thank you, Mommy; for being my cheerleader, for the home-cooked meals and lay-in-bed-days and come-cry-on-momma moments. Thank you, Daddy; for giving me my name, for bragging about me to any and everybody you meet, for just being you.

And you know what? Thank you to me; for sticking it out, for staying alive, for digging my heels in and *insisting* even when others tried to persuade and dissuade me. Thank you, Yah Yah, for being stubborn, for having a vision of yourself in the future, and for chasing that vision.